PULLED BY THE TAIL

CELESTIAL MATES

NANCEY CUMMINGS

FOREWARD

Wife Wanted: Aristocrat Needs an Heir. Fertile Females Only.

A clerical error matched Georgia to the wrong alien. It'll take months to get their marriage annulled, so she's stuck in a grand house that's falling down on a backwater planet with a massive brute of an alien who likes books more than people. But the more time she spends with Talen, the more she questions if their marriage was a mistake.

All Talen has in the universe is his family. When his brother's latest scheme delivers a human female to his door, technically his wife, he refuses to turn her away. She's part of his pride now and he knows that her luscious form and biting wit is vital to his future. He'll win her heart and convince her that nothing about the heat between them is a mistake.

CHAPTER 1

GEORGIA

Sunshine,

I regret to inform you I have a scheduling conflict and cannot attend your meeting this afternoon.

-Kevin

"Benign," the doctor said.

Georgia sighed with relief; she had never heard such a sweet, perfect word before in her life. Benign. Thank God. For the last week, she'd been living on tenterhooks, unable to sleep due to worry and unable to concentrate on anything beyond "what if."

What if the polyps were cancerous?

What if she had cervical cancer like her mom?

What if they didn't catch it in time?

"So, what's next?"

The doctor leaned back in her chair. "I'd like to start you on a course of progesterone. That should get your hormone levels balanced. The regime will be two weeks on, two weeks off. The hormone won't affect your ability to have children," the doctor said in a warm, reassuring tone.

"Okay," Georgia said, unsure of her ability to remember to take a pill every day for two weeks, then skip the pills for another two weeks. She'd have to get a pillbox.

That's how the whole mess started. Georgia's cycle had never been predictable but at least it was light and pain-free. Until it wasn't. Slowly, so slowly she hadn't noticed, her cycles grew more troublesome and erratic until she reached the point where she couldn't leave the house due to heavy bleeding for weeks. Not days. Weeks. Clearly, something had been wrong and silly Georgia didn't realize until she was in the thick of it.

Fortunately, her best friend, Freema, a med school student, found her a good doctor who listened to her symptoms. With her family history of cervical cancer in mind, they promptly eliminated possibilities. After blood tests, thyroid tests, and an ultrasound, what remained was cancer and the suspicious little polyps inside her uterus.

"...but you might want to consider any children sooner rather than later."

The doctor's words snapped her back from her daydreaming. "But I'm only twenty-eight."

Only twenty-eight and already her body had betrayed her. This time the polyps were benign. What if next time it was cervical cancer? She could lose her uterus and even her life. Georgia had vague memories of her mother going in for a partial hysterectomy when Georgia was young. Mainly she remembered sitting in the hospital cafeteria with her elderly neighbor, eating ice cream and crying because she was so scared. The neighbor's solution to everything unpleasant was ice cream, a bad habit she picked up and explained the extra pounds she carried on her hips.

"So, you're saying I should have a baby now while I'm still able?"

"I'm saying with your family history of cancer, you should consider your options."

While she still had options.

"I see no reason, medically, why you cannot conceive now, but if you decide to wait, you could consider freezing your eggs and other treatment options."

Expensive options, the doctor meant.

"And don't overlook adoption. That love is just as real as a child that grows in your belly."

"Yeah, I mean, of course." She liked the idea of adopting or fostering. Having gone into the foster system after her mother's death, she knew the pain of being an unwanted, unadoptable child. If she could give a kid a home, she would, gladly. "It's just a bit sudden. I don't have to make any decisions today?"

She just found out she didn't have cancer—thank God—and she was unprepared to figure out how to afford a baby or foster a kid. She needed to be married first. That was the plan.

"Of course not. Let's see how you respond to hormone therapy."

With a prescription in hand, Georgia made her way to the pharmacy and then to the apartment she shared with her boyfriend, Kevin.

Things with Kevin were fine. Not amazing, but not bad, just fine. That was good, right? A stable relationship with no surprises. Sure, it was boring, but boring was good. After an unstable childhood—not to speak ill of her mom, who did the best she could—paying the rent on time, holding down a nine-to-five job, and never having to worry about the utilities being shut off was wonderful.

Boring was just another word for stable and stability was fantastic. No one embodied stability more than her Kevin.

But were they ready for children? They lived together, sure, and hadn't encountered any major problems, but a baby? Agreeing on what pizza to order or what show to watch in the evening wasn't the same thing as raising a child.

She had some time. Not years, like she originally envisioned in her master life plan, but she didn't have to jump on Kevin's dick and get knocked up today.

Yes, Georgia had a master life plan. Her first draft had been written in glitter gel ink when she was twelve and determined not to end up like her parents. She'd been updating it ever since. Graduate high school, done. Don't get pregnant as a teenager, like her mom. Georgia didn't even date in high school, avoiding the temptation of sex and opportunities for surprise pregnancies. College, done. She traveled out of the country, got a small tattoo on her shoulder, and even had an anonymous one-night stand, all according to the plan. Moving in with her boyfriend right out of college was on schedule. Maybe she should accelerate the schedule and bump up married at thirty to twenty-eight?

Having a list of her goals kept her on track. The big picture vanished too easily in the day-to-day. Like now. Having a baby before thirty wasn't in the plan but what if the plan was wrong? What if she waited and then couldn't have a baby?

She needed to think this over, preferably with a big slice of chocolate cake.

Her phone buzzed with an incoming message. *Well? Don't leave a girl hanging.*

She smiled and typed a quick reply to her friend, Freema. *No cancer!*

Thank you, sweet Jesus! Celebratory drinks? Strawberry and margarita emojis followed. Freema loved her boozy strawberry drinks.

I'm exhausted. I didn't sleep, she replied.

Take a nap. Let me know if you change your mind, Freema wrote.

Georgia wouldn't change her mind. She wanted to curl up on the sofa and watch something mindless with people decorating cakes poorly. That sounded amazing.

"Sweetie, I'm home," she announced, tossing her keys on the table next to the front door. Immediately she noticed the extra set of car keys, which were not hers or Kevin's. "Do we have company?"

No one replied but she heard music from deeper in the apartment. Georgia followed the noise, opening the bedroom door to find Kevin balls-deep in the new intern.

Boring, predictable Kevin was fucking the intern. How cliché. How uninspired. Georgia had to laugh. Kevin's pale, hairy butt was laughable, too.

The intern finally noticed Georgia standing in the door and screamed.

"The intern? Really, Kevin? Is she even legal?" Georgia knew the young woman's age to be at least eighteen, probably closer to twenty, but still.

"What are you doing home?!" Kevin jumped away from the woman like distance could erase what Georgia saw. "You're supposed to be at the office until five."

The intern grabbed her clothes from the floor and rushed by Georgia.

"I had a doctor's appointment, which I told you about this morning. Oh, and it's not cancer. Thanks for asking."

"There you go again, always sniping at me."

"Don't turn this around on me. You were fucking the intern!"

Kevin ignored what she said. "So, you're fine now?" He stood with his hands on his hips, his dick flagging, way too confident for a guy with a scrawny, pale, hairy ass.

"Fuck, you're not even wearing a condom," she said. So gross. Thank God she had insisted on protection with him. Still, she added getting a check-up at the clinic to her list. Getting a funky sex infection was not part of the master plan, but here she was, staring at the unimpressive, unprotected dick of her asshole boyfriend, not knowing where he put that thing.

She did know he wouldn't be putting it in her again. Ever.

"But you're fine?" he asked, and Georgia got the distinct impression he wasn't concerned about her health.

"Yeah, no cancer."

He flashed a confident smile that made her skin crawl. "She didn't mean anything, baby. I just needed a backup plan if you were sick. I didn't want to get stuck, you know?"

If she was sick… His words turned her stomach. "So, you'd trade me in? Ditch me when I needed you?"

Exactly what happened to her mom. She grew sick and her dad vanished. Her parents had a rocky relationship to start with, on-again and off-again, but her dad always came back. Eventually. Usually broke and needing a place to crash, but he came back. Until her mom had cancer, and he disappeared for good.

Fuck. Despite her carefully monitored plan, she ended up with the same type of man as her father. Fuck a duck.

"How many?" she asked.

"Just the one. Just Janice."

"So, this is the first time?" Not that it made it better, but she was trying to wrap her head around when boring, reliable Kevin found time to screw the intern.

"Well, not the first time, but she's the only one."

"How long?"

"It doesn't matter, baby." He flashed his charming smile, but Georgia saw it for the superficial facade it was.

"How long?!"

"Since October."

Since she got sick and went in for testing. That creep. He tossed her aside the moment her body failed to meet his standards of perfection.

"Get out," she said.

"You're not upset, are you? Where's my Georgia sunshine?" He cupped her face. The pet name used to make her heart flutter, now it made her nauseous.

Georgia stepped back. "I said get out, Kevin."

He huffed, like he wanted to argue, but pulled on his jeans. The whole situation was so strange. They never argued and until a few minutes ago, she would have sworn that Kevin would have never cheated. He was too boring.

"I'm leaving, but just to check on Janice. You're not kicking me out," he said.

"Yes, I am. Don't bother coming back."

"My name's on the lease."

"I'll get the locks changed," she said. Immediately.

"I'll get the landlord to let me back in," he retorted.

"Don't you have a backup apartment with Janice, since you're so worried about being stuck?"

Kevin drew himself up to full height, a move that might have been impressive with his average build and narrow shoulders if he had scruples or even the smallest bit of dignity. "I paid for the deposit on this place. It's mine. If you can't see your way around this one little indiscretion, I really think you should leave."

"Fine."

"Fine," he said in a mocking tone. His smirk said that he expected to find her on the sofa, waiting for him, when he got back. He slipped on his shoes, grabbed his keys, and stood at the door. "Don't eat all the ice cream while I'm gone. You've really let yourself go, Georgia."

"You did not just call me fat," she said as the door swung shut. She stood there in disbelief. "He called me fat."

He fucked the intern, blamed her, made a jab about her weight as he left to chase his mistress, and expected to find her waiting for him when he got back. No doubt on the sofa, eating directly out of the ice cream tub, because that's what chubby chicks did.

Georgia looked around the apartment. When Kevin said he wanted to move in together, she'd been thrilled. He purchased most of the furniture and furnishings, but that made sense. He made more money than her and could afford to upgrade to the leather sofa and the side tables with the marble inlay. Everything had been arranged just so and kept pristine with zero clutter. Kevin didn't like clutter. They decorated with a trendy gray and white color scheme. Excuse her, *French* gray and origami white. It was bland. Safe.

Boring.

Fuck boring and especially fuck Kevin.

Part of her wanted to take a knife and ruin the fine-grain leather on the sofa, to destroy Kevin's favorite lounger, but she didn't have it in her. She wasn't a vandal. Knowing Kevin, he'd send her a bill.

Okay, she ruled out property damage. Revenge would have to be less physical and more intangible.

Like frozen fish fillets in the heating vents. Concerned with his heart and omega-three fatty acids, they stocked the freezer with a variety of fish. She didn't particularly enjoy fish but she choked it down because that's what a good girlfriend did, right?

She refused to be Kevin's good girlfriend anymore.

Georgia grabbed a bag and stuffed it with the first things

she grabbed from the closet. She'd crash with Freema for a few days until she could find a place of her own. She had money. She had a job, even if it was a job in Kevin's office as his subordinate.

Yeah, she'd need to find a new job, too.

She dumped her toiletries into the bag and couldn't think of another reason to stay. She'd be back in a few days with Freema to fetch the rest of her stuff, unless Kevin changed the locks, and then she'd put the fish in the heating vents.

"WE'RE OUT OF STRAWBERRIES, so it's just a plain daiquiri." Freema set two tall glasses down on the coffee table.

"Lame. I was promised strawberry daiquiris." That wouldn't stop Georgia from drinking her plain daiquiri, though.

"We drank all the rum, too, so I used the whiskey," Freema said.

"That's not a daiquiri." She didn't think it was anything. She took a cautious sip. Tart and sweet, it burned down her throat. Georgia sputtered but swallowed the awful concoction. "This is terrible. You ruined really good whiskey."

"No one likes whiskey and we're too drunk to go to the store or a bar. They won't serve us." Freema leaned against Georgia, holding the vile drink like it might explode. The glass tilted to its side. Spilling was a real possibility.

Georgia grabbed the glass and set it back down on the coffee table. "We're not that drunk." Probably. She'd been crashing on Freema's couch for a week, too down in the dumps to do much of anything. She quit her job, so she did that. She showered, but only because Freema sprayed her with air freshener. Subtle, her friend was not.

That morning, they went to Kevin's apartment and cleared out the rest of her stuff. She half expected to find her books, clothes, and favorite coffee mugs already packed in boxes and Janice moved in. Instead, nothing had changed, like Kevin expected her to come crawling back. After packing up her meager possessions, they stole Kevin's expensive bottles of whiskey and rum.

All things considered, Georgia was proud of how maturely she handled the situation. She didn't destroy Kevin's property or dump dog poo on the carpet and start up the floor cleaning bot to smear the poo everywhere. She considered it but didn't do it. See? Mature. She only took two little bottles of alcohol. He owed her.

Just before she left the apartment for the final time, she set all the televisions to Spanish and hid all the remotes. She wasn't *that* mature.

To celebrate, Georgia and Freema were determined to get falling-down drunk, watch bad movies, and eat pizza and junk food until they were sick. Or fell asleep. Whatever happened first.

"We're going to be so sick tomorrow," Georgia said. Her

tolerance for alcohol had seriously diminished. In college, she could stay up all night, drink, eat junk, get only two hours of sleep, and be fresh as a daisy. Now? One beer was her usual limit. Anything more and she had a headache for days. She was so not looking forward to the morning.

She stuffed a handful of chips in her mouth, to soak up the booze.

A knock sounded at the door.

"Pizza's here!" Freema jumped off the couch and raced to the door, sliding across the floor in her socks. "Um, Georgia. It's for you."

Kevin stood in the doorway, wearing a wool coat more expensive than her monthly salary, and looking around Freema's small apartment with a judgmental frown.

"What do you want?" Georgia crossed her arms over her chest, aware that she was braless—girl's night in, after all —and a cold breeze came in through the door. She didn't want Kevin to think her nipples got hard just because he showed up. It was cold, dammit.

"This is where you've been hiding?"

"I'm not hiding," she replied before she could think better of letting Kevin direct the flow of conversation. That's what he did: steered her down a path until she agreed with everything he said, even if she disagreed. All their past arguments fell into that pattern. It had to stop. "What are you doing here?"

He reached into the inside pocket of his coat and withdrew an envelope. "I thought I'd drop off your last paycheck," he said, voice cold. Georgia reached for the envelope, but he drew it back. "By the way, starting a rumor about Janice in the office was highly unprofessional."

"It's not a rumor if it's true." She shrugged. See, she could be cold and unfeeling too. "The director wanted to know why I was leaving. I didn't mince words." She had been fairly blunt stating that she no longer felt comfortable working with her ex-boyfriend while he was fucking the intern.

"I'll have to mention it if anyone calls for a reference," Kevin said.

Georgia narrowed her eyes, not sure what game Kevin played. Did he want an apology? A blowjob for a good reference?

"No, I don't want a blowjob," he said.

Shit. She must be drunker than she thought.

"I've had enough of your unenthusiastic blowjobs to last a lifetime."

"Well, it's hard to get excited about sucking your dick when you fall asleep."

"Sunshine, I don't know how you expect me to be excited when you look like *that*." His gaze swept her from head to toe and from the sour look, he found her lacking.

Georgia blushed. She knew she wasn't a supermodel, but he had to have found her somewhat attractive. They hadn't had sex in months, even before the breakup, but she had been ill. Between the near-constant bleeding, the fatigue, and the stomach cramps, she hadn't felt sexy in a long time.

"Oh shit. That happened? Sorry! I'm not listening," Freema said, slamming two pillows on either side of her head.

Yeah, that happened. She had his pecker in her mouth, giving it her all, and he fell asleep. He wasn't drunk or anything; he just wasn't interested.

Georgia saw the entirety of their relationship. She had predictable sex with her boring boyfriend. They had a boring, predictable life where the most exciting thing was a new bagel place opening on the corner. That life was as gray and bland as the color scheme in their apartment. She deserved better. They both did.

Kevin actually did them a favor. Huh.

"Have you been to the apartment yet?" Georgia tried to ask casually and not darting her eyes side to side like a guilty person. Freema coughed dramatically. Yeah, not such a smart question.

"Why?"

"No reason. I got my stuff and left my key." True enough and not a complete lie.

A figure appeared behind Kevin, holding two pizza boxes.

"Look, we're in the middle of stuff here. I appreciate you dropping off my last paycheck." Georgia snagged the envelope while the pizza guy distracted Kevin, then signed for the delivery. "Thanks! Have a good life," she sang in a far-too-chipper voice, slamming the door shut.

Abruptly, she opened the door again on Kevin, who had not moved. She shouted, "Florida is the sunshine state. Georgia is peaches!" Another slam, this one final. She'd never see Kevin again, God willing. "Fucker," she muttered.

"He's the worst," Freema said, opening the box and helping herself to a slice of barbequed chicken. "We totally need to find you a rebound guy."

"I don't want a rebound guy." She wanted pizza and maybe more whiskey. Her needs were simple.

"You do. Everyone does. It's like dating law."

"Oh, well if everyone does it," she said, adding extra sarcasm to her voice. The sarcasm must not have been obvious because Freema jumped up from the sofa and raced to her tablet computer.

"Let's sign you up for a dating app," Freema said.

"I don't think that's a good idea."

"Pfft. It's the best idea we've ever had. Oh, Celestial Mates. Find your perfect match. Look at the hot guy." Freema shoved the screen in Georgia's face. The blue-skinned Fremmian model had no shirt, appeared to be covered in glistening baby oil, and flexed his biceps for the camera.

"Um, he's blue. Is this an alien hookup app?"

"Don't be narrow-minded. Blue guys need loving, too. Besides, that's just the sugar to lure you in. The profiles are totally average."

Georgia grabbed the tablet and scrolled through the sample profiles. "They're all aliens. This *is* an alien hookup app."

Freema snatched the device back. "Don't be such a xenophobe. Have you ever dated an alien guy?"

"I'm not a xenophobe," she protested. She hadn't dated anyone of extraterrestrial origins but not because she wouldn't; she just hadn't been asked out. "You know Kevin was my only boyfriend."

Freema stuck her tongue out and made a completely mature retching noise. "Such a waste. We have to get you out there and getting some. How about this guy?" turning the tablet to face Georgia, a golden-skinned male with four arms filled the screen.

"A Gyer? I don't know."

"What's wrong with a Gyer? They're hot. All those hands. Yum."

"They're not, you know, binary." The Gyer did not have distinct male or female genders. They were equally capable of becoming pregnant and also impregnating a partner. Maybe. The details were fuzzy.

Georgia really should have paid attention in her Comparative Biology course in college, otherwise known as Alien Banging 101. The class in a nutshell: humans like to fuck, have fucked every alien they've encountered, and can have babies with most of those aliens. Basically, humans were slutty when it came to aliens.

"Do you think they're, umm, compatible?" Georgia asked.

A grin tugged at Freema's painted fuchsia lips. "God, I really want to find out. I can think of lots of things to do with four hands."

"Gross!"

"For hugging." She rolled her eyes dramatically. "Pervert. Okay, profile picture. I got this old one from last summer when we went to the beach."

"Not the bikini." The floral two-piece looked so pretty in the store and Georgia thought it flattered her curves, but Kevin didn't like her showing so much skin. She spent the day covered up with a towel rather than enjoying the sun.

Freema never had those worries, being thinner than Georgia and infinitely cooler. She wore her blonde hair in twin buns, streaked in pastel-colored hair wax, and her friend totally pulled it off. Georgia? She had a hard enough time finding jeans that fit her hips without leaving a gap at the waist. She'd never tried trendy hairstyles, electing to play it safe with the same old haircut.

"Yes, the bikini. You looked super cute with those high-lights," Freema said.

Georgia absently touched the end of her hair. The golden blonde highlights had grown out long ago and hovered at the bottom of her mid-length chestnut hair. "You think I should get highlights again?"

"Yes. It's not even a question." Freema continued to fill in personal data in the app. "Tomorrow, let's have a girl's day and spoil ourselves. Facials. Manicures. Massages. The works."

"Sounds brilliant." She took a slice of barbeque chicken. As she chewed, she grew curious as to what Freema was writing on her behalf. "What does it want to know now?"

"No peeking! It's a surprise."

"But you're talking about me." She reached for the tablet with greasy fingers.

"Nope." Freema sprang from the sofa, clutching the tablet. "We're going to find you a perfectly disreputable bad boy and you're going to bang your brains out. Doctor's orders."

"With tattoos?"

"At least three."

She'd never dated a bad boy before. That wasn't part of the plan, but the plan failed her. Going off-script terrified her but thrilled her to her core. "Let's do it."

Talen

MR. T. ACHAVAL,

Your presence is requested on the 30th level, in the private gaming rooms. We wish to discuss your brother. Please visit the concierge at your earliest convenience.

-Noxu Station Management Team

"You what?!"

"It's a sure thing," Quil said, tail curiously still.

Talen stared down at his elder brother. Quil's tells were so obvious. How did everyone at the card table not know Quil lied? His body practically screamed that he played a poor hand and winning was far from guaranteed.

Take care of your brother, his mother commanded the last time he saw her. Never mind that Quil was the elder and by all rights, he should be caring for Talen, not the other way around, but their mother had been a practical female and didn't expect miracles.

It had been twenty years since an assassin took Talen's parents from him, but he tried his best to abide by his mother's words. Talen tried to take care of Quil, but his older brother made it so hard.

"We only have each other in this universe," Quil said, resting a hand on Talen's forearm. Invoking the words of their nursemaid—the female who smuggled the young males off Talmar and raised them as her own—was a dirty trick.

"The ship is our home," Talen said. His ears pressed flat against his head and his tail twitched in agitation. His claws itched just below the surface at his fingertips. "You're gambling our home."

"And Lerrence is gambling his family's ancestral estate."

Quil's greedy eyes flash as he took a sip of his drink. The dark amber liquor complimented his pale amber complexion. "Besides, the collateral had been certified by the casino already. It's too late."

With a growl, Talen knocked the glass from his irresponsible brother's clutches. He knew how he appeared, a large brute about to lose what little control he had.

The liquor splashed a Corravian male seated at the table. "I say! Watch yourself."

"Forgive my brother. He's in a mood," Quil said, laying on the charm thick and easy.

"I'm not *in a mood*. I'm furious." Quil rolled his eyes, which only ratcheted up Talen's fury. "The ship is our transportation, our livelihood, and our home. How could you be so reckless?"

"That rusted old beast?" The seated Corravian male snorted. "I'll be paying the junkers to haul it away."

"You're Lerrence, then?" Talen knew the male's identity. They had played cards before, in another gambling hall. Of course, Quil had lost spectacular sums of money to the male, no doubt boosting the male's confidence about a win.

"And that estate is nothing but a money pit. I'm doing you a favor taking it off your hands," Quil said, taking his seat at the table.

"Yes, and your ship is bringing down the property value of the entire station. I'm surprised you can even afford the docking fees," Lerrence retorted, his tone practically dripping with money and privilege.

"I don't like this," Talen growled. His fingers flexed, claws extending and retracting. The crowd of spectators around the table took a collective step back.

"As the gentleman said, it's too late now. The bet is placed and the collateral certified. The only way to finish this is to win," Lerrence spoke with the confident tones of a male used to winning. Of course he was. He lived in the luxurious sky palaces above Corra, where the ultra-rich fled when ecological disaster struck their homeworld. They lived the literal high life in orbiting stations, indulging in every available vice while the less monied struggled on the surface.

Not that life on Corra proved to be a hardship. Talen had grown fond of the planet on the far edge of the galaxy. It was free from many of those pesky Interstellar Union rules and regulations, and the provinces had contained the mornclaw problem. Well, the civilized regions were secure from the monstrous creatures that wrecked the Corra ecosystem and slaughtered nearly half the planet's population. He was sure the money pit Quil gambled everything for was far from civilization and infested.

Judging by Lerrence's smug expression, of course it was. They really would be doing him a favor if they won the property.

"I need a drink," Talen growled, snagging a glass from a passing tray.

Lerrence rolled his eyes at the uncouth behavior and then

picked up his cards. Those very same cards would determine whether Talen rested his head in his familiar bunk that night or hustled to find a new berth. He had little but he had his own ship and a trade. He'd rather be in his bunk, reading, than scowling over Quil's shoulder.

Lerrence motioned to the dealer for another card and examined it with an impassive expression. Quil, however, practically shouted his distress with his flattened ears and twitching tail.

"You bet everything on a bad hand," Talen muttered. He didn't have to see the cards to know the truth.

"Not now, dear brother. I'm working," Quil hissed.

"You're losing." His frustration grew. With his jaw clench, he was surprised the entire room couldn't hear him grind his teeth.

Quil ignored his obvious agitation and motioned to the dealer.

"I won't let you ruin us," Talen said, grabbing Quil by the ear and yanking him to his feet. "We're leaving. Now!"

Large Tal males in expensive suits moved to block the door. If they had any loyalty to the planet of their shared origin, they gave no sign of it.

"No one leaves until we finish our game," Lerrence said.

Talen curled back his top lip in a hiss. He sized up the guards, believing he could take one, perhaps two. Larger than the males and with military training, he had an advantage, but if Lerrence alerted the station, soon every available pair of fists on the payroll would be involved, and that was a fight Talen could not win.

So he resorted to verbal fighting. "Typical. Rich Corravian sources his protection off-world. How much does he pay you to pretend you're not disgusted with him?" They gave no indication of hearing him, let alone of being affected by his barbed comments. He turned his ire to Lerrence. "And you! Fleecing my brother. You know he's terrible and you know our pockets are empty. How dare you accept such a bet? Is your pampered life so empty that you have to torture a stupid male for entertainment?"

"Stupid? Hey now," Quil said, taking offense.

Tough. Talen called his brother a lot worse.

Talen turned to Lerrence, knocking his tumbler of no doubt expensive alcohol into the male's lap. He jumped to his feet and a casino employee appeared out of nowhere with a towel. "Watch yourself! You damn hot-headed fool."

"And what happens when you take our home? You plan to make us beg? Grovel for your amusement?"

"You Tal are all alike," Lerrence sneered. "Happy to spend money like there's no tomorrow, full of growls and threats when it's time to pay the bill. Your kind is good for nothing but being hired muscle, and even then, I wouldn't put it past you to steal the silverware. Everyone knows the Tal are nothing but thieves."

Talen tossed a scandalized look to the two Tal males at the door. "You let him talk about your people like that?" A shifting of weight from foot to foot was the only indication of unease. "So, it's like that then," Talen said, disappointed that negative Tal stereotypes thrived in the modern world.

"You bore me," Lerrence said. With a flick of a finger, the nearest guard grabbed Talen and shoved him out the door.

"You think you're better than me! Because you have money and pedigree." Over the guard's shoulder, his brother gave a mournful shake of his head. Before he could continue his rant, the door slammed in his face.

Finally.

Talen ran a hand through his hair, unconcerned about making a mess of it. His hair refused to cooperate, always appeared tousled. He had started to wonder what he had to say or do to get thrown out of the private room. Smash furniture, perhaps. Marks like Lerrence usually had a pricklier disposition. The first insult, and they tossed Talen out on his tail. That was one advantage of size: no one wanted to see him angry.

He sauntered up to the nearest bar and ordered water. The next bit required a clear head.

He didn't know what Quil saw in Lerrence's parcel of Corra, but his brother wouldn't let an opportunity pass him by. They had encountered Lerrence before and knew enough about the male to know he played a decent hand but had a cocky attitude. Talen played a solid if unremarkable hand and won consistently enough to barely notice. That was the second advantage of size: no one ever suspected Talen of being more than dumb muscle.

Quil, however, was all flash. He lost in spectacular fashion, always paid his debt, and got invited to the exclusive tables. Once the marks—and to be honest, Quil always knew who could afford to lose the most—were well and truly comfortable, all but ignoring the poor sucker losing a fortune while gloating and congratulating themselves, Quil would place an impossible wager.

Why not take the fool's money? Or his ship? Or anything else he owns in the universe?

Quil won. He always won. Talen played the furious brother, upset at the gambling losses, and used his bulk to create a distraction. With attention diverted elsewhere, Quil cheated.

No one should be surprised, least of all the people at the table with Quil. They were all cheats. Stations like this one, Noxu, were tax dodges for the ultra-rich, so that was the first cheat there. The same tax-evading ultra-rich snobs avoided rebuilding their homeworld, instead chasing pleasures in a floating palace. Their lifestyles cost a fortune and only the smallest percentage ever funneled back to planetside. Moreover, Corra could not afford to police Noxu, instead relying on private security to keep the peace.

Stations like Noxu were fiefdoms, ruled by kings and aristocrats. There was no justice for the everyday person. Crimes committed by the wealthy were swept away but crimes against them—mostly theft—were pursued to the point of obsession. Stories of a maid caught with stolen jewels or a footman caught in bed with an heiress filled the news cycle.

Talen did not worry about Lerrence crying to the media once he realized he'd been conned. The brothers counted on embarrassment to keep him silent. Lerrence would be more likely to sic his private security on them. Talen's biggest worry was making it to the ship and warming up the engines for a quick exit.

He had a book, a murder mystery, waiting in his bunk. The story just got to the good part and he had his suspicions as to the identity of the murderer. The family had secrets and secrets always clawed their way out of darkness into the light.

He felt a heavy blow connect with his shoulder before that person hooked their arm into his elbow and took off at a run.

"What are you still doing here?" Quil's eyes had a manic gleam to them.

Talen didn't ask if there was trouble. The brothers wouldn't be running for any other reason. They dashed through the crowd, nimbly avoiding security by ducking behind a row of slot machines. The bright lights and constant noise provided enough cover for Talen to weave his way across the casino floor and reach the exit.

The concourse left them too open. Talen ducked into a service corridor that ran behind the shops and would bring them nearly to their ship.

"I never thought I'd be glad you memorized the station's layout," Quil said.

"Always have an exit strategy." Talen knew his elder

brother often acted first and worried about the consequences after, which was why he took it upon himself to over-prepare.

The ship's engines were already online when the brothers arrived. A four-armed copper-skinned male moved from the pilot's seat.

"You moved my settings," Talen complained, taking the chair from Charl. He disliked the distance of the chair from the console, as Charl always moved it back due to his freakishly long arms. He'd have to fiddle with the seat before it felt correct again.

"I did not," Charl said, dropping into the co-pilot's seat. As the ship's engineer, the male rarely sat in the cockpit, let alone the pilot's seat. "Security put out an alert for two Tal males, so I thought you'd appreciate a quick exit."

Talen grumbled, unwilling to admit the male was correct.

"The alert described the males as particularly handsome, yes? That's how you knew it was us," Quil said, taking the third seat. Technically, the seat was for the weapons specialist, but they rarely had reason to use the ship's weapons.

Charl snorted, two hands fastening the safety harness and the other two punching in a destination. "The usual?"

"Yes," Talen said at the exact moment his brother said *no*. "Let's get out of here first, before they lock the docking clamps." The engines whined and the ship slid gracefully away from the dock.

Then lurched to a stop.

"Too late," Charl said.

"Did the alert use our names? How did they identify us?" Talen spun his chair to face his brother. "You didn't use our real names, did you?"

"Of course I did. Couldn't have the deed made out to someone who doesn't exist."

"Quil," he growled in frustration. That was so typical of his brother.

"Relax. It's not like I used our real-real names."

His claws itched and burned, yearning to break free and dig into his stupid brother's stupid face. They couldn't afford to lose time fighting but it would only take a moment to scratch that cocky expression off Quil's face and make him bleed—

Quil seemed aware of Talen's mood and jumped up. "I'll fix it. Just be ready to fly."

Talen growled but turned back to the console. Using the monitor, he watched Quil opened the hatch, attach a safety tether and lean over the edge. "Be ready," Quil said over the ship's comm. Then Talen witnessed his brother take a drill to the tether and disable it in a highly illegal and destructive manner to the station's property.

"You're paying when the station sends the repair bill," Talen muttered into the mic.

"Go."

The ship pulled away. As it crossed the haze barrier that kept the atmosphere in, the hull sealed shut. The station sent several requests to return to dock and cut off the engine. Talen muted the comm.

"That's a violation of IU protocol," Charl said. They had served in the Interstellar Union Navy together and usually, Charl's instance to still live as if they were bound by IU regulations didn't bother Talen, but it rubbed him the wrong way today.

"Get off my tail."

"Don't snarl at me. I'm not the one who got caught cheating at cards."

Talen held his tongue. Charl tolerated Quil and his unorthodox recreational activities, but Talen knew his brother irritated his friend.

Good thing they spent so much time together in a tiny ship.

The males managed to avoid each other, despite the size of the ship. Charl spent most of his waking hours in engineering or maintaining the ship's systems. With the ship's age—decades beyond the time most vessels were put into retirement—the repairs were never-ending. Quil spent the majority of his time drumming up business to haul cargo and the occasional passenger. Cheating at cards was strictly recreational.

Quil's stunt today still confused him. He had no idea why Quil would take such a huge risk and use their actual names.

The wayward brother returned, tossing himself into a chair with a dramatic sigh. "Your distraction was flawless but apparently there was a camera just over my shoulder," Quil said.

Talen calmly set the destination, their usual retreat after a job, and then leaped from his seat toward Quil. He grabbed his brother by the throat, tail lashing viciously behind him. "What was that?"

Charl cleared his throat. "Right. I'll be down below, watching the engines make pretty colors. Try not to kill each other."

Quil tossed Talen a charming smile, the one he used to open doors, ease doubts, and convince people he was a harmless fool. "I know you're upset—"

"You used your real name. Of all the irresponsible, foolish risks to take, I don't understand. How could you be so selfish?"

"I can explain."

"Do more than explain." Talen's thoughts crowded with the worry that Quil's actions put their small family—technically his crew but in reality, his family—at risk. All they had in the universe was each other. How could he?

Quil's legal name, linked with a good image of him, could tie them to everything they left behind on Talmar. If that happened, they would need to do more than lie low for a few weeks at Curiosity Terminal. The station didn't verify ship information when it came to berth and manifest reporting was voluntary. It was the perfect place for those who played fast and loose with the law to pass the time. Outside of Interstellar Union space, warrants were rarely enforced, but the live-and-let-live attitude of the station management was no protection against a hungry contractor looking to collect a bounty.

"I'm tired," Quil said.

"Then take a fucking nap—"

"No, Talen, look at me. I. Am. Tired. Of this life. Of the ship. I can't do this anymore."

Talen looked at his elder brother, truly looked at him. Despite being younger, Talen had never been the little brother. He stood a good four inches taller than Quil and the years in the IU Navy put solid muscle on his broad frame. Quil could never be described as delicate, but he had a slender, runner's build. Quil enjoyed good food and wine, to the point of over-indulgence, but kept off the adverse effects with running. Every day, he ran on the treadmill in the makeshift gym in the cargo bay. He ran to the point where Talen heard the whirr of the machine as constant background noise, claiming it helped him think.

But dark circles hung under his eyes. He tossed smiles around with ease, but they didn't reach his eyes. Talen couldn't remember the last time Quil had genuinely smiled, or laughed, for that matter. Maybe that time they toured the royal gardens on Fremm, but that had been years ago.

"How long have you felt this way?"

Quil rolled a shoulder. "I'm not sure. It crept up on me. Besides, we have other factors to consider. You surely have noticed that life on the ship is growing harder for Bright—"

Talen's tail lashed with annoyance. Yes, the ship was designed for a younger person. Yes, their adoptive mother was advancing in age. Yes, the ladders used between the ship's levels were too much for her aging joints, effectively confining her to one level. "Then you want to sell this parcel of land and upgrade to a larger ship?"

Larger ships came with additional expenses. Their current crew of four lived comfortably—excluding the ladders and Bright's joints—on the ship. The size of their vessel was just large enough to go anywhere, even long hauls in deep space, and small enough to dock anywhere without racking up enormous fees.

"No, I want us to live there," Quil said.

"In a house?" Talen hadn't lived in a stationary building since before he joined the IU Navy. How could he sleep without the constant background noise of ship engines?

"Yes, a house. Many people live in houses. It's all the rage nowadays."

"Smartass," Talen grumbled.

"Imagine having a home and a mate," Quil said, sliding an arm over Talen's shoulder, like the male had no sense of self-preservation. "Imagine Bright sitting by the fire with a kit on her knee. Telling stories of Talmar."

"I didn't know you were the sentimental type," he said, shaking off his brother's arm. "Why not just purchase a house? Why this one in particular?"

"The moon violet."

A flower. Of course. Quil had an extensive botanical collection in his cabin and had annexed parts of the ship, turning it into a garden.

"You swindled a man's property away because of a flower?"

"It's a rare specimen only found in certain locations, including Lerrence's land. No one is preserving the habitat. No one even cares that the entire species could be lost."

"Then we'll go to the planet's surface and collect your specimens."

"No, that's not the point. That's not what I want." Quil ran a hand through his hair, ruining his perfect coif. "Don't make a decision right away. Let me show you the property."

He sat at the console. Half the screen went dark and images of a rundown house replaced navigation charts. Stone with a slate roof, Talen saw only an unending list of repairs and renovations. The house was a pit they would pour the remaining portion of their inheritance into. "Perhaps it looks better in person," Quil said.

CHAPTER 2

GEORGIA

Ms. Phillips,

Thank you for submitting your application for our rental property. Unfortunately, without solid credit history or current proof of income, we are unable to rent to you at this time.

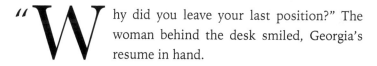

"hy did you leave your last position?" The woman behind the desk smiled, Georgia's resume in hand.

And the interview had been going so well until then.

Georgia sighed, digging down to find the strength and give a bland lie about wanting new challenges, or a position with room for growth. Whatever she did say, she absolutely could not, under any circumstances, tell the truth.

But why bother? The moment they checked her references, Kevin whispered poison in their ears and convinced them not to call her back for a second interview. That was the only reason she could think of to explain how she could have interviewed every day last week and not a single one considered hiring her. Georgia shared her theory with Freema last night and while her friend didn't outright call her paranoid, it was strongly implied.

"Well," Georgia said, "I felt a bit restricted in the last office. The company culture didn't agree with me." Great, that made her sound like a fussy diva. She'd have been better off with a wishy-washy response about wanting new challenges and growth.

"Really? I always found that company to be quite excellent. It's one of my favorite poaching grounds." The woman made a note at the bottom of Georgia's resume. The frown told her that the interview was all but finished.

"Does this company allow supervisors to have personal relationships with their subordinates? No? That seems wise, because I dated my direct supervisor, we lived together, and found him screwing the intern in our bed," Georgia said, having nothing to lose. "I'm sure you can imagine why I felt I couldn't continue to work in that type of environment." She gathered her bag and stood. "Thank you for your time. I completely understand if you go in a different direction."

The non-drama llama direction. Shit, even she wouldn't hire herself after that.

Five minutes later, the dark gray sky finally dumped the rain it had promised all morning. Lacking an umbrella—of course—Georgia ducked into a coffee shop. The cheery holiday music playing did not match her mood. She scraped together enough coins from the bottom of her bag for a small caramel latte and dumped two packets of sugar into the brew. Then, deciding that her miserable day deserved something nice, she added two more packets to her bomb of sugar and caffeine.

Despite the disastrous interview, she left with her head held high. Of course, pride didn't put money in the bank, and her account felt empty.

For the last month, she'd been living on Freema's couch. She honestly had expected to find something—anything—by now. Her bestie's one-bedroom apartment wasn't made for two people and they were wearing on each other's nerves. Freema worked odd hours at the hospital thanks to her med school residency. She'd come in at two in the morning, starving, and make a racket in the kitchen.

Georgia didn't feel as if she could complain about her interrupted sleep when she ate Freema's food, used her hot water, and couldn't contribute to the bills. She did keep the place tidy and tried to do as much of the cooking as possible, avoiding complete mooch-hood. Still, they were two adults used to having their own space. Georgia seriously considered taking what remained of her savings and finding her own place, but what she could afford terrified her, and she wasn't that desperate. Yet.

The last month burned through her modest savings with one emergency after another. First, she woke up one rainy morning to find four flat tires on her car. A new set put a nice dent in her account, but then the battery went, followed by the alternator. Fixing the car was non-negotiable. How could she get a job if she couldn't get to job interviews?

While the car was in the shop, she had to take the bus. While she checked the phone for directions, someone bumped into her and the phone took a dive into a puddle, because it was raining—of course it was. The phone didn't recover from its brief nautical excursion and even the cheapest replacement set her back a bit, but she needed a phone for the job hunt.

And the job hunt... Yeah. She fucked up today but as long as they kept checking her references, and Kevin badmouthed her, she'd never find a job. Leaving the job off her resume made a suspicious four-year gap. Maybe she could find someone else at the company to list as her supervisor? No, if she planned to doctor her resume, she should at least use Freema, who would sing her praises.

Had it gotten that bad? Having her best friend pretend to be her boss just to get a job, any job.

Depressed at the thought, she checked her messages. A response from Celestial Mates sat at the top of her inbox.

She remembered signing up for the dating app. The next morning, hungover, she canceled her account. At least she thought she did. There was probably a box she didn't check or a button she forgot to press. The last thing she needed was dating drama. Kevin embarrassed her more than broke her heart, letting herself be played like that, but the idea of moving on made her nervous.

She'd just send a quick reply and set Celestial Mates straight—

A Tal male, with light amber complexion with darker stripes, grinned up at her. He had fine features, dark eyes framed with dark lashes, and russet hair that sat in an unruly mop on his head. Those eyes though, they weren't quite human, and she felt as if he stared out of the screen directly at her.

Georgia blushed. He had to be the single most beautiful man she'd ever seen.

Tranquility Achaval.

This guy needed a mail order wife? Really? She felt confident that he could get a date easily.

She read the brief bio, which explained that he lived on Corra, a planet on the edge of nowhere, ran a bed and breakfast, and wanted an heir. Huh. So there weren't any women on Corra? Or no women there were willing to make babies with him? Maybe he just had a thing for humans.

She scrolled back up to his image, trying to discern why a striking man such as him needed a matchmaking service. The photo told her nothing. Rereading the bio told her nothing more than he lived on a remote planet, ran a bed and breakfast, and wanted a family.

Isn't that what she wanted? A family with a responsible partner? She could picture an idyllic life in a B&B, chatting with guests, and chasing after the little ones.

That sounded good, actually.

She went back to the photo. He had a charming smile and Georgia felt the desire to get to know him better, but

Celestial Mates wasn't a dating app. There was no casual dating or even a get-to-know-you. She had to make a serious commitment, a leap of faith.

The smart thing to do would be to delete the message and forget the beautiful alien man with a charming smile.

The rain showed no signs of letting up. She should get home now before traffic turned into a nightmare. It rained sparingly in Southern California but when it did, the city came to halt. She rushed out, oblivious to the rain. It drenched her with a cold that settled into her bones. Once in the car, she shivered and rubbed her hands together until the heater finally warmed the space.

Her options were running out and she didn't know how much longer she could abuse Freema's hospitality. Going off to marry a stranger on the far side of the galaxy seemed like overkill but, honestly, why not? Her evil ex would continue to torpedo her job prospects. Her bank account had hunger pains it was so empty.

But Freema…

Georgia had no family to speak of, but she had an amazing and supportive friend. Then again, Freema had always talked about going to an off-world colony after she finished her residency. A lot of colonial governments paid bonuses for skilled professionals to emigrate, especially doctors.

All that was a year away, but Georgia didn't think Freema would change her mind. She talked about it too often.

Her gut said to take a chance on the Celestial Mates

match, her perfect match, but her gut also thought moving in with her boyfriend and taking a job at his company was a grand idea. She couldn't trust her gut.

Back at the apartment, she made a lasagna from scratch and waited for Freema to come home.

"Something smells amazing," her friend said, dropping her rain-soaked coat at the door.

Georgia went to the kitchen and served up two helpings. She must not have looked the part of a happy homemaker because Freema laid a hand on her wrist. "What's wrong? Is it the job hunt? Don't worry. You can stay here as long as you need, roomie. Especially if you keep making me lasagna," Freema said.

"I need to pick your brain."

"Well, that sounds ominous."

Georgia pulled out her phone. She explained the message from the agency and all the reasons to take a chance.

"This is him?" Freema grabbed the phone and examined Tranquility's photo. "He's almost too pretty."

"I know, right? I keep wondering what the catch is."

Freema stared at the photo. "Too lazy to date or too busy. I say go for it."

"For a guy who's too lazy or too busy to date?"

"He wants a family and he's upfront about it. Besides, if it doesn't work, get a divorce and come live with me."

"But you won't be here by then," Georgia said. Corra was

far away, like a six-month journey away. By the time she got there, Freema would already have her bags packed. Her residency ended in eight months and she'd been shopping around offers for placement on a colony. A decade practicing medicine on a colony meant total debt forgiveness. Freema had been talking about that plan for years, since their freshman year of college.

"So come with me," Freema said with a shrug. "You can be my office manager."

Georgia looked at Tranquility's photo again, willing it to whisper all his secrets and tell her what to do. "I've never had such a difficult time making a decision."

"It's a big one."

"I want to say yes. I feel like I need a fresh start, but I'm scared."

"You'd be silly not to be a little scared," Freema agreed.

She took a deep breath. She wanted a family but even if the worst happened and she lost her fertility to cancer, there was adoption. Her kids didn't have to have her DNA; she'd love them with her whole heart. Could she love Tranquility? Celestial Mates thought so.

Saying yes was a risk but it felt like the right move. Plus, she had a backup plan. If the match didn't work out, she'd go to Freema.

"Any idea where you're headed?" she asked Freema.

"I got a few offers, but I haven't agreed to anything yet." Freema finished the last of her lasagna and reached for

Georgia's hand. "It's going to work out. I have a good feeling about this."

"Okay," she said, all the breath leaving her body in a rush. "Okay. I want to do it."

Talen

WELCOME to your new home on Corra!

Our beautiful homeworld offers limitless opportunities for the industrious immigrant.

- Corra Immigration Affairs

THE PROPERTY DID NOT APPEAR MORE attractive in person. The honey stones glowed in the morning light, which was about the only appealing feature Talen could find. When he looked at the sprawling house—more a manor, really—the inevitable and enormous heating bill, the roof in desperate need of repair, and a hundred fucking broken windows, crowded his imagination.

Quil bounded across the lawn in long strides, toward the tumbledown building, bubbling over with excitement.

In the three weeks since winning the property from Lerrence, they kept a low profile in the Terminal. Quil only played fair at cards, no hustling, Charl took the time to install necessary upgrades to the ship, and Talen splurged and booked a room for Bright. As much as he hated to admit it, Quil had been correct. Climbing up and down the ladder in the ship was too much for Bright's aging hips and knees. If they were stuck at the station for weeks, she should at least be able to go out and enjoy all the station offered, rather than be confined to the ship.

Her silvery hair caught the morning sunlight and Talen hadn't noticed how gray she had become. In his mind, she still towered over him with infinite strength and even more patience. Had she always been so small and slender? When had the warm amber of her complexion and hair faded to gray?

She hobbled, the arthritis in her hips and knees hindering movement. Talen held out an arm to her as they traversed the uneven ground. Bright was the first name he ever spoke and her presence formed his earlier memories. He had only a vague impression of his parents. When he thought of his mother, he thought of Bright. There was nothing he wouldn't do for her if she asked.

How long had the climbing the ladder in the ship been painful for her? She fell six months back and badly bruised her knees and hips. Luckily, she suffered no fractures. Even as Talen carried her up and down as needed, she never complained about the unfriendly accessibility of the ship. That fall had to have been the genesis of Quil's scheme.

Quil had been correct to say that living planetside would be easier for her and it rankled him that Quil saw it first. Talen had never been one to anticipate the needs or wants of another. He was more the type who, once he had been steered toward a problem, threw himself at it with a single-minded focus until he fixed the issue, be it a faulty engine, a face that needed to be punched, or a sprawling house with broken windows.

Damn Quil.

The inside of the house proved the building to be in better condition than Talen feared. The house had not been abruptly abandoned, but closed, as if the original owners planned to return. Heavy canvas tarps protected furniture from dust and falling plaster. Water damage, vermin, and simple age damaged the majority of furnishings in the house, but he felt some could be salvaged. Delicate porcelain dishes sat stacked in cupboards, coated with a thick layer of grime but in otherwise perfect condition.

Paint peeled away from the plaster walls. A few sections were lost to moisture and mold and needed to be removed. Vermin lived in the walls. Talen could hear their little claws scrabbling about.

Portions of the floor buckled from water damage, but those boards could be replaced. The subflooring felt solid. He inspected the floor joists in the lower levels and found them to be sound.

Quil rushed them through the house, throwing open the doors to reveal room after room filled with moldering old furniture. Leaves, dirt, and other debris scattered across the floor. Animals had nested in a few closets, leaving behind bones and other filth.

The sound of claws in the walls drew Talen back. He assumed it was vermin but it could be mornclaws. The aggressive pests arrived on Corra—no one knew how but speculated that a clutch of eggs arrived with a cargo vessel —and devastated the Corravian environment. They had no natural predators, bred quickly, ate almost any animal, and slaughtered huge portions of the population.

No. Those did not nest in houses. They buried their eggs in grassy fields, the more vegetation the better.

"Vermin. The place requires an exterminator," Talen said, wondering how much of the dirt on the floor was scat and if he could slip on gloves and a mask without his brother mocking him. Let Quil laugh. He had never been bitten and suffered rat-bite fever or had to recuperate in an understaffed and overcrowded naval hospital.

"We'll get a *wuap*. They make good hunters," Quil said.

The house had enough room for them all, more than enough. They could each have their own suite of rooms and still be able to comfortably put up a dozen guests and a herd of vermin-hunting *wuaps*. Talen had no idea why they needed so much space. He had lived the last decade of his life with all his possessions fitting into a duffel bag. What would he do with a suite of rooms? All he required was a bed and a footlocker.

Quil's excitement grew as they ventured further into the house, but the repair costs kept racking up higher and higher in Talen's mind.

"It's not perfect, I know, but can't you see the potential?" Quil said, standing in what had once been a library

Windows lined the far wall. Unfortunately, storm damage had broken half the windows. The library overlooked what had once been a charming garden but was now little more than an overgrown wilderness. Uncontrolled vines, heavy with perfume, pressed right against the glass and broke through into the room in several places. Sunlight filtered through the greenery, flooding the space with a soft light.

The room hurt Talen's soul. Soggy books sat on the shelves, swollen and smelling of mold. A few books had obviously been chewed on by vermin. He couldn't imagine that the remaining books were rare or valuable. The library had obviously built by someone who loved books and Talen wanted to believe that they took the most precious books with them when they abandoned the property. Still, most books were digital and physical copies grew scarce. How could they just leave all those books to rot?

The stairs to the upper level of the library looked like they would crumble to dust with the slightest bit of weight. Talen squinted, trying to see into the shadows of the upper level. Shelving lined the walls and he could see the binding of several books.

He needed to save the books that could be salvaged. The rank stink of the room made him sneeze but he could never forget the scent. It would haunt him.

Damn Quil for knowing exactly how to manipulate him.

Mentally, he already segregated the books into various categories: acceptable, damaged but salvageable, and those without hope of saving. Yeah, Quil knew all his buttons.

The outdated kitchen was fully furnished. Charl pulled

out a set of tools—from where, Talen had no idea—and got the stove in working order.

Finally, they entered what had been the conservatory and Talen understood. Barely visible, black and white tiles peeked out from under the layer of dirt that carpeted the room. Half of the glass panes had been broken, exposing the room to the elements, and the surviving plant grew in a riot of greenery. A thick vine twined around the exposed skeleton of the windowpanes, up and over like a canopy, and exploded in pale violet blossoms. The floral scent overpowered the space, mixing with the pungent aroma of soil and decaying leaves.

Quil ignored the show stopping blossoms and fell to his knees in front of a low growing plant with broad silvery-green leaves. "Oh, look at you lovelies—"

"You planned this whole thing," Talen said. They had targeted Lerrence, not out of a sense to right a wrong or even to liberate some credit from the arrogant man, and practically stole the man's property because Quil wanted a plant.

"The moon violet, still thriving. You're gorgeous. Yes, you are," Quil said to the plant, reverently stroking the leaves.

"I wish someone would look at me the way he's looking at that plant," Charl said, sharing a sentiment disturbingly close to Talen's own thoughts.

Bright found a stone bench, brushing off the surface before lowering herself with a sigh. The light pooled at her feet and the air warmed with the sun overhead. "How much work is it to get this place habitable?" she asked.

"It's habitable now," Quil said, rising to his feet.

"If you don't mind a lack of heat and running water," Charl said. "I suppose we could live on the ship until I got the basics working. The roof seems solid enough, but we might have some surprises the next time it storms. Let me take another look at the boiler in the basement."

Talen grabbed Quil by the elbow and pulled the male to the side. "All this for a plant?"

His brother yanked his arm away. "Not just any plant, the moon violet. Very rare and only found in a handful of locations."

"And here."

"Yes! Aren't they beautiful? They blossom under the moonlight, you know. The soil has to be just right. The fact that they've survive here, abandoned, is miraculous. This house is a miracle."

"This house is a money pit," Talen said.

"This house is our future."

Talen disagreed strongly but Quil kept talking. "I know we'll sink most of our money into repairs."

"Our inheritance." The compensation they received from a second cousin for their parent's stolen estate and bank accounts. The brothers went missing after their parent's assassination and were presumed dead. After a decade, they had been legally declared dead and a cousin inherited what should have been Quil's. Talen didn't particularly miss having a house and land, or a title, but he knew it bothered Quil, who had always loved the gardens.

Had the political climate allowed for Quil to inherit, rather than be smuggled off-planet to save his life, he would have made a fine lord of the manor.

Of course, the brothers weren't dead, and the cousin's lawyers found them in due course. The brother received a payout for signing an agreement to never return to Talmar and never use their birth names. Some males might be disturbed by turning their backs on their heritage, but it was all ancient history to Talen. The planet of his birth had treated his family cruelly and he felt no great love for Talmar.

"Yes, and half that money is mine. I let you buy the ship," Quil said. "We'll do what we need to get this place presentable, then offer rooms as a bed and breakfast. We won't be able to restore all the rooms at first, so we'll have to do it as we go. Did you know there's a hot spring somewhere on the grounds? Guests will like that."

"Wait, a bed and breakfast? You're joking." Not once, in all the years, had his brother ever expressed an interest in playing host. Gambler and gardener, yes, but not a host at a B&B. "You don't have the temperament for it," Talen said.

"*You* don't." Quil rested a hand on his chest and said with all sincerity, "I am charming as fuck."

Talen huffed, unmoved by his brother's dramatics.

Quil continued, "But I know what you're saying. I'm going

to be too busy in here. I think it's too late to plant for the spring, but I'd like to see what the grounds look like in the summer, anyway, before I plant."

"You're not listening to me at all." Frustration edged into his voice.

"No, you're not listening to me," Quil said, finally turning his full attention to Talen. "I want this. When you came back from the Navy, you weren't yourself."

"I was—"

"I know, I know, and I don't blame you. The only thing that made you seem half-alive was leaving port. Always had to be moving, could never let the ground grow cold under your feet, so I went with that. We made a tidy profit, had a few laughs, and that was good enough for a time."

"Half-alive? Was I that bad off?" Talen knew his behavior after being discharged had not been optimal, but he thought he was better off than half-alive. It was just... he couldn't pin it down, exactly. The universe was vast and he wanted to see as much as possible. Staying in one place made him restless. Anxious. If too much time passed, he found himself looking over his shoulder, which was unfounded and paranoid, adding to his frustration. Better to move on and not think too hard on it.

"So, we did your thing, and it had some fun, but I'm tired. I told you the truth about that, and Bright is getting older," Quil said.

"I know." He noticed how she climbed the stairs slowly

and needed to rest frequently. "But you think this big house is the solution to that? She'll wear herself ragged trying to run the house."

"Then we'll hire help. A place this size needs staff."

"And Charl? You plan to give him a recommendation and drop him off at the next port?"

"He's family and welcome to stay. This place has more than enough projects to keep the cranky bastard entertained."

"You want to demote our engineer to a handyman?"

"Estate manager, then. It's a promotion. What do you think?" Quil spread his arms wide and grinned, surrounded by the chaotic greenery of the conservatory. His tail swayed from side to side, pleased with himself.

Bright enjoyed the sunshine and the flowers. Charl was having the time of his life grubbing around, inspecting the inner workings of the house. Talen had lost the fight. This ridiculous scheme proved good for his family.

"Is this what you truly want?"

A smile tugged at his brother's lips, a true smile and not the charming mask he slipped on. "Yes, very much, but what do *you* want, Talen? And do you think you can find it here?"

Talen took a long moment to consider. He joined the IU Navy to see the universe. But the only locations he ever saw were the bowels of an interstellar cruiser or a military base. The only exotic location he ever experienced was a steaming jungle full of mud and vermin.

He had also wanted to help civilians but found the vague assistance that the military delivered to be unsatisfying. They protected ships in the depths of space from pirates, yes, and had deployed to conflict areas, but Talen never felt the situation improved for all the muscle and ballistics the military employed.

"I want to help people," he answered. "How can I do that here?"

Quil scratched behind one ear. "Why do you have to be so noble? It's damn inconvenient."

Talen tilted his head back and squinted in the sunlight that filtered through the dirty glass and the floral canopy. He had spent so much of his life off-planet, be it on ships or stations. Living on the ground, under an open sky, without the constant background hum of engines and circulated air, made him feel exposed.

His mother's last words came to him. Take care of each other. They were all they had in the universe.

Quil could be such a manipulative bastard.

"Why couldn't you just discuss this with me ahead of time?"

"I've been telling you my plan for ages, but you never listened," his brother said.

Had he failed to notice? Was he too wrapped up in himself to hear what his brother had been trying to tell him?

Probably. Selfishness and single-minded determination were flaws they shared.

He could do this, indulge Quil if that's what his brother wanted. Having a home with a mate and kits still felt restrictive but he could be an uncle. He'd like that very much. Plus, it would take years to fill that library. His meager collection would fill a shelf, maybe two. The anticipation of hunting for books, talking with other collectors, lazy evenings reading in a comfortable chair—he selfishly wanted that.

"Three years is a good run," Talen said. "We've been lucky, but our luck would run out sooner or later."

"I knew you were a reasonable male under all the huffing and snarling," Quil said, slapping Talen on the back.

Talen gave a low warning growl, ears twitching like an irritated male who knew he was about to be bankrupt. "I don't have the temperament to be a host and you're already obsessed with your violets."

"Moon violet, and yes, that's why I already signed up with Celestial Mates. I thought a human female would be good. Nothing says you have a successful business like a human. Stars know they're not much good for anything but looking pretty. And the best part is that my new wife is already on her way."

CHAPTER 3

GEORGIA

Tranquility,

Hello! I'm Georgia, your match from Celestial Mates. Writing this feels super awkward but I wanted to take the opportunity for us to get to know each other. After a few medical appointments, vaccinations, and some paperwork, I'll be on a ship headed to Corra in three weeks.

So, five things about me.

1. My perfect date night is watching a film and staying in.

2. My favorite color is blue.

3. I'd tell you my favorite book, but I can't pick. I've got a top ten, though.

4. Some people try to call me Georgie, but I do prefer to be called Georgia. Do you prefer your full name, or do you have a nickname?

5. I'm grumpy in the morning before I've had my coffee. I'm so not a morning person.

Care to share five things I should know about you?

—Georgia

I t took six weeks from signing the contract to setting foot on a ship. First, she had to attend mandatory counseling to "identify coping strategies when making life-changing decisions." Basically, the agency needed to know if she was crazy. Medical exams were scheduled and she had a weekly appointment for vaccines. Not fun but better than getting the Dagoba Flu or bleeding from her eyes. No joke. Eyeballs. Bleeding.

Yeah, the agency made her watch a very explicit video about alien viruses and bacteria. She'd take the needle jabs and feeling lousy for a day or two over bleeding from places not meant to bleed, thank you very much.

Between medical appointments, she had to sit through training modules about the alien cultures she'd encounter at the end of her journey. The computer tracked eye movement, so it knew when she failed to read or pay adequate attention to the video. Nothing like having the machine snitch on her. At least there wouldn't be a quiz at the end.

Through it all, the one thing that made it tolerable was knowing that Tranquility went through the same counseling, medical exams, and education modules. The agency guaranteed that he would not welcome a disease-ridden lunatic into his home, and she had the reassurance she wouldn't be stranded on a planet, alone with an abusive germ factory.

The moment the shuttle left Earth's orbit and she felt the release of gravity's grip; she knew every hoop the agency made her jump through was worth the trouble. This was everything she wanted.

Talen

THE LEVEL of satisfaction Talen gained from working on the house surprised him. He never thought of himself as mechanically inclined—that's why he hired Charl—but he couldn't deny the warm pleasure of having tangible results at the end of the day. His body ached. Life in the military shaped his body for a specific purpose. Manual labor used him in new ways, breaking his body down and reshaping it.

Each night, he soaked in a cool bath—the hot water boiler proved unreliable—and slept harder than he had in years, since basic training. Each morning, he got up and did it again, working through the heat of the day.

The enormous scale of the renovations the house required weighed on him. The house was simply too big for four people and they could not, without blowing through their entire budget in an instant, renovate the entire property. They had to choose, which Quil resisted but Talen enforced. Quil's conservatory sat at the top of the project list, but it was not more important than a new roof, working plumbing, safe-to-operate appliances, and vermin-free rooms.

Talen and Charl started by cleaning out the section of the house they planned to live in. With the debris and vermin eradicated, they tackled the ancient plumbing. The house had clean water, thanks to a natural spring, but it also had leaks.

Charl understood how the guts of a house worked and spotted problem areas before they became disasters. Hot water remained a luxury with the unreliable boiler that needed to be replaced twenty years ago. In a water-damaged ledger, Quil found a reference to a hot spring and grotto on the grounds, but he had yet to locate it.

Quil's conservatory required special high-strength, impact-resistant material for the glass panes, which ate a considerable chunk of their savings. Considering the wind speeds in the storms that Corra experienced, they would forever be replacing broken glass. It was smarter and more frugal in the long run to buy the durable material, regardless of expense.

The wrought-iron frame of the conservatory had badly rusted and needed to be replaced. For one harrowing day, the entire structure swayed in the wind and Talen thought it would collapse. Fortunately, the glass panes added necessary stability and they avoided disaster.

They used the same material for the windows in the library. Talen packed away the contents and sent them away to be restored, if possible. His gut told him that most of the books were beyond saving, but he let the professionals make that call. Every single book went, no matter how swollen with water or chewed by vermin.

Talen sold the ship. Paying for docking fees at a station seemed ludicrous; it was better to sell and sink that money into the house. Surprisingly, he didn't miss the ship. He missed the noise of the engines and the rattle of the air vents, but he didn't miss stooping for the low doorways, squeezing into the tiny cleansing stalls, or rationing water. He had lived in the ship since leaving the Navy, but it wasn't his home.

Quil, Bright, and even Charl were his home.

He had not lived on a planet for years.

After the first week, he felt the itch to leave. As a kit, they never stayed in one location for long, always one step ahead of those who might want to do them harm. As time passed, when they had not been murdered in their bed, the sense of urgency faded but they still continued the pattern of never staying in one place for long. He had never questioned that urge before.

Quil had arrived at the need for a planetside house in a roundabout way, but he had been correct. The house was what their little family needed. Talen found he took an inordinate amount of pride in making the building habitable for his family. Under an inch-thick layer of dirt in the foyer, he discovered a mosaic floor with dark navy stars embedded in a creamy field, which reflected the vaulted ceiling of navy with painted gold stars. He enjoyed uncovering the house's secret treasures.

The roof, though, was a special kind of hell. Badly damaged, little could be salvaged of the traditional slate tiles. Whole sections of the roof had rotted away. If Talen did not step carefully, he could put a foot through it. Steeply pitched, the roof required athleticism and an unfailing sense of balance. Morning dew made the tiles slippery and treacherous but after a day of soaking up the heat of the sun, the tiles were hotter than a supernova.

Talen mopped his brow with a cloth. The summer sun beat down and the roof offered no shade. "I hate this roof."

"You'll like not having the rain on your head," Charl replied.

They had been lucky with a lack of summer storms, but their luck could not hold. One day, a storm would roll over the horizon, steal the sun for days, and bring down a fury of hail and cold rain. Talen and Charl worked day in and day out on the massive structure. The project would have been finished by now if the roof had a uniform design. Each section was unique, and each gable had its own measurements. Each new area required measuring and custom cutting tiles to fit.

"If we were smart, we could have just put on a flat roof and be down with it," Talen muttered.

Charl sat down next to Talen and handed him a cold bottle of water. "I remember someone insisting on traditional aesthetics."

"That someone was an idiot," Talen said.

"That was you, yes?"

Talen growled, ignoring his friend. Charl chuckled into his bottle. He had insisted on replicating the original roof out of a misguided idea that if they were going to do something, they would do it properly. He had been so naive then, unaware of how much a complete pain-in-the-ass working with the tile would be.

"Next roof," he said, "is tar paper."

"This roof will last a hundred years, so I don't think it'll be your problem," Charl said.

"So practical. I knew there was a reason I liked you." Talen stretched out on the roof, letting the heat of the tiles soak into his tired muscles. That morning, Quil had left on a supply run while they used the last of the boxes of tiles. Talen and Charl had done as much as they could until Quil returned. He should climb down, clean up, and see if Bright needed any assistance, but his bones did not want to move.

His stomach decided for him and rumbled.

After stowing away the tools, he took a frigid shower and followed an enticing aroma into the kitchen. Bright set a plate of sautéed vegetables in a creamy yogurt sauce over rice in front of him. The meal was too heavy for the summer heat, but Talen scraped his plate clean, using thick slices of bread to gather up the last bits of sauce.

"Don't eat too much. You'll make yourself ill in this heat, Talent," Bright cautioned.

"Yeah, Talent," Charl added, barely pausing as he shoveled food in his maw.

"What about Charl? He ate twice as much," Talen complained in a masculine and not childish at all tone.

"If I get sick, I'll just use my other stomach."

"You're making that up."

Charl shrugged, his massive shoulders heaving. "Am I?"

"How many stomachs do you have then?" Talen challenged. Charl forever made outlandish claims about his innate Gyer abilities. True, the male had remarkable hand-eye coordination. He'd need to with four hands, but a fair majority of the boasting was just a male stroking his own ego.

"Three. One for everyday consumption, one for toxins and poisons, and another for dessert."

See? He couldn't expect Talen to take him seriously.

"Three? Is that where you put all my cooking?" Bright poked Charl in the stomach but the large male laughed. "Now get out of my kitchen. Go on."

"Yes, *Talent*, back to work," Charl said in a sing-song voice.

Talen growled a warning but Charl ignored him, as always. He knew he behaved like a whining kit, but he loathed being called Talent because it was a stupid name. Only Bright called him that and he could not correct her without a lecture about how she smuggled him and Quil off Talmar at great personal risk and raised them as her own, with no money and no resources.

His name was Talen and he had gone by that moniker for years. It sounded like another word for claws and that suited him just fine. *Talent*, however, as a name, was remarkably uninspired.

Quil, short for Tranquility, was the epitome of 'cranky baby christened by exhausted parents.' The name reflected his parents' mindset at the time and their desperate prayer for a bit of rest. What did his parents hope to gain with talent? That their youngest son would excel at something, but they didn't particularly care what? Talent was a placeholder name, a kit's name that no grown male should carry.

As an adolescent, he intended to change it. Every day was a new name, a new identity, but nothing suited him. Talent, as much as he loathed it, was one of the few remaining gifts from his parents and he found himself reluctant to part with the moniker.

His feelings were complicated and refusing to look closely at them did not make him an overgrown kit. He was a busy male with no time for navel-gazing. Quil could mope about their lost family and childhood; Talen had work to do.

He and Charl prepped the hallway for painting as they were stalled on the roof until Quil returned with supplies. Charl used his many hands to fill in any holes in plasters and sand the surface smooth.

The sun eased closer to the horizon and the shadows moved across the floor. Quil had been gone too long for a simple run into town and that made Talen nervous. The nearest town, Drac, was mid-sized and had no casino or gambling hall to lure Quil into temptation.

But it did have several bars.

Fuck.

Quil had to be at a card table, fleecing the locals. Talen knew it in his bones. They didn't need that kind of trouble. If Quil's starry-eyed notion of a bed and breakfast was to ever turn a profit, they could not afford to turn the local population against them. They no longer had the option of hopping in their ship and sailing away to another port.

Fucking hell. Could Quil ever think of anyone but himself? How could he be so selfish? Then, with dread tugging on his tail, how could he have let Quil go into town on his own? He knew better.

Talen needed to find Quil. He needed to get this situation under control. For one day, just one day, Talen would like his older brother to behave like a grown-ass male and not require constant supervision.

At last, just as they finished for the day, a vehicle arrived.

Back before dinner, he couldn't have possibly gotten into too much trouble.

Talen ambled toward the vehicle, ready to unload the cargo.

Quil stood proud, the last rays of the summer sun casting a golden glow over him. Talen noticed what he had on his arm.

Double fuck and all the trouble in the galaxy.

"What did you do?"

. . .

Georgia

TRANQUILITY,

Tomorrow's the big day! I don't think I'll be able to sleep tonight.
—Georgia

THE SHUTTLE LANDED on a raked gravel drive. The hatch opened and fresh air flooded the cabin. She breathed deep, enjoying how the scent of fresh-cut lawn overpowered the oil and engine aroma of the shuttle. Her day had started early with her ship landing before dawn. With hours to wait until she caught a connecting shuttle, she wandered the spaceport, choking on fumes and the unique scent of stale coffee and unwashed travelers.

She was tired down to her bones and nervous. She wrote faithfully to Tranquility, hoping to develop some type of relationship before they met face-to-face. Six months was a long time to travel, but her actual time spent aboard ships was only half that. The other half of the journey had been spent waiting at stations and ports to catch a connecting ship. She spent nine days at Aldrin One, which was technically still in Earth's territory.

Fortunately, she had no shortage of interesting things to see or food to try. Once she made it on board, entertainment options were limited, but she filled her tablet with books and movies.

Unfortunately, somewhere along the way, she picked up a bug that morphed into an upper respiratory infection. She suffered for days in her cabin, congested and coughing, reluctant to see the ship's medic. They weren't human and the captain might want to ditch her at the nearest port like she carried a plague instead of the common cold. Once she put on her big girl panties and visited the medic, a course of antibiotics sorted her out.

The agency covered the cost of the trip—which explained why it was so slow with so many gaps in connections—and allowed a daily stipend. Her messages were filled with photos of the new and weird surroundings and short little anecdotes about the joys of traveling.

Tranquility replied initially but his responses slowed to an eventual nothing. She worried that he changed his mind or if he suffered an accident. He would have sent a message, something, even if only a brief, "In the hospital."

If he was able to send a message. Corra was a dangerous planet. He could have passed away and no one thought to tell her.

The dark thought spoiled her mood. Was he waiting for her? Or would she arrive and find herself a widow?

Freema, however, kept up her correspondence. Each day had a new message, even if it was only a brief, "I miss you." Near the end of her residency, Freema often repeated that when she accepted a post on a colony, there would always be a place for Georgia.

Having a fallback plan helped to calm her nerves. If it didn't work out, if she couldn't get along with Tranquility or he was deceased, then she'd lick her wounds, go live with Freema, and become one of many human colonists seeding the stars.

No, she scolded herself. She wouldn't start this new chapter of her life with one foot already out the door. She made a commitment and would see it through.

Her journey was at an end. Just outside the shuttle, her future waited.

She blinked in the afternoon sunlight. Cold air braced against her exposed skin. Winter firmly had its grip on this part of Corra and all her winter gear was packed away. The climate on ships and stations had been strictly controlled, and maybe even a little on the cool side, but she had never needed anything more than a cardigan or light jacket.

The house stole her attention and she forgot all about the cold. Constructed on honey-colored stones, it stood warm and glowing in the sunlight. The doors and windows were semi-circles, a traditional Corravian style she recognized from her reading. Half of the windows were boarded up; the wood painted beige to blend with the stones. The house was massive. Not a castle, not by a long shot, but much grander than any place she had ever rested her head. Despite this, the house still held a warm and inviting air.

The door opened and Georgia's body snapped to attention, exhaustion vanishing. A coppery bald head peeked out before vanishing again. Before she had a chance to worry that Tranquility forgot about her arrival, the door opened again, and a grinning Tal male strode forward.

With an easygoing smile on his face, she recognized him immediately. Tranquility. He hadn't forgotten after all.

He held out his arms like he greeted an old friend. Georgia dropped her duffel bag to the ground, ready to run forward and embrace, just like in the movies.

A woman with vibrant chestnut hair styled in loose, perfectly placed curls, joined Tranquility and wrapped her arms around his waist. She stretched up on her tiptoes and placed a kiss on his jaw. The message was clear as she marked her territory. "Who's this, honey bear?"

CHAPTER 4

GEORGIA

Freema,

That offer still good?

-G

The woman's smile hit her as hard as a punch to the gut. She was stunning, Georgia thought, like a slimmer, more glamorous version of herself.

Somehow, while Georgia tried to process the situation, more people joined them. The shuttle pilot unloaded the last of her bags and shoved a tablet toward her for her signature. She took the pen but didn't sign. Not yet.

"Georgia! At last!" Tranquility's smile didn't budge but now, all too late, she realized it did not reach his eyes.

Feeling disconnected from her body, the confusion of

several people talking all at once washed over her but did not penetrate the fog in her mind.

Abandoned again. Like always.

Vicious doubt clawed at her, whispering all her worst fears. *Replaced, again.*

"What's going on?" she said, finding her voice at last.

"Yeah, honey bear, what's going on? Who is she?" The woman pressed herself closer to Tranquility.

"Yeah, honey bear," another Tal male said, his voice mocking. He folded his arms over his broad chest and frowned. He shared more than a passing resemblance to Georgia's match. This had to be the brother, Talent. He gave his brother such a scornful look that Georgia felt he was on her side.

"I'm Georgia, Tranquility's match. His mate," she said, only to be met with silence. Three sets of eyes stared at her blankly, like she spoke a foreign language. Had her translation chip failed? No, it worked flawlessly for months. She shifted nervously from foot to foot. "From Celestial Mates? We're, um, married."

The blonde narrowed her eyes. "No, I'm married to *Quil*," she said, stressing the abbreviated name.

Now it was her turn to stare blankly. "I don't understand. The agency sent me. We were matched."

Tranquility—no, Quil—ran a hand through his hair and had the decency to look ashamed. "Well, you see, there was a change of plans—"

Quil kept talking but his words didn't penetrate the static buzzing in her head. Minutes ago, she had been worried that Quil had died and left her a widow. Instead, she had been left at the altar. Humiliation burned through her.

"I decided to marry Fiona, but don't worry, I'm not abandoning you," Quil said. A bitter laugh tore from her throat. "You can marry my brother, Talen. He's not much to look at, but he's hardworking and loyal. You can be happy with him. What do you think?" Quil paused, tail swaying behind him like he genuinely expected an answer.

"I don't know—" She felt faint. Never in her life did she feel like she would faint, but her equilibrium had been thrown off, perhaps from the new gravity, but that didn't make sense because the ship had adjusted to Corravian gravity weeks ago. She wondered what a panic attack felt like.

The world spun and she didn't think she could be upright for one more moment.

Talent laid a steady hand on her arm. She leaned into him for his warmth, and she was so cold and her legs just couldn't function anymore.

What a fucking mess—but what did she expect? She ran away from her messed-up life on Earth and just found herself a new mess. God, she was a worthless idiot.

"Are you well?" Talent asked.

"No, not at all," she muttered. She wanted to hide and bury herself under a pile of blankets, to forget the humiliation of this moment.

"I don't know what he's playing at. I'm sorry."

The sincerity in his voice pulled her from her spiral of doubt and despair. Her head snapped up, finally noticing the man who held a gentle arm around her waist. He had warm, honey-colored eyes that looked down at her with concern. His complexion was a deep amber with dark stripes. One bisected his right eye, which made the eye seem brighter somehow. His russet hair had a patch of white that started at his crown and fell forward in a careless tumble. She was certain that was the only careless thing about the alien male.

His ears, triangular with a small tuft of hair at the tip, moved forward, waiting for her response. He smelled of spice, citrus, and harsh chemicals, like paint remover, a surprisingly pleasing combo.

His lips stretched back into a grin, no doubt to put her at ease, but the white fangs peeking out negated any sense of comfort. Those wickedly sharp teeth stole her focus.

She opened her mouth but only emitted a squeak. Any possible response emptied out of her head and he was the most terrifying and sexy man she had ever seen.

"She's for you," Quil said, dragging her attention back to the luminous smile on his pretty face.

The contrast between the two brothers could not be more obvious. They shared similar features—coloration, careless hair—but their similarity ended there. Quil was empty charm and just a bit sleazy.

How did she ever allow that smile to charm her?

Talen seemed solid and reliable, with sincerity in his awkward and just a teeny bit terrifying smile.

"For me?" The question rumbled out of Talent, low and menacing. He sounded about as thrilled as she felt, meaning not thrilled. At all. Zero titillation happening at the moment.

"A mate! A pretty little human. Only the best. What do you have to say? You don't need to thank me," Quil said, tail waving and his entire posture announcing loudly that he did, indeed, expect to be thanked. "You're speechless, I know. My generosity astounds even myself."

Talen moved swiftly, striking Quil in the chest and grabbing him by the ear. The male folded in half, hissing in pain. He struggled to pull away but when Talen snarled, Quil stilled.

"What are you doing to Quil-boo? You're hurting him," Fiona wailed. She pounded on Talen's arm, her fists practically bouncing off his sculpted biceps.

He ignored her and focused his attention on Quil, tugging his ear until he knelt on the ground. "You are selfish and dishonor our family," Talen growled. "I am ashamed to call you brother."

"Talen—"

"No! You think of only yourself. You wanted that damn plant and we allowed you to uproot our lives to satisfy your whim. You wanted a mate and I thought nothing of it when you brought that one home. All this time you had two mates. You plan to start your own harem?"

Georgia coughed. A harem? Not happening.

"The contract with the agency was vague—" Talen gave another harsh tug and Quil whimpered. "Check the contract. It does not say that she's mated to me, just an Achaval male."

The blonde continued to pound on Talen, who continued to ignore her. This was chaos. She just needed peace and quiet to think and check that damn contract, and possibly send a strongly worded message to Celestial Mates.

"Enough," Georgia said.

Everyone ignored her. Fiona cried. Talen growled. Quil groveled. A Tal female arrived, her complexion silvery in the fading sunlight, and she scolded the brothers like a mother. She had to be their mother. Judging by the tired slump in her shoulders, she was too used to Quil's... whatever this disaster was. Shenanigans sounded too lighthearted.

Mischief.

Yes, that was the word. Quil's mischief.

"I said *enough!*"

The crowd fell silent. Talen stepped away from Quil, who rubbed his ear with a frown.

The older woman took Georgia by the hand. "You must be tired. Let's get you settled into your room, put something warm in your belly, and we can sort everything out in the morning."

"Sounds good," Georgia said, finding herself nodding. She

suspected that woman's soothing, motherly tones would make her agree to any suggestion.

"Talen, put this young female in the room next to yours. I'll send up a tray." The older woman turned her attention to Quil. "And you. Is this how you behave in front of guests? Get out of my sight before I decide you're not too big to take over my knee."

To his credit, Quil's tail went limp and he looked ashamed.

Talen grabbed her bags and escorted her into the house. The foyer had a grand entrance with an elegantly tiled floor and a vaulted ceiling painted to resemble the night sky. Leafy potted plants softened the space, as did the obvious age and wear of the building. They went down the hall, up a staircase, and around several corners. Georgia paid little mind to their route, knowing she would be turned around in the morning, but instead noticed the thin tread on the carpet and the cracks in the plaster walls. The further they drifted from the public part of the house; the more obvious the building's age became.

She wondered if the house even had a central computer to manage daily functions and utilities. She had never lived in a place without a computer to schedule cleaning bots or wake her every morning. Asking if the house was as primitive as she suspected would make her seem spoiled, so she kept her mouth shut. Manually setting her own alarm wouldn't kill her.

"Here." Talen opened a heavy wooden door and stood to one side.

The room was gorgeous, and she wasn't just saying that because she spent the last six months in ship berths and tiny space station hotel rooms. Spacious, the plaster and timber room were painted a mellow white that suggested age, despite the scent of fresh paint. Soothing tones of blue and a complementary gray dominated the decor while a heavy four-poster bed crowded the room. Opposite the bed was a window with three intersecting half-circles. A padded window seat, perfect for reading, was tucked under the window. The interior wall held a fireplace, already crackling merrily, shaped with a circular arc that mimicked the windows. A comfortable-looking high-backed chair sat by the fire, next to a delicate side table. A large armoire and vanity flanked the bed.

The room had two doors, facing each other.

While she explored, Talen held himself in a rigid stance with his arms behind his back that screamed military.

Georgia opened one of two doors, discovering the cleansing room. Across the room, the other door revealed another bedroom suite, decorated in darker greens and browns.

Talen cleaned his throat. "I apologize. Our rooms are connected. I never questioned why Quil was so keen to finish this one, but now I know."

"The paint's barely dry," she said.

"It's had a few days to dry but I laid the carpet this morning."

"No, what I mean is that he's known about me for six

months and you had to rush to finish my room. Oh," she said, suddenly realizing. "This wasn't my original room. I assume Fiona has a connecting room with Quil."

Talen's ears lay flat, betraying his embarrassment. "The door locks—between our rooms. I won't disturb you." She made no quick response and the moment stretched out between them. He cleared his throat again. "Would you like a bath? Something to eat or drink?"

"I don't think I have the appetite."

As if on cue, a knock sounded at the open door. A Gyer male, copper in his complexion, carried a tray laden with a bowl of soup, a thick slice of bread, and a steaming mug of tea. He set it at the small side table by the fire and left without saying a word.

The aroma of fresh-baked bread made her stomach rumble. Talen's lips tugged up at the corners and his tail swayed behind him.

"Maybe a little something to eat," she admitted.

From her vantage at the table, she spied a large soaking tub in the cleansing room and temptation briefly raised its head. Washing off the stale funk of the ship from her face and body sounded good, but she was tired. With her luck, she'd fall asleep in the tub and drown.

Talen left her to finish her meal and returned with the rest of her bags. She felt guilty having him cart them all the way through the maze of the house when she wasn't staying.

She left Earth on good faith that the agency had found her

a perfect match. Within the first ten minutes, she got the measure of Quil Achaval and found him severely wanting. Fiona could keep him. She wasn't interested in a cheat and a liar. Had he changed his mind, why not tell her and save her the journey? He was thoughtless and selfish and inconsiderate and so much more that it made her heart hurt.

No, wait. That's heartburn.

With a frown, Georgia rubbed her chest. She only ever got heartburn when she was stressed. She dashed off a short message to Freema, basically saying that she arrived, and her heart got stomped. More to follow.

"Do you need anything else?" Talen asked, standing by her luggage.

"I think I just need to lie down for a bit." Her emotions went from excitement to confusion and humiliation, followed by disappointment, frustration and, inexplicably, attraction.

"We'll talk in the morning. If you need anything, I'm on the other side of the door," Talen said, casting one long look at her. As his eyes swept over her, she felt the heat in his gaze. A blush rose to her cheeks, but he left before she could say anything more.

She washed her face in the bathroom and brushed her teeth. When she returned to the bedroom, a housecat-sized creature nestled on a pillow atop the bed. It had iridescent blue and green feathers with a long tail but no wings.

Georgia sat cautiously on the edge of the bed. It had to be a pet, right? Wild animals just didn't wander into houses and make themselves at home in beds. "Hey, pretty. What are you doing here?"

The animal lifted its head, blinked sleepy hazel eyes at her, and stretched out a paw. Casually, it flexed claws and yawned, revealing a mouth full of needle-like teeth.

"Okay, whatever you are, you can defend yourself. Understood."

Then it went back to sleep.

Georgia slid under the blankets, careful not to disturb the creature that claimed half the bed.

Shamefully, her mind kept replaying the look Talen gave as he left the room. She wanted to convince herself that the look was a look of longing and not concern, but she found she couldn't lie to herself. That look was all about pity, and maybe a little shame at his brother's behavior. Whatever she had seen, she imagined the heat in his honey-colored eyes. It was probably indigestion.

Yup, a bit of bad beef or whatever they ate on this planet. The faster she got off this backwater rock, the better.

Talen

THE SEVEN VIRTUES ARE HUMILITY, *patience, kindness, justice, fortitude, and prudence.*

But Grandfather, that is only six.

Above all, the most cherished virtue is practice. The virtues only hold meaning if they are practiced.

-Traditional Tal proverb

TALEN CLOSED the door to his bedroom and found the air stifling. He threw open the window, but the cold air gave him little relief. His skin felt too tight and his tail would not stay still. It brushed against his legs, twitching in agitation.

He counted the seven virtues, willing them to instill a sense of peace in his restless soul. He counted again, nose twitching with the damp notes of snow on the air.

A mate. His brother gifted him a mate.

His stomach rolled at the notion because people were not possessions to be given as *gifts*. Quil's thoughtlessness horrified him. The look of utter humiliation on the female's face haunted him. His brother did that, stole the female's joy and replaced it with empty promises, and it shamed Talen. How would he make this right?

Resting on top of the bed, the cold air washed over Talen, but he knew he'd never fall asleep, despite his bone-deep exhaustion. He was forever cleaning up Quil's messes. He spent so much time and energy reacting to his brother's schemes, trying to mitigate damage, and draining himself, that he had no idea what he wanted for himself.

Damn Quil.

He should let his irresponsible, impulsive asshole of a brother deal with this disaster of his own making, but he dreaded discovering how Quil would rectify the situation.

No doubt he'd do something stupid and impulsive, thereby making everything worse. Talen fought his instinct to jump in and fix it. If he did that, Quil would never learn and Talen would spend the rest of his days trailing after his brother, sweeping away trouble.

But the female had been hurt. She did not cry but her eyes, a curious green, told that she would do so in private. He politely ignored her swiping at the damp corners of her eyes, understanding she had suffered enough humiliation for one day. He could not ignore her situation. He had to make it right because he knew Quil would not.

This was pointless. He needed his sleep. Tomorrow promised to be a very long, very annoying day.

Talen rolled out of bed, intent on a soothing cup of herbal tea. The rest of the household was asleep or in their rooms as he prowled through the darkness.

With a warm mug of tea, he entered the library. Moonlight shone through the window, casting light and shadow on the floor.

He enjoyed the library and looked forward to the day when he could fill the bookshelves with actual books. His father had been a historian and Talen remembered the grand library of the family's estate on Talmar. The space seemed massive to him as a kit, with the floor-to-ceiling shelving of neatly arranged books. He loved spending sun-filled days in the room, sprawled on the carpet reading or drawing on loose paper, while his father worked. He had only been a young kit and did not comprehend everything he read, but he enjoyed the feel of books, holding knowledge in his hands. He studied illustrations, finding atlases and star charts interesting but not nearly as fascinating as the photos and illustrations in a history book.

Perhaps, if his parents had not been assassinated, if the Talmar civil war had not come, he would have followed in his father's scholarly footsteps. Quil had always been the heir and studied how to manage the estate from their uncle, Forthright. Agriculture and maintaining a relationship with tenants may not have been Quil's passion, but he had a keen interest in the gardens and grounds, even then. But all of that was another life and it was pointless to speculate on what-ifs.

He took a jeweled flower blossom out of the display case. Carefully winding the clockwork mechanism on the underside, he set it on a table. The first notes of a Tal lullaby rang out and the blossom slowly opened. The device glowed with an internal light, casting a prism of rainbows through the cut crystal of the flower's petals. Once the blossom opened fully, a figurine of two entwined dancers emerged. They spun with mechanical precision as the music played.

Talen cradled the warm tea and watched the colorful lights from the music box play across the ceiling. Normally a source of comfort, the music did nothing against the tension coiling inside him.

He spent so much time reacting to Quil that he forgot himself. It wasn't healthy. When his mother instructed him to take care of his brother, this couldn't be what she meant. He wished he had a lifetime of memories to trawl, searching for some scrap of wisdom. He had only been a kit—eight years old—when that life of privilege ended. The gaps in his memories continued to grow while the memories themselves faded with the passing years. All he had was hurried goodbyes and an ornate music box.

The music box had been a courting gift from his father to his mother. Crafted by a renowned jeweler and encrusted with gems, the costly device received more admiration for its expense rather than its artistry. That fact did not paint his parents in a flattering light and Talen sometimes wondered if he would have been as concerned with appearance and conspicuous spending as they, had they lived.

They had not been bad people, but they had been flawed. As with many of the aristocratic families murdered during Talmar's civil war, they sort of had it coming. They weren't outright villains. His father spent his days in scholarly research, leaving the management of the estate to his brother. His mother served as a member of Talmar's parliament. But they spent staggering sums of money, seemed to care only for their pleasure, and that made them easy targets.

As a child, though, he understood none of that. He had been fascinated with the flower-shaped music box and played it nightly before bed. The melody lulled him to sleep and the fact that it had been in his bed was the only reason it came with him as they fled Talmar. Bright had gathered him up, blankets and all, and carried him on the shuttle. Only later, when they were safely in orbit, did they discover the music box as it fell out of the wad of blankets.

It stayed with him, the only tangible link to his parents and former life on Talmar. The music box could have been sold for a small fortune and they would not have had to stay in dilapidated stations.

Sentimental fool.

He couldn't deny it. The scraps of his personal history were so few that he clung to the pieces he had. Quil knew this and exploited it at every turn.

The music box wound down, the last notes fading into the silence of the house.

"I thought I'd find you here," a familiar voice said.

Talen drained the last of the now-cold tea. "I'm not in the mood for your nonsense, Quil."

"But you are in the mood for nostalgia." Quil turned over the music box, inspecting it carefully. "This could be in a museum."

Or a bank vault.

Talen took the precious device and locked it back in the display cabinet.

"I have a gift for you," his brother said, producing a flat box.

Talen instantly knew what the box contained. "Do not

think you can buy my forgiveness with gifts, especially that kind of gift."

Quil cracked the lid, displaying the flexible claw caps inside. "You must be responsible and think of protecting your mate. Humans are delicate and their skin is not as thick as ours."

He meant that literally. Tal skin was durable and resistant to casual contact with claws. It took effort to shred a Tal skin with claws alone. Humans, however, could be shredded to ribbons before a Tal realized they even touched the human. He had served alongside enough humans in the Navy to see it happen during hand-to-hand training. He never had a human bedmate, but he could imagine the consequences of claws unsheathing in a moment of passion.

Quil had no shame.

"I do have experience in these matters," Quil added, making the moment worse in every possible way.

Humility, patience, kindness, justice, fortitude, and prudence.

And practice. I do not wish to gut my brother. Not really.

"I do not need a sex talk from my brother," Talen said, taking the box and ignoring Quil's idiotic smirk. He left the library, Quil following close on his tail.

"Are you no longer speaking with me?"

"I'm tired," he said.

"Then stop prowling the house and find your bed."

"No, I'm tired of *this*." He paused, motioning between himself and his brother. "I am not helping you when I fix the trouble you cause."

In a rare moment of openness, Talen saw unease on his brother's face, only to be quickly replaced with a nervous smile. "Of course that's helping me."

"No, you are a grown male. When our mother told me to take care of you, she did not intend for you to always be a kit."

"I am not a kit," Quil said, showing the first signs of exasperation.

"If you behave like a spoiled kit, you are a kit, no matter your years." His tail lashed violently behind him. "And I have spoiled you, but this must end. Tomorrow we will rectify what you have done to the human female, but that will be the last time I scurry behind your wake of chaos. No more."

Quil's ears moved forward and then back. His posture became more guarded and closed off. "Will you stay?"

Talen wanted to reassure Quil that they were always brothers and would always be together, but the words never came. "I don't know."

CHAPTER 5

GEORGIA

G,

I'm not saying that as a medical professional, I could end a certain two-timing cat bastard's life and make it look like natural causes because that would be unethical. Plus, leaving an electronic record of such a boast would be dumb. Beyond dumb. But I am saying that I have certain skills and righteous fury.

Let me know what you think.

-Freema

Georgia barely slept. She couldn't fault the enormously comfortable bed or the snuggly, plush blankets. Other than a few creaks of the floorboards in the hall and the groan of wind outside the windows, the house was quiet during the night. She just couldn't turn her brain off.

She kept running through scenarios, trying to wrest some

control over the situation. The one thing she knew for certain was that no matter what the contract said, if it was valid or not, she didn't want to be married to Quil. They were finished.

Freema's invitation to life on a colony sounded like her best bet, but that was still a few months out. Plus, she'd need to foot the transportation bill to wherever Freema settled. The agency—and by extension, Quil—paid for her travel to Corra. She had some funds but not enough to get back to Earth, probably not even enough to get off Corra.

Right. She needed a job and a place of her own. Staying in Quil's house wasn't an option. She didn't want to see his smarmy, slippery smile or his side chickie's better-than-you sneer.

Rolling onto her side, she buried her head under the pillow.

He got tired of waiting. How was that possible? He knew the distance before he signed the contract. The whole situation reminded her of Kevin's unwillingness to be a supportive boyfriend when she was sick.

No, she mentally corrected herself. He was never a supportive boyfriend. Pity she didn't see it. He just didn't want to be associated with having a sick girlfriend, like her illness tarnished his reputation.

Georgia never considered herself a doormat, but two men just walked all over her like she had "Welcome! Please wipe your feet" printed on her forehead. Something about her must attract assholes. Or, more likely, she desperately wanted to be loved and accepted so she willingly turned a blind eye to romantic relationships.

She rolled onto her other side. The enormous empty bed stretched out before. She hated wallowing in self-pity. She wasn't a doormat and deserved to be treated with respect.

Tomorrow would be better. It had to be.

Finally, after drifting in and out of a stress dream where she had to repeat high school—despite her protests that she went to college and had a degree—the silvery light of early dawn spilled through the window.

She showered and dressed, hoping that would revive her tired self, before checking her messages. Freema responded, outraged and sorrowful for Georgia's predicament. She may have offered to commit a little light murder, which warmed Georgia's heart. Then she looked out the window and discovered snow.

Actual snow.

"Holy hamburgers," she said, jamming her feet into her boots. She had never seen snow in real life. Her hometown sometimes dipped into the freezing temperatures in winter but never for more than a few days and never had it snowed in her lifetime.

Bundled up with two layers and a jacket, she navigated her way through the maze of the house down to the ground floor. She didn't find the front door but found the kitchen, which opened to the outside.

It appeared to be a small garden nestled against the house, with empty box planters near the doors and shrubs along a stone wall at the foot of the garden. Treetops poked over the wall. A gate hung partially open and Georgia couldn't resist.

An inch-thick layer of snow covered the ground, dusting the shrubs and the tops of the trees. Her breath hung in the air like smoke and her boots made a pleasing crunching noise on the gravel path, despite slipping. Snow continued to fall in fluffy, wet flakes and Georgia tilted her head back, letting the snowflakes melt on her face. Her nose went numb from the cold and she was certain her boots weren't waterproof, but it was marvelous.

The gate creaked opened and Georgia stood at the edge of an expansive lawn. Rolling forested hills surrounded the house on either side, blanketed in snow. When the shuttle landed yesterday, she didn't have the opportunity to appreciate the view.

The world was fresh and calm in the morning light and she stood right in the middle of a living, breathing Christmas greeting card. She'd be okay. She wasn't desperate or without friends. Life kept giving her lemons, but she'd handle it because lemonade was delicious as fuck.

"Human? Are you lost?"

Georgia turned toward the Tal female calling her from the kitchen door. "Why would you think I'm lost?"

"I'm certain I don't know, but perhaps because it is snowing and you're standing there like you've never seen snow before," the woman said, shoulders pulling back. The words

Pulled by the Tail

may have been sharp, but the tone held the infinite patience of a parent trying to explain to a child why they shouldn't touch the hot stove. Georgia instantly liked the woman.

"But I've never seen snow before," she said.

"Now come inside. It's too cold and you're hardly wearing anything."

Georgia looked down at her bare hands and shoved them in the jacket pocket. "Fair enough."

"Foolish kit," the woman said, pulling Georgia into the now-warm kitchen. The layout and appliances were older, but they gleamed from care and pride. A skillet sizzled on the stove and smelled delicious. The sensation of being at home settled over her like a warm blanket.

"Let me see what you've done." The woman grabbed Georgia's hands and turned them over, inspecting her. "Are you supposed to be this color?"

"Um, yes. I'm pale."

"But this is pink. And here, too." The woman grabbed her by the cheek and squeezed, just like she was a child.

"From the cold. Let go." Georgia rubbed her tender face. "I'm fine. I'm wearing a coat."

The older woman sneezed lightly; her ears pressed back against her head. "This is not a proper coat. If I hadn't found you standing on the lawn, you'd be frozen to death by now. Sit down and let me get you some tea. That will warm you up." The woman continued to mutter about high-maintenance humans as she filled a kettle and set it to boil.

"I don't think I caught your name," Georgia said.

"Bright." A plate of eggs and what appeared to be bacon arrived at the table, along with toast and a bowl of sugar. A box of tea and a mug of hot water soon joined. "I suppose you'll be here from now on. We'll need to get you proper clothes for the winter."

Georgia packed her winter clothes but knew her Southern California wardrobe wouldn't suffice. "I need gloves, a hat, and a scarf, I guess." She wiggled her damp toes. "And boots."

"Shameful," Bright muttered, bringing over another serving of bacon. The meal was delicious, and she ate with an appetite that surprised her. This seemed to please Bright, who poured herself a cup of tea.

"This is marvelous. Thank you."

"Guests normally eat in the dining room, but I think you must be family now," Bright said.

A clank and loud bang rang out, sounding very much like hammering. Bright's ears twitched but said nothing as she stirred her tea.

The hammering continued. She pulled out her tablet reader and checked the time. Most sensible people would still be asleep. She'd rather be asleep. "Bit early for that," Georgia said.

"The kits like to get an early start on the day."

A bell added to the noise.

"That'd be guests at the front desk," Bright said, unconcerned.

"Shouldn't we see what they want?"

"I've never troubled myself."

Georgia followed the bell to a counter in the foyer. Fiona spoke with two Corravian men and a woman. Georgia remembered something from the informational packet the agency sent, that Corravian biology required two males to fertilize a female, so marriages were trios. The repeating trinity design in the house's architecture fell into context.

The trio appeared disgruntled and disheveled, like they hurried out of bed. "The noise is unacceptable."

"You want hot water this morning? You're going to have to put up with the noise," Fiona said.

"What I want," the man said, "is a refund from this farce of an inn."

A dark look settled on Fiona and she opened her mouth to speak. Whatever she was about to say, it wouldn't be good for business. Georgia might not know much about the situation she landed in, but she understood customer service.

"Good morning," she said with breezy cheer. "I see you found our guest robes. They're lush, aren't they? So soft and cuddly."

The Corravian woman stroked the sleeve of her robe. "I suppose."

"I apologize for the noise this morning. We're in the middle of our soft opening and, obviously, we're still working out the kinks. These historic homes always require a little bit more and the hot water never goes out at a good time. How about I take 50% off your bill for the inconvenience of our growing pains? Would that be acceptable?" She nodded and the trio nodded along with her, forgetting their complaint, given the significant discount.

"Well, nothing is perfect. It's a lovely house," the woman said.

"It snowed overnight and the view is amazing. How about breakfast? The kitchen is open and I'm sure we can whip up whatever you like," Georgia said, leading the trio to the dining room. Or what she hoped was the dining room. The room had a long table, chairs, and a pot of tea already waiting.

Georgia felt the need to reward herself with another cup of sugary tea and possibly more bacon, when Fiona grabbed her by the arm, her nails digging through the sweater. "What was that? You think you can take my place?"

"It's called customer service." *Bitch*. Georgia yanked her arm away. "And don't touch me."

"I didn't need your help and you gave away half our fees."

"Those guests were about two seconds away from not paying a cent, so you're welcome."

Fiona huffed. "No one asked for you to be here."

"Quil did." The reply came out quicker than her decaffeinated brain worked.

Fiona cast a critical eye over her appearance, sweeping from head to foot and back again, sizing up the competition.

Right. Like Georgia wanted that piece of shit Quil.

Ugh. That attitude would not help her now.

She took a deep breath and reminded herself that only yesterday, Fiona's world was rocked just as hard as hers. "I know we're both upset. Yesterday we got a shock, but let's remember that we're not the enemy. Quil—"

"Don't you dare say anything nasty about my honey bear."

Not my enemy, not my enemy. Not my friend, but not my enemy.

Georgia fought the urge to sneer but continued in a measured, even voice. "He signed a contract to marry me and then turned around and married you. He played us." Quil deserved their anger, not each other.

"What seems to be the matter, females?"

Speak of the devil.

Georgia's back stiffened at Quil's voice. She had all night to think of what to say to him, but her mind went blank.

He went to Fiona and pressed a kiss on the top of her blonde head and Fiona giggled, then shot Georgia a sharp look.

"He's no prize, so you can stop acting like I'm trying to steal him," she said.

"Well, what else am I supposed to think when another woman shows up on my door, claiming to be his first wife?"

"We'd have to be divorced to be his first—" She stopped herself, refusing to be drawn into dramatics. "We shouldn't be fighting each other. We should be united against him."

Both their eyes turned to Quil, with enough awareness to look uncomfortable. Then he tilted his head to the side and gave a grin full of mirth. His posture changed and she couldn't say how, but he radiated confidence and good humor. The ears with little tufts of hair at the tip completed the image of a perfect little scamp.

Georgia knew that as soon as he opened his mouth, he'd spew such utter bullshit, and she'd want to believe him, because this man knew how to manipulate people.

"Stop," she said, holding up a hand. "I'm not interested in whatever you have to say."

"If you weren't interested, you'd walk away."

Ugh. And where did he propose she go? With what money?

Never mind. She wasn't going to let him distract her.

"I'm disappointed, Mr. Achaval," she said. "Six months ago, we signed a contract. It was no easy thing for me to do, to leave my planet, my friend, and everything familiar. I hope you appreciate that, but it's been six months. Minds change. Circumstances change. You could have, at any point in the last six months, told me that you had doubts or wanted out." She kept her voice even, an impressive feat considering how her heart raced and she wanted to grab his adorable little tufted ear and snatch it off his head. "Six months I've been writing you, and you used to write me back."

Fiona gasped. "Boo! You never."

"Did you get tired of waiting? Bored? Meet someone?" She tossed Fiona a glance. "The decent thing would have been to tell me. I would have been upset, yes, and disappointed, but I'd get over myself. Instead, you stopped all communication. Do you know I was actually worried about you? I thought you were dead." She pressed her index fingers to the corners of her eyes, horrified to find them wet. He didn't deserve her tears. "Or injured or something prevented you from replying. I honestly thought I was a widow. I never imagined that you'd abandoned me before you even had a chance to meet me."

Fuck. Her fingers came away wet and the tears rolled down her cheeks.

"Sorry," she muttered. All her emotions threatened to bubble over, a toxic mixture of self-pity and heartbreak. People left her. That's what happened to her. Her father. Her mother. Kevin. And now this clown. Anger was so much easier to process than this misery.

"I want to stay logical to get through this, but your suggestion that I hook up with your brother was incredibly hurtful. I'm not a…" she searched for the correct word but settled with, "a party favor for you to pass around. I don't think I like you very much and I think we need to speak with a lawyer."

The little-boy-mischief-maker facade vanished and for a moment, Quil was just Quil, vulnerable and uncertain. "I'm sorry I hurt you."

"How long did you wait before you replaced me?" She wanted to ask why Fiona, what drew him to her, and how he could so easily forget the commitment he made to Georgia, but those questions remained unspoken.

"Three months."

Right around when his messages stopped coming.

A throat cleared behind them. Talen stood at the foot of the stairs. From his expression, he had clearly heard everything. Just as well. Georgia wasn't in the mood to repeat herself.

He pointed toward the kitchen. "Tea. Food. Then we read this blasted contract."

Talen

"I'M NOT an expert in contracts, and this was written in Terran first, then translated," Talen said. He highlighted a passage in the contract. *T. Achaval.* "But the contract used the Terran spelling of Quil's name. How Quil could have signed something so sloppily written, I'll never know," he said.

Quil grumbled in protest. "I don't read Terran."

"It's in English," Georgia said. "And why does that matter?"

"Because in the Tal language, Tranquility and Talen are nothing alike. They use entirely different letters." He leveled his gaze on Quil. "Which means this liar here knew enough English to find a loophole."

Found out, Quil shrugged. "The contract is not specific. It says 'T. Achaval,' which could be you or me. Really, the outrage shouldn't be why I exploited a loophole but who put the loophole there in the first place. Celestial Mates has a lot to answer for, if you ask me."

Talen cuffed Quil behind the ear. He squawked in protest and rubbed the side of his head.

Bright dished out crispy pieces of smoked bacon and toast, moving down the table one by one. When she reached Quil, she passed him by, sniffing loudly.

"But I'm hungry," he complained.

"Make your own. I only cook for good kits, not spoiled brats," she said coolly. When she finished topping off mugs of tea and ignoring Quil's groans of hunger, she prepared a cart for the dining room. Quil jumped up to help, opening the door and pushing the breakfast-laden cart.

"We need a lawyer to get this mess annulled," Georgia said. Dark circles hung under her eyes. She looked like she hadn't rested in days.

He admired the sure way she handled the three disgruntled guests. He made a note to talk with Charl about starting work later when they had guests in the house. More than the easy way she defused the tense situation, he enjoyed watching her lay into Quil. His brother deserved every word, but she had never been overly harsh. Her hands had trembled as she spoke, betraying her true rage, but she never resorted to name-calling. This female intrigued him.

"I agree. We need a lawyer. I'll make some calls," he said. The nearest town, Drac, was large enough to offer most basic services. The nearby mines powered the economy and the population steadily grew.

"Are you done? I'm bored, honey bear." Fiona scooted her chair closer to Quil.

Quil looked toward Talen before answering. "I have to go into town with Talen and Georgia."

"Drac is boring too. There's nothing to do there." Fiona rolled her eyes. "Let's go to the city, just you and me. We haven't had any time together." She not-so-subtly touched Quil's tail at the base. He jolted upright.

Talen focused on his tablet, pulling up contact information for lawyers in Drac. He did not need to see his brother get his tail pulled.

"I must attend this meeting—"

Fiona brushed the tip of Quil's tail against her lips and he suddenly lost the ability to speak.

"Soon. I will book us something as soon as possible," Quil said, taking Fiona's hand and herding her out of the room.

"Well, that was gross," Georgia said caustically.

Talen's laugh caught him by surprise. "And I'm sorry this happened to you."

"Yeah, well, that and five dollars will buy me a drink."

CHAPTER 6

TALEN

Talen,

Can you pick up an order for me from the general store while you're in town today? And you should get some proper winter gear for the female. I don't know what the weather is like on Earth but I'm amazed humans have survived this long. They don't seem to have any common sense when it comes to snow.

-Bright

Talen found a lawyer with an open appointment shortly before noon. Fortunately, the meeting was brief but, unfortunately, it did nothing to resolve the tension sitting heavily in his gut and he understood exactly why that lawyer had an open schedule.

Quil, Georgia, and himself had crowded around the lawyer's desk. Fiona briefly protested at not being involved, worried Quil would run off with another woman. Honestly, given his track record, she had every reason to worry. She waited in the lobby, turning up the volume on a talk show playing on the view screen.

The lawyer read over the contract. "I'm afraid I'm not qualified to have an opinion on a Terran legal document."

"It is a simple matter. That name is not specific. It needs to be annulled," Talen said.

"But it is signed by both parties." The lawyer, a Corravian male, sat back in his chair.

"So, I'm married to Quil?" Georgia asked.

"Like the good male said, the name is not specific."

"What does that even mean?" she muttered.

"I'm afraid I'm not qualified to have an opinion," the lawyer said smoothly.

Talen despised lawyers.

Georgia twisted her fingers into the ends of her hair. "Basically, I'm fucked, and no one even bought me dinner first."

His ears flicked forward. He knew she spoke in frustration and was not literal, but he felt the need to clarify, "No one has fucked the human female."

"Not true. Quil screwed me over pretty hard yesterday." Her gaze caught his. The irritation was evident, but he saw nothing of the tired defeat he witnessed last night.

This female had fire. Had they met in any other circumstances, he would be drawn to her.

"If the union has been consummated—"

"No one has fucked anyone," Talen snapped at the lawyer.

"That was a figure of speech. A human idiom. My apologies," Georgia said. "Can you at least advise me on my options? The man who signed this contract married another woman, using his full legal name."

Quil sat calmly, as if he and his actions were not being discussed.

"You could contest the second marriage, possibly have it dissolved," the lawyer said.

She waved her hand dismissively. "I have no desire to be married to Quil after what he did. I want to be not married. How can we make that happen?"

"Just for my own clarification, you are Tranquility Achaval," the lawyer said, facing Talen.

"No. I am Quil. That's my brother," Quil said, finally involving himself in the conversation.

"You want to marry the brother instead of Quil?" the lawyer asked Georgia.

"I don't want to be married to anyone. I want this to go away," she said.

"Not being married will jeopardize your citizenship application and you'll have to contact a lawyer on Earth. I'm not—"

"Qualified to have an opinion, yeah. I heard," she followed. "What can we do about the citizenship application?"

"Well, immigration to Corra is very generous. Most aliens are sponsored for citizenship through their employers or marriage to a Corravian citizen. Are you a citizen?" He directed the question to Talen.

"Um, yes." Purchasing property was the fastest way to get citizenship and Quil and Talen put both their names on the deed. Corra was a planet rich in natural resources but poor in its number of inhabitants. The planet's local population had never recovered after an environmental disaster two generations ago and the government did everything to attract immigrants. When Talmar fell into civil war, a significant amount of people fled to Corra.

"If you marry Ms. Phillips, her citizenship can no longer be challenged," the lawyer said.

"I don't—" She rubbed the bridge of her nose. It was curiously flat, not as wide as his own nose. How could she breathe with that tiny thing? "How about a tourist visa? Or something short-term?"

"An employer can sponsor you."

"I don't have a job at the moment," she said.

"I suggest you find one. Corra is ripe with opportunity for the enterprising soul," he said, sounding just like a tourist brochure.

"Yeah, pass. I'm not sure I want to stay." Another rub to

the bridge of her nose. "Are you qualified to send a strongly worded letter to the matchmaking agency?"

With a strongly worded letter sent, Quil and Fiona departed for a getaway to the nearest city, and Talen took her to a Talmar café for lunch. "After we eat, Bright gave me a list for the general store. Do you need anything?"

She nodded. "A few things, yeah. What's good here?"

"Everything is good here. Have you had Tal food before?" The owner was a remarkable chef but also had a notoriously prickly disposition. Talen had once found a sauce to be too salty, said as much, and she tossed him out of the café on his ear.

"Yes, on Earth. It was probably Terranized." She scrunched up her nose, which he found endearing. "Earthified? Not authentic is what I'm trying to say." She opened the menu. "This is going to sound ignorant, but are there foods a human should avoid?"

"Other than small variations in taste receptors, most sentient lifeforms are able to consume the same food without ill effect," he said, pulling the clinical passage from a corner of his memory. The Navy required certain education modules of all enlisted sailors. Apparently, more of it stuck than he realized.

"I see someone took Comparative Biology."

"Alien Nookie 101," he confirmed, using the sailor's slang name for the course.

She laughed and for a moment, unhindered glee transformed her. Yesterday, she had appeared worn and tired.

In the morning, lack of sleep and stress hung about her. Nothing about her appearance had struck him as particularly attractive until that moment of laughter when she became riveting. Her eyes flashed green and he wanted to hear more of the melodious sound.

Georgia selected a grilled poultry dish served over a bed of rice. He ordered the same, only spicy, with a basket of warm bread and two sweet yogurt-based drinks. The sweetness helped with the heat, if Georgia found the dish too spicy. When their meals arrived, the trivial conversation went to the wayside. She took a cautious first bite and nodded, taking the next bite with relish, which pleased him.

"What's yours like? Is it hot?"

He shook his head, a gesture he had seen many humans use. "You would not like it. Too spicy."

"You don't know what I like," she said, spearing a piece of meat on her fork. She popped it into her mouth before he could protest. "It's not so bad. A little warm." Then her eyes went wide, and she frantically reached for the drink.

He huffed with amusement. The delicate column of her throat as she took a long swallow caught his attention, causing him to avert his eyes. His admiration was inappropriate and unwanted.

"A little spicy," she admitted.

He pushed the breadbasket toward her. "Bread helps as well. What are your plans? Will you return to Earth?"

"With what money?" She tore off a piece of bread,

consuming it bit by bit. "I just spent the last six months traveling. I really can't stomach the idea of more time on a ship. Can you imagine spending an entire year of your life like that?"

"I can and have." She gave him a questioning look. "I served in the IU Navy, then ran cargo until Quil got the estate," he explained.

"I thought you might be military," she said. "Anyway, I don't have the money for a ticket home."

"Can your family assist?"

"No family. My mom passed away a long time ago and my dad ditched us."

"That sounds lonely. My family is small, but they mean everything to me," he said with sincerity. "What are your plans?"

"Find a job, earn enough money to get off-planet. I have a friend who's moving to a colony in a few months. I'll join her there." She paused and then asked, "Is it okay to stay for a few days? I know what you said this morning, but—"

"The offer stands." It'd be poor manners to turn her out and she needed a warm place to stay while she searched for employment. He scratched behind an ear, taken with a notion. "Work for me."

"No," she said quickly. "I don't want your pity."

"Hear me out. The way you handled those guests this morning was perfect. I need someone who can manage visitors, because I'm busy with repairs and renovations. Honestly, I've needed to hire a house manager for some time. I can give you room and board and fair wage."

The more he spoke, the more his need for Georgia to manage the bed and breakfast side of the house became obvious. Quil was consumed by his plants and Fiona proved useless for making guests feel welcome or managing the lodgings. He and Charl spent all their time restoring and maintaining the estate. Bright spent her time cooking for the family and guests.

She hesitated to answer, and Talen suspected the source.

"It's a big house. You can go days and days without seeing anyone you don't wish to see," he said.

"I'll see him at meals."

"He spends more of his time in the conservatory and often eats in the kitchen." Then he said, "I can put a bell on him."

She smirked and shredded the piece of bread, considering the offer. "I'm not completely broke, you know. I can afford a hotel while I'm job hunting."

He spread his hands wide, turning them palm up to demonstrate his sincerity. "Understood, but I do need a house manager and I've already seen your skills."

"Fine," she said. Then, her green eyes narrowed. "But this is temporary, just until the contract is annulled, or I can afford a ticket off-world."

"A reasonable position," he agreed.

"And I'm leaving if things get weird."

"Define weird."

She huffed out a breath. "We," she said, gesturing between them, "are not married. That door between our rooms stays locked. And if fuckface tries anything, I'm out."

He assumed fuckface's identity to be Quil. "Agreed."

They returned to their meals. Eventually, Georgia broke the silence. "Did Quil inherit the estate?"

"He won it in a card game," he said without hesitation. It never occurred to him to dodge the question or offer a vague answer.

She said nothing but popped another piece of bread in her mouth, studying him with her keen gaze. "You're not pulling my leg, are you?"

Pulling her—

He gulped down his drink, trying to finish the thought. Did humans do that? Was it a sign of sexual attraction, like pulling a tail? His tail had been neatly wrapped around his leg but now it beat an intrigued rhythm against his leg. He was a brazen flirt and Quil would tease him mercilessly if he found out, but Talen realized he did not care. This female stirred curiosity in him, reaffirming his earlier notion that had they met under different circumstances, he would pursue her.

Perhaps Quil had not been wrong to force them together.

"No, I am not. Do you want me to? I know what you said about the door between our rooms remaining shut, but we are two adults with healthy appetites—"

She blinked at him, her gaze a verdant green and clueless as to his meaning.

"Do you not want me to pull your leg?"

Her eyes went wide. "Holy shit, no. No. Do you think I'm flirting? Because that just means 'joking around.'"

His tail stilled and he kept his posture relaxed. "As you say, but I like the idea of flirting with a pretty female who is technically my wife."

"I am not your wife. I don't care what that contract says, and I was not flirting," she said. Her voice took on a harder tone, almost angry but firm, and her eyes seemed to grow brighter. He liked this new passion in her as much as he liked her laughter.

"In my culture, it is traditional for a male to keep a harem and to gift a bride from the harem to another male," he said, waiting to draw out more of that passion.

"No offense, but some aspects of your culture suck."

"That idea is old-fashioned, and you only find it lurking in the strictly traditional families," he said.

He hadn't taken offense but now he had to know what she believed about his people. The negative stereotypes surrounding the Tal outnumbered the positive by a fair margin. In the Navy, he heard enough slurs to last a life-time, "fleabag" and "kitty cat" being the mildest. While he acknowledged that the position his brother placed her in was unfair, he would rather give her the money for a ticket off the planet than constantly be listening for muttered insults. "Do you have a problem with the Tal?"

"As a whole, no. In particular, yes," she said.

Talen leaned forward. "Yesterday, surely you thought we were nothing but flea-bitten criminals and con artists. It must have crossed your mind."

Her nose scrunched up again. "You mean on the worst day of my life, did I think that? No. Sorry to disappoint you. I was far too busy wallowing in my own misery to think poorly of your culture or people."

He grinned and his tail waved playfully. This irritated, sharp-tongued mood was so much more interesting than the sad and tired mood of yesterday.

"I can guess the Tal you think poorly of in particular," he said. Quil. It was always Quil between them.

"Obviously." She sipped at the glass of water. "Look, I don't have a problem with the Tal in general, but I can't guarantee I'll be able to put aside my feelings about you-know-who. I'll keep my head down and work. When I have enough for a ticket, I'll leave. But if that's not good enough, tell me now and I'll find something in town."

He had no doubt she could find work in Drac or a neighboring town. Corra had a surplus of vacant job postings. "No, I want you."

She raised her eyebrows.

"To stay. I want you to stay," he amended. "As I said earlier, the house is large enough that you can easily avoid sources of irritation. But I think I'd like to see you use that sharp tongue of yours on him."

She snorted, then covered her mouth and laughed. Color rose in hers, a soft pink that flushed against her pale skin. "I'm sorry. You're being all serious and really nice, but that phrase doesn't mean what you think it means."

He turned over the words in his head. No. They were innocent.

"I think I'm going to like you," she said.

"Agreed."

"But you should totally put a bell on him, though."

Georgia

CELESTIAL MATES

To Whom it May Concern,

Suck a bag of dicks. The entire bag.

Sincerely, Georgia Phillips

THEY STOPPED at an all-purpose general store. While Talen picked up an order, he told her to grab what she needed. She chose a pair of gloves that looked like they would fit her and a scarf. Those would tide her over until she could get better boots for the cold and a coat with her first paycheck. Besides, she wasn't going tromping through the fields. She worked in a hotel.

Talen took one look at her modest purchase and shook his head. He had her try on coats, raising and lowering her arms to check the fit. He kept adding socks, shoes, and personal care items to the purchase until Georgia had to protest.

"It's fine," he said, putting the whole pile on his tab.

"Another human," the clerk, a Tal woman, muttered as she rang up the purchase.

"No, it's not fine. I can't afford all this," Georgia said.

He shrugged, like money meant nothing to him. "I know where you work. I'll take it out of your salary if you like."

"But I don't need all this stuff." Shoes with extra-traction soles for the snow and ice? Sure. A heated blanket? That sounded amazing but she'd double up on blankets if it got that cold.

"Listen, you don't know how tenacious Bright can be, but she told me to get you outfitted, so that's what I'm going to do," he said. She opened her mouth to protest but he continued, "Whether you like it or not. It'll be easier, for both of us, to let Bright have her way. I don't want a week's worth of burnt meals or, even worse, porridge."

"It's that bad?"

The recollection made his tail jerk. "I was a stubborn kit and she fed me nothing but porridge for a month, morning, noon and night. She won. Bright always wins. So, right now? Let me spend money on you, Georgia. Bright will be pleased, you'll be warm, and I'll eat proper food. Yes?"

"This is not a gift," she said, not asking a question. "You will take this out of my pay." Again, not a question.

"You're bossy. I like it."

"It's the pants. They're bossy." She put a hand on her hip and cocked it dramatically to the side.

Where did the flirting come from? Probably not the best idea but, honestly, she was so out of practice that this heavy-handed flirtation was as good as it got.

He looked at her, as if waiting for the punchline of a joke.

Oh no, he wasn't flirting. He was serious. Embarrassment flooded her. "Yeah, umm. Bossypants? It's a joke. Maybe it doesn't translate."

"That's a shame, because those look amazing on you. I like them."

She shouldn't be blushing at the way his fangs peeked out when he said he liked her bossypants.

What was this? Her emotions were all over the place. Hooking up with Talen would be trouble. So much trouble. The agency warned her about this. Well, not this specific situation, but the giddy, flirty feeling now that she was at the end of a long trip. She was excited and hopeful.

New gravity, solar radiation, and even oxygen levels affected her body and that body wanted to jump into bed immediately. The agency cautioned against that. She needed time to get to know her match. Even though messaging was encouraged, they were strangers. Familiar strangers. The agency recommended dating and discussing expectations and desire around sex.

The agency could suck a bag of dicks. They knew nothing. They matched her with a guy who ditched her before she even arrived. So much for her perfect match.

Georgia kept stealing glances at Talen as he drove back to the house. He had been patient and understanding, even generous.

Easy on the eyes too.

Frankly, he was everything she hoped to find when she got off that ship. Too bad what she found was the other brother and heartburn-inducing chaos.

"You want the grand tour when we get back?" he asked. Despite never taking his eyes off the road, she got the feeling he was very aware of her and her less-than-polite staring.

"It's dark. Will that be a problem?" The sun had set. Before she left the shuttle yesterday—had it only been yesterday?—she'd been informed that the season was late autumn and to dress according to the weather. Too bad her Southern California wardrobe didn't have a cold setting.

But when had doing the responsible thing ever worked out for her? She dated one guy in college, moved in with him, and planned her life around him, and he ditched her the moment she became less than perfect.

Maybe rebound sex was what she needed. No strings. No feelings. Just fucking. That's what Freema tried to talk her into. Do something wild. Enjoy herself. Get over this dry spell. It'd been a year since the last time she had sex, so the dry spell was more significant than she wanted to admit.

"You don't happen to have any tattoos, do you?" Georgia asked.

"I do. I got it in the Navy."

Oh, he was a deliciously bad idea that she wanted to lick.

Sex now was a bad idea. Sex with her boss was a very bad idea.

Then again, she wasn't staying. Just long enough to afford a ticket back to civilization or wherever. Six months at the most. She could have casual sex with no commitment. Probably. She'd never done that before because it hadn't been part of the plan. The only thing she'd ever done that wasn't part of the plan was sign the Celestial Mates contract.

She shivered, like she had been doused with cold water. Okay, that was a terrible example. Her one spontaneous leap of faith didn't turn out the way she wanted, but neither had any of her careful designs.

"Are you cold?" Talen reached over and adjusted the scarf, covering the back of her neck.

"Keep your eyes on the road," she grumbled, totally not rubbing the back of her neck where his fingers brushed against her. The lights from the vehicle illuminated fluffy snowflakes that fell in a flurry, coating the pavement.

Sex only complicated things. She had enough complications to last a lifetime.

CHAPTER 7

GEORGIA

Freema,

There is no coffee in space. Stay on Earth! It's not worth it. Also, send coffee.

-G

The day started way too early. No guests were staying in the house, so construction started a split second after dawn, and Georgia needed caffeine to deal with the racket. Unfortunately, whatever was in her mug might have been brown and hot, but it was not coffee. The tea Bright favored tasted of grass and berries. Not the worst thing but also not coffee. Had she known the dire extent of the caffeine situation, she'd have picked up coffee, or the Corravian equivalent, at the general store.

Georgia frowned at the cup and added another spoonful of

sugar, hoping the muck wasn't the Corravian equivalent. Earth coffee was a fairly unique crop and early colonizers brought the bean with them, planting, harvesting, and creating a lucrative industry. Getting good coffee shouldn't have been difficult. Even with Corra on the fringes of charted space, it should be available, just expensive.

"Glaring at it won't make it taste better," Talen said. "Did you sleep poorly?"

"The opposite, actually." She covered a yawn with the back of her hand. Yesterday had been emotionally draining and she went straight to bed after dinner. Curled up under the self-heating blanket, she slept solidly until hammering and banging woke her. "I'm just missing coffee. My brain doesn't wake up until my second cup."

"That is an addictive beverage for humans, yes? Will you have withdrawal symptoms? Do you need a medic?"

"Are you even serious?"

He waited, hands pressed flat on the table, ready to spring into action.

Totally serious, then.

"I might get a headache from the lack of caffeine, but I'll be fine. No medical intervention needed." She pulled out her tablet and jotted down a note. She had a feeling that she'd be taking a lot of notes today. "But I'll figure out how to source a decent brew."

"Fremmian kava is often available in town. I believe it has levels of caffeine you would find acceptable."

"Noted." She wrote down the item. "I'm ready for my first day of work, boss."

"Let's start with a tour. As you can see, the kitchen is classically appointed and maintains the historic character of the home," Talen said loftily.

"More like we don't have the budget to modernize. Don't look at the refrigeration unit funny. It's temperamental." Bright entered the room, carrying a basket of laundry. Talen sprang to his feet and took the burden.

"*Temper*-mental. Funny," Georgia said. Her brain hadn't warmed up enough for wordplay, but she recognized a good game when she saw it. Heard it. Whatever. She needed coffee, dammit.

"Lack of funds. Historic preservation. It's all how you look at it," Talen said. He vanished through a door, presumably to the laundry room.

Thirty minutes into the tour and it became obvious that the historic character of the house was due entirely to the budget, or the lack thereof.

The public-facing rooms were gorgeous and freshly painted. The native wood flooring, a pale cream, had been polished to a luminous sheen. It looked stunning but Georgia suspected it was a bitch to keep clean. Every little speck of dirt would show. The furniture was sparse. What was present was heavy in an older fashion but in good condition.

The drawing room, the dining room, parlor, and the study blended together. The library was noteworthy because it had no actual books. Talen said the collection was out for restoration. He glowed with the obvious pride he took in the house as he explained the original state and what work had been done. Georgia couldn't help but catch that same pride and excitement.

The ceiling was a deep shade of twilight blue. Gold painted stars scattered across the surface, forming alien constellations.

"Is that real? I mean, are those actual constellations?" she asked.

"The constellations are real but it's also a story. I researched the design while it was being restored." He pointed to the center design. "That is the princess. Her father set three impossible tasks to win her hand." The golden stars formed a cluster, but Georgia could not see a princess in the abstract shape. Talen continued, "Two males initially competed against each other, then worked together to win the princess and became friends in the process. Their quest is in the corners of the room."

"And those are in the night sky?"

"Yes, but not at the same time. Some are seasonal," he said.

Other than the princess being a prize to be handed out—Georgia still felt some kind of way about that—it was a charming story that unfolded across the stars in real time.

The conservatory was a lush explosion of greenery and rich, earthy scents. Plate glass formed a dome, opening directly under a vivid blue sky. Snow collected at the seams in the glass, drifting in the wind.

"This has to be stunning in warmer weather, but I'd worry the glass will break," she said. She could imagine the cacophony of a hard rain pounding against the glass. Or dense fog slithering by. Or the shake and sway of the glass dome in a windstorm.

Standing next to her, Talen tilted his head back, sharing what she imagined. His tail swayed, lightly brushing against her. Heat radiated off him like a furnace. She wore her new thermal undershirt, a sweater, thick woolen socks, and her new boots, but she still felt the cold. She wanted to curl up next to him and soak up his warmth.

"It's beautiful and terrifying," she said.

"That sums up Corra." He stepped away, suddenly aware of how close they stood. "The glass is rated for space travel, so you need not fear. It'll hold."

"Sounds expensive."

"Better than replacing broken glass every other storm."

Four guestrooms had been refurbished but remained sparsely furnished and not terribly luxurious. Georgia made notes to combine some furnishing into a luxury suite and leave the other rooms as economy options.

The private rooms, however, were less impressive. They were clean and structurally sound. As they ventured further into the house, it became apparent that the estate was falling down around their ears. Talen and Quil had no doubt poured a fortune into saving the house, but they needed another fortune and a small army of laborers to finish the job.

He peppered the tour with the history of the house. It was once the estate of an old Corravian family, the kind with a long pedigree but dwindling bank accounts. The house had been abandoned in the ecological disaster a hundred years ago. Huge portions of the population were killed by the mornclaw infestation and entire towns vanished.

Eventually, they went into the lower level of the house, which housed the heating and cooling system. She knew nothing about the mechanics of a house, utilities, pipes, and whatnot, but everything looked dated. Judging by the way her shower groaned when she turned on the hot water, it barely worked, too. So, another fortune to get all that up to snuff.

She eyed the hard-packed dirt floor in the basement. The mornclaws buried their eggs, which could lie in wait for years before they hatched.

"I've never seen the creatures, but the Watchtower thoroughly swept the house and grounds," he said. "There are no mornclaws here."

"What would it take to pour a concrete floor? Just to be on the safe side." In case the murder bugs tunneled under the house.

"If you fill out a service request, our crew will get back to you in three to four months," he said.

"Are you teasing me?"

"A little." His tail swayed behind him, obviously having a

good time. "A new floor will have to wait until the spring. I don't trust all the pipes to survive the winter and I'd rather not dig up a new concrete floor to replace the plumbing."

"Fair enough."

With the house explored—but Georgia made a note to investigate the third floor and attic—they ventured outside to the grounds. Snow covered the lawn in a smooth blanket and softened the features of the garden.

"There are three cottages on the property that are not fit for habitation at the moment. Stables, also not fit for beast or person," Talen said, approaching an L-shaped building with wide, rounded doors and a roof missing large sections.

"Do you plan to have horses?"

"Absolutely not. I know nothing of animals, but it seems like a waste to not utilize this building." The door groaned loudly in protest as he pushed it open.

She blinked, adjusting to the darkness. The sun streamed in through the hole in the roof, lighting up dust motes as they drifted. The space smelled musty, like moldering hay, but not rank like mold or... Well, a hundred other very gross and disgusting things that can happen to a building when it's been abandoned. Talen was correct; the old stables could be converted and repurposed.

"I'll put it on the list and brainstorm." She wanted a feel for how the house operated before she made changes. New managers who mucked things up just because they had something to prove and felt the need to leave their mark had never impressed her.

They walked through the garden. Several beds had been trimmed back for the upcoming cold season. Shrubs bent under the snow and late autumn plants had wilted in the cold. In the distance, the trees lost their leaves.

"Feels like we skipped autumn and went straight to winter," she said. Her boots crunched on a snow-covered path. When the snow melted, the garden path would be a muddy mire. She made a note to investigate ordering gravel for the garden. Guests wouldn't like slogging through the muck, and she didn't want to deal with mud being tracked into the house.

"Winter comes fast and lingers," he said. "Snow this early is typical and we can look forward to more snow for another four months."

Was it too soon to develop cabin fever? Georgia felt the snowy walls closing in.

They walked around to a flagstone veranda tucked between the house and the conservatory. It would be perfect for outdoor entertaining if the stones weren't buried under a layer of dirt and weeds. A broken balustrade skirted the patio, giving it a graceful outline. Arched doors opened onto the veranda, but the glass was filthy. Georgia rubbed at the glass with her gloved hands and peered through the least grungy bit but couldn't make out the interior. She needed to figure out what room had access to the neglected veranda.

Another item added to her list.

They followed a stone walkway away from the house, past the stables. The ground sloped down, and the walkway became a series of steps. The slick stones grew treacherous, but the new boots never slipped.

A small stone building sat at the foot of the hill. The round building did not appear to have a roof.

"Another building to be converted?" Her hands flexed, automatically reaching for a non-existent railing. Mentally, she added that to the list as well.

"No, this one is acceptable as is," Talen said. He held out a hand to stabilize her, which she took gratefully.

Palm-to-palm, the gloves prevented skin-to-skin contact. She focused on her feet as she traversed the last few steps. At the bottom, Talen continued to hold her hand. She glanced up, their eyes catching, and the moment stretched out between them, warm and sweet like toffee.

"Your face changed color," he said. "Are you cold?"

"Umm, a bit." She snatched her hand back and pressed it to her face, desperately trying to cover a blush.

"You'll be warm soon. Come along."

The building had no door. Dried leaves scattered through the entrance. Georgia made another mental note about cleaning the building out.

Humidity hit her first, instantly bringing sweat to her brow. Unzipping her coat, she detected the unmistakable scent of sulfur. She stripped off the gloves and wool hat, stuffing them in the coat's pockets.

A round pool took up the center of the room. Sunlight glimmered on the shifting water, sparkling like diamonds. The edges of the room remained shrouded in shadows, but pale flowers clung to the rough-cut stone walls.

"Our own, private thermal bath, fed by a natural hot spring." Talen sat at the edge of the pool, then removed his boots.

"This is gorgeous," she breathed.

Talen stood and shucked off his trousers and shirt.

Georgia turned around quickly, finding the flowers and the wall to be suddenly fascinating. She heard a splash and a chuckle.

"Come and warm up. I won't bite," he called.

"No. I'm good." She kept her eyes focused on the wall.

"Soak your feet. I can tell they're hurting you from your walk."

"New boots, that's all. I'm breaking them in." And blistering her heels.

Soaking her feet did sound tempting. She sat at the edge of the pool and kept her eyes downward. More splashing. She refused to look. The brief glimpse she saw of the tightly corded muscles and the flex of his thigh—

Not going to look.

"Are you shy?"

"I'm not shy," she said.

"Then you should come in the water. It's the best way to warm up."

"No thanks." Not without a swimsuit and not with an audience. She'd rather avoid displaying all her jiggly bits. "I don't want to walk back all wet," she added, which was a perfectly plausible reason and not a cop-out.

"Next time." He heaved himself over the ledge and flopped onto his back. Naked. Wet. Next to her.

She scooted over a foot or two. He chuckled. That fucker enjoyed teasing her.

"It's not funny. This could be sexual harassment," she said.

He rolled toward her, his dick resting heavily on his thigh. "Why? I haven't asked you to do anything."

Oh, but the things she wanted to do to him, her boss and husband by technicality.

She looked up at the circular gap in the roof. Vines hung down, reaching toward the warmth of the water. "Other than skinny dipping."

"My apologies. The Navy beat any scrap of modesty out of me." He sat upright and draped his shirt over his crotch. A ship's anchor with a star decorated his right bicep. "Acceptable?"

"Very. Thank you." She kicked her feet, trying hard not to think about his tattoo or that flimsy piece of cloth over his dick. It was a nice dick, with a generous girth but not so much that it'd make her clamp her thighs together and wince. A ring of soft, flexible spines was under the head, but she knew to expect that from the reading materials the agency supplied her. She'd never seen an alien dick before. Honestly, she'd never seen anyone's dick but Kevin's, at least in the flesh. She'd seen plenty in porn and had watched human-Tal videos—for research—during her long trip and Talen's looked better than anything on film.

Stop thinking about his dick. Stop.

She coughed, clearing her throat. "Is the pool open to guests?"

"Not yet. Some of the steps are loose and uneven. It's not safe," he said.

"The steps could use a railing, too. We don't need any slips or falls."

"I planned to do that in the spring. Charl and I spent a solid week just clearing leaves and debris from the water."

She shivered at the thought. "I'm surprised you even bothered. It had to be disgusting."

"Hmm," he said, stretching out onto his back and tucking his arm behind his head. "I found some old photos of the pool, so I knew its potential. Winter is long and cold here, and the temptation of a thermal bath was too good to pass up."

Georgia didn't think she'd trudge out to the pool in a foot of snow, but on a day like today? Yes. It was perfect.

The silence stretched out between them in a perfect, golden moment, at ease with the lapping of the water.

"So, all of this from a card game?" she asked, breaking the silence.

"For those," he pointed to the flowers clinging to the stone walls. "Moon violets. They are very rare and only found in a few locations. They only bloom in the dark."

"They're lovely." They seemed to thrive in the warm, humid air.

"Quil nearly pissed himself when we finally found this place." Talen's laugh was low and rumbling. "He's a plant enthusiast. Has been since we were kits."

Georgia thought back to the lush conservatory and the potted plants in every room of the house. "He must be happy here."

"Like a *wuap* in mint."

Georgia didn't understand that phrase but let it slide. Context told her enough. "I think when you finish the repairs, the house will be quite the draw for guests."

"It has to be," he said, still staring upward. "No one travels to Corra for a holiday, but I think we can get enough trade from nearby towns. Drac's population has doubled in the last five years. We're close enough for a quick getaway but isolated enough to feel like a destination. This house was built for entertaining."

She saw that, in the way the rooms flowed into one another and partitions could be removed to make the spacious rooms even larger.

"The house has debt, which we're responsible for when we took ownership," he confessed.

"What kind of debt? This place was abandoned."

"For almost a hundred years," he said with a nod. "Unpaid taxes, mostly. I don't want you to think we're paupers. We have a sizeable inheritance. *Had*. I've sold assets but that money went directly into the house. The accounts aren't in the red and we have enough for the major repairs, but we need to turn a profit by spring. Tomorrow we'll look at the accounts and you'll see for yourself."

"You don't have to—"

"A manager needs to understand the financial situation. I don't trust Quil not to cheat the vendors, so I've been doing the books myself but there's no time. Busted pipes seem more important than sorting through invoices and billing."

"I'm going to disagree with you there." She'd use her office ninja skills to whip things into shape. "And thank you for being frank. Do you have the budget to pay my salary?"

"I'm counting on you being an investment. You're going to help me pull this house together."

"You have a lot of faith in a woman you don't really know," she said.

"I have faith in my mate," he replied.

"I'm not your mate."

"If you consider it from a certain vantage, you are." That teasing tone returned.

"If that certain vantage is a misogynistic notion that women are property, then you can go fuck yourself."

He laughed, the burst of amusement echoing off the stone walls. "I do like you."

Talen

CURIOUS KITS SHOULD NOT COMPLAIN when they find themselves in endless trouble. That is the price of curiosity.

-Persistence and the Secret of the Shadowed Hill

GEORGIA TOOK the chaos of running the house and shaped it into order. He showed her the household accounts, vendors and invoices, upcoming bookings. The disorganized pile of unpaid invoices frustrated and shamed him. He had no idea they had not paid their bills. When they ran cargo—which felt like a lifetime ago, not merely a year—shippers were also trying to screw them out of paying the bill. He knew exactly how frustrating it felt not to be paid for his labor and he hated that he inadvertently did just that.

Fiona was meant to help with the business end to free up his time for the very necessary renovations, but the female couldn't be bothered, it appeared. Talen knew that if he asked her to explain herself, she'd either claim she was bored or burst into tears. He never knew what to expect with his brother's mate.

Happily, Georgia seemed undaunted by the mess. She asked relevant questions, often wanting very explicit details, but she never asked the same question twice. She made notes, organized the invoices by most-urgent to least.

Georgia gazed out the window, a mug of coffee in hand, as the morning light pooled around her. A light layer of snow fell overnight, dusting the ground, and the sunlight seemed brighter as it reflected off the immaculate surface. What struck him was how obviously she belonged there, at ease in the quiet of the morning, before the hectic rush of the day. Ideally, she'd be sipping tea in his bedroom, wearing nothing, perhaps a blanket wrapped just so to expose her back and the fabric would gather just above the luscious curve of her ass—

Talen adjusted himself. She affected him. He hardly knew her, but his body craved her, which was a new experience for him, having always needed an emotional connection before he felt physical attraction. He couldn't explain the greedy way his eyes drank in her form, loving every curve and the thickness of her hips and thighs. She was built for a male like him. More than that, the way she lifted her stubborn chin and looked him in the eyes, unafraid. He stood a head taller than her, outweighed her with muscle mass, had claws and fangs that could shred her thin human skin, but she never held her sharp tongue and told him what she thought of him, which wasn't much.

He knew hardly anything about Georgia Phillips, but he wanted to know everything.

"Good morning. May the day bring you good fortune," he said. She muttered a reply. "That was barely comprehensible. Is that your first cup of coffee?"

"Oh, fuck off," she grumbled.

"As I suspected. I will refrain from conversation until you are sufficiently caffeinated."

She wrinkled her nose at him, which he found endearing beyond explanation, and drained the mug. He paid handsomely for the coffee, which she assured him was vital to her health, and it pleased the feral part of his brain that wanted to feed and provide for his mate.

"Have you eaten?" he asked.

She shook her head. "Fiona's having a meltdown about not getting an invitation to some party. Or maybe she did but has nothing to wear. I wasn't really listening. All I know is you don't want to be in the kitchen right now."

He agreed. They could eat in town if hungry. "Dress warmly today. We're going to the market."

The bookseller only made it to Drac's open-air market once every two months. He could download digital books to read, and did, but he enjoyed the tactile feel of a paper book.

The bookseller's stall overflowed with tables and boxes of treasure. His heart sped up at the sight.

"Are we looking for anything in particular?" Georgia

crouched down to examine a box filled with mystery novels. She thumbed through the copies, not pausing to read the blurb.

His tail twitched with irritation. "Do you not like books?"

"I like reading. I just never felt the need to clutter up my space with books. Seems inefficient when I can have thousands of books on a single device." Her words hurt him. Caused actual, physical pain.

"So, you're not perfect after all," he said with a dramatic sigh.

The look she tossed him stole his breath, her keen green eyes glimmering in the sunlight. "You thought I was perfect?"

"I'm looking to build a collection for the library," he said, sidestepping the question. "A casual mix of genres, I think, for the guests to enjoy." Not to mention the history volumes he asked the bookseller to track down, and a few more specialized titles.

She browsed the tables but never picked up a book. The behavior puzzled him and then he realized. "You don't read Corravian?"

A pink flush spread across her face.

Apparently not.

He looked at the tables, noticing for the first time that most of the books were written in Corravian, followed by Tal and Fremmian. He could speak and read in all three languages, but he had traveled extensively as a youth, an age that made language acquisition easier.

"The translation chip doesn't work on written stuff," she said. "Only audio. I have a Tal and Corravian grammar primer but it's so dull. I thought I'd pick up the reading comprehension by immersion."

"I did not mean to shame you."

"Not everyone picks up languages quickly. I'm working on it. That's all."

"Grammar readers are incredibly tedious. Let me find you something better." He scanned the tables, searching for the perfect book.

She picked up a book, seemingly at random. "It's amazing how you can tell the genre, even if you don't understand the language. Blue-gray cover. Haunting landscape. No people. This is a mystery or a thriller."

Talen recognized the author's name. "A mystery."

She crouched down next to a box on the ground and thumbed through the books. With a grin, she held up a red volume with two Corravian males embracing a female. Neither man had a shirt and the female was clearly enjoying her predicament. "This one's a romance," she said. She glanced at the cover again, "Actually, I think I'd like to read this."

He found the perfect book and held up the faded cloth-bound volume in triumph. *"Persistence and the Secret of the Shadowed Hill*. It is written in Tal. Now we need something in Corravian."

Georgia took the book and flipped through the pages. "This is a children's book."

"Not just any book. My favorite," he said.

"Your favorite kid's book."

"My favorite book," he repeated. He took the volume from her hand and flipped until he found a favorite passage. "It is about a young kit who suspects that the adults are keeping secrets, which they are. She and her friends investigate and solve the mystery. It is very exciting."

She gave him a dubious look. "A kid sleuth? That was your favorite?"

"You will read this." He handed the book and the next in the series to the bookseller. He read and re-read the series until his well-loved copy of the first book fell apart. Digital books were acceptable, but nothing captured the pure joy of reading under the covers of his bed, unable to sleep while the mystery remained unsolved. "The story is engaging, and the language is not too challenging."

"I'm not judging you," she said.

She was absolutely judging him.

"What was your favorite book as a kit?" he asked.

"Oh, you know, orphan boy goes to magic school. Shenanigans ensue. I think every kid loves those books. It's like Earth law."

He scoffed. "Orphans. All Earth stories are about orphans. Can humans write about anything else?"

"It's a time-honored literary convention," she said.

"It is improbable. There is no family? No one to care for a kit?" How could an entire family abandon a kit? His own family was small, but he would never willingly leave any of them. As much as they tried his patience, they carried his heart and would until the light left him.

Georgia grew silent, walking to another table. Her posture changed. Human body language was so difficult to read without a tail or ears, but she seemed rigid, defensive. From what was she defending herself?

Talen looked around the market. They were ignored in a crowd of people. The only answer was him. She needed to defend herself from him.

"Georgia? My mate?" He approached cautiously, ears flat and tail tucked tight to his body. He'd crawl to her on his hands and knees if need be.

"I'm not your mate." She swiped at her eyes. "Dammit. I'm not crying."

"You are distressed."

"No shit." Another swipe, this time with the cuff of her sweater. "I'm an orphan. I mean, my mom died when I was sixteen, so it's not like I was a little kid."

"You were a kit." She had told him this once before, at the bookseller's stall in the market.

"Legally, but I was very much on my own. As for my father, I haven't seen him for thirteen years, so he might as well be dead."

"Is he imprisoned? Why was he prevented from coming to you at the death of your mother?"

A smile born of pure anguish crawled across her face. "He might be in prison, I don't know. He left us. He didn't want anything to do with his sick wife or his kid. I can't believe I'm all teary-eyed about that bastard. It's not like, you know, things were great when he was around. He made Mom so sad. We were better off without him." She took a shaky breath. "I haven't thought about him in years." She sniffed, her nose pink but not entirely from the cold. "Ignore me. It's the solar radiation levels or something. Too much oxygen in the atmosphere."

Talen stood next to her. If she were Tal, he would curl his tail around hers in a sign of comfort. "How do humans give comfort?"

"You mean a hug?"

"Yes. I want to hug you," he said. "May I?"

"Knock yourself out, fuzzy britches."

He folded her into an embrace. Initially, she stood stiffly, as if enduring his touch, and then she slumped and melted into him. "I am an orphan, too," he confided. "My parents died when I was eight."

"That sucks," she said, voice muffled by his coat.

"It is hard for me to remember them now. Quil remembers them better than I. My father was a scholar. I believe I have my love of books from him," he said, not entirely understanding why he felt the need to share such personal information. Best not to think too hard on it.

She stirred, pulling away. The dullness in her green eyes alarmed him, like he was witnessing the light leave her and he desperately needed to bring that light back. Instinct told him to kiss her, to claim her mouth and pour his light into her. He did not care if he dimmed as he needed her to shine.

The civilized part of his brain cautioned that she might not appreciate all the things his body wanted to do to hers, not yet. Instead, he reached for a tool he suspected she would appreciate.

"Fuzzy britches? Really? My posterior is not fuzzy," he said.

She laughed, the sound delighting his soul.

Georgia

SOME TRUTHS ARE UNIVERSAL. *Pests are one such truth, as unfortunate as that may be.*

-Guidebook to Life on an Alien Planet

THE POUNCE of little feet on the bed jolted her awake. The cat-peacock creature, either the same one that curled up on her bed to sleep or another, had a wiggling, squeaking rodent in its mouth.

The cat-peacock looked at Georgia, fanned its tail in a brilliant display of colors, and dropped the rodent.

On her bed.

The mouse scurried up the blanket and over her legs.

Georgia thrashed and screamed, jumping out of bed and pulling all the blankets with her. She landed hard on the floor, fully awake and certain that the mouse was in her hair. In a panic, she batted at her hair.

Someone pounded on the door.

The cat-peacock gave a malicious murder cry and pounced. She woke in a nightmare of claws and feathers and squeaks and screams.

The door smashed open.

"What has happened? Are you injured?" Talen stood in the doorway, wearing only boxer briefs. His chest heaved, the striation pattern across his chest and shoulders moving with each breath.

"The thing has a *thing*!" She pointed at the cat-peacock, currently batting at the rodent.

The small creature gave a squeak and dashed under the bed. With a blood-curdling yell, Georgia scrambled back into the bed, clutching the blankets to her.

"Humility brought you a present." He sounded pleased.

Pleased.

"That thing dumped a mouse on me when I was asleep," Georgia said.

"That thing is a *wuap* and you'll hurt Humility's feelings."

He crouched down and peered under the bed. "Who's a good hunter? You. Yes, you are," he crooned.

"Don't encourage it. Just get rid of it."

"You'll give Humility a complex. *Wuaps* are very sensitive to the emotions of their people and she's our best hunter. We don't want her to feel unappreciated."

Humility hissed and the mouse squeaked. Something thumped under the bed. Georgia stuffed her fist in her mouth to preserve what little dignity she had. Mice didn't normally freak her out, but this was an alien mouse, it could be venomous for all she knew, and she did wake to see it dangling out of the jaws of Humility, feet scrabbling at the air, squeaking and twitching.

"This is a nightmare. I'm still asleep," she said.

Humility bolted out from the bed, tumbling across the floor with the said rodent in her mouth. Then, pretty as you please, the *wuap* jumped back into the bed, tail feathers fanned, and swallowed the mouse whole.

Georgia jumped off the bed and wrapped her arms around Talen. Slowly, he brought his arms around her in reassurance.

"She won't hurt you," he said.

"That's the most barbaric thing I've ever seen."

"It's not so bad."

"Looked plenty bad to me," she said. "It toyed with it. That's cruel."

"You should see footage of wild *wuaps* hunting. They toy with their prey, too."

She knew that Earth cats toyed with their prey before the kill, too. It was one thing to know that intellectually, it was another to hear the frightened little squeaks of a mouse having a mousy heart attack.

"Wild *wuaps*?" she asked.

"About this big." He gestured to his knees.

"You know what? I don't want to know. Don't tell me." The domesticated version of the *wuap* was the size of a large housecat. She didn't need to picture a feathery murder machine the size of a pony.

Humility sat on the bed, cleaning her paws.

"Can we trade beds tonight?" she asked. Not a drop of blood had been spilled on the bed, but she couldn't stomach crawling back under the blankets. At least, not until the bed had been stripped and everything washed on hot.

"You can sleep with me," he said, not teasing her for being squeamish.

CHAPTER 8

GEORGIA

Freema,

It's only the one tattoo, but it's military, so that's worth three at least.

-G

Days blended into weeks and Georgia learned the rhythm of the house. A woman came in from town three times a week to clean. Bright served as housekeeper and cook, managing two meals a day. They were on their own for lunch. Talen and Charl handled general maintenance and repairs. Construction on the house would go faster if they hired laborers but after Talen's frank discussion about their finances, she understood the slower pace to be a frugal decision. Quil concentrated on his plants, which meant he mostly left her alone, only occasionally wandering through the house with a bag of potting soil and a trowel. She had no idea what Fiona did and preferred to keep it that way.

The house had six *wuaps*, the species of the cat-peacock creature that feasted on a mouse in Georgia's bed. Each had their own personality. Justice insisted on sleeping in Georgia's bed each night. A cushion by the fire was insufficient, nor was an appropriately sized pet bed. Humility brought in a steady supply of dead rodents, leaving the offerings at the foot of the main staircase. Patience prowled the outdoors and only came in when the weather turned wet. Kindness was nothing but a bunch of lazy bones loosely held together by feathers and spent all her time napping in the sun. Fortitude followed Georgia with curiosity but scurried away when she tried to pet him. She had yet to see the mysterious sixth *wuap*, Prudence, who was reported to be shy.

Georgia never thought of herself as a cat person—or a cat-peacock person—but she liked it when Justice jumped up on her lap when reading or curled up on the bed each night. She didn't care for it so much when she found a partially eaten mouse in her slippers.

She worried about the spring. At the current pace of construction, they wouldn't be ready. They only had three rooms ready for guests and three, even if they were occupied every day, would not pay the bills.

Spring also brought other considerations, such as groundskeeping. The grounds were extensive and overgrown. Quil would need at least another person to help him tame the gardens, lawn, and environs.

If guest occupancy increased, then they needed to hire additional housekeeping, and possibly a kitchen assistant. Bright never complained, but Georgia saw how stiffly she moved and climbed the stairs. No doubt Bright would blame the cold rather than age if anyone ever fussed about her. Georgia kept her mouth shut and added a note about hiring assistants for Bright.

The first task on her list was to sort out the broken windows. The house needed to make a good first impression, not scare away guests with the promise of drafty rooms. A conversation with the contractor revealed they were waiting on the windows to be delivered before they could install them. With another call, she discovered the windows would not be delivered until the invoice was paid.

Georgia shifted through a pile of invoices, bills, bank statements, and other paperwork, before she found overdue notices, and not just for the windows. Talen had admitted that he loathed the bookkeeping side of managing the house and had asked Fiona to take on that responsibility. All evidence pointed to no one paying any bills for months, thankfully due to neglect and not lack of funds.

Georgia took three days to sort through the mess and paid the most pressing accounts. She set up a desk in the study but Quil also had a desk there. On an average day, she didn't see him, which suited her just fine.

They played a cat-and-mouse game of exiting a room when the other entered. If he prowled into the study and propped his feet up on his desk, she had a dozen other irons in the fire that needed attention. There was always something going on and some days she walked miles in the house.

Avoidance was a normal, healthy way to deal with unpleasantness. Lots of people said so. Probably.

Okay, she was being a coward, but she had nothing more to say to the man who left her at the altar. They would never be friends, so she bit her tongue and kept quiet. The last thing she needed was for the Achaval brothers to realize they didn't need a sarcastic, cranky woman hanging around their house, making snide comments and eating their food. Better to keep to herself and avoid trouble.

Trouble, however, liked to fuck on her desk, she learned one afternoon.

Run off her feet dealing with the damn windows again, she ducked into the study to grab her tablet. There she saw Fiona bent over her desk—not Quil's—being pounded merrily by the man who had his own perfectly good desk.

No amount of soap and furniture polish would make that desk clean.

Ever.

So that was how she came to share the old housekeeper's office in the basement with Bright.

Under the kitchen was a labyrinth of disused servant quarters, storage, scullery, laundry, and even a wine cellar. The room was dark, despite the narrow windows near the ceiling, but it was quiet. Bright rarely ventured in except to drop off receipts for food deliveries or cleaning supplies, and to bring her a cup of tea. It was the perfect work environment.

Freema continued to write, encouraging her to be spontaneous and do "something stupid" and wanting pics of Talen's tattoo. The girl had no boundaries.

Other than the eyeful she got her first day on the job, he kept his distance and kept his clothes on.

If she kept her head down, she'd be on a ship, heading off-planet in no time. That was the plan. Every night when she crawled into her gigantic, empty bed, she reminded herself that even if the plan bored her to tears, it was the smart thing to do. She didn't need spontaneity. She tried spontaneous once, and it didn't work out.

A knock at the office door yanked her out of her ruminations.

"So, this is your subterranean lair," Talen said, his amber gaze taking in the simple room. The wall could use a fresh coat of paint, but she wasn't staying, so it seemed like a waste of time and paint. A rug on the floor and more lighting would make the room cozy, but, again, she wasn't staying.

"It's tolerable."

"Tolerable. High praise indeed." He poked at the window frame of the lone window, high in the wall. "It's drafty and cold. This is unacceptable."

"I have a space heater and it's quiet." No one ever ventured down the stairs except Bright, and Georgia had her self-heating blanket wrapped around her shoulders like a shawl. She loved that thing.

"We're playing cards and need a fourth," Talen said.

"I don't play cards."

"I'll teach you."

The moment stretched out between them. She couldn't help but think that he was sort of perfect, exactly the type of guy she hoped to find waiting for her when she got off that ship, but she shouldn't get involved. That wouldn't be fair to either of them. She wasn't staying. Five more months and she'd be on a ship, headed toward a colony.

"I'm tired and we've got the window installation to deal with tomorrow," she said. One hundred and twelve windows in total and a crew of four. The work would take at least three days if the weather cooperated. If the winter storm came through as predicted, the work would be delayed. All guest bookings had been canceled until the work was finished. "I think I'm just going to finish this and go to bed."

"If you change your mind, we're playing for bragging rights. Someone is too full of himself and needs to have his ego deflated."

"Maybe next time," she lied.

"Next time," he said, tossing a warm smile.

Gah, she was such a weenie. The hot, friendly guy she secretly thought was perfect wanted to spend time with her, and she hid underground like a troll because she was a coward.

This was fine. This was the plan.

She certainly didn't feel pangs of envy when laughter drifted down the kitchen stairs into her subterranean lair.

Her plan sucked balls.

Talen

TALENT,

I am alarmed at the flirtatious nature of your relationship with Georgia. I did not bring the female to Corra or this house, to have you drooling after her like a kit who just discovered what his cock is for. It's deeply embarrassing to witness your amateurish moves. Sometimes it is like you have never spoken to a female before.

I understand that this may not be entirely your fault, as military service kept you in the company of females of an equally blunt and boorish nature.

I am available to provide tutelage. I do so only out of a sense of familial obligation and a desire to shield the family name from dishonor.

You carry my heart,

Your Elder and Superior Sibling

THE WINDOW INSTALLATION started just after dawn

and continued until the storm loomed over the foothills, turning the sky an ominous gray. This winter storm promised significant snow and high winds. The workers left at mid-afternoon, leaving ample time to arrive safely in their home. They would return in two days if the roads were passable.

The new windows had shutters that oscillated closed like the lens of a camera. Those secured automatically. The older windows, especially the broken ones, had to be secured by nailing plywood over the vulnerable glass. Wind speeds in a storm topped out at just shy of the fantastic. Any stray debris, even as small as a pebble, would shatter the window and send glass flying. By the time Talen, Charl, and Quil secured all the windows, the sky was completely dark.

Bright called them into the kitchen for the evening meal.

"Where's Georgia?" he asked, noticing the empty spot at the table. The female avoided socialization, at least when Quil or Fiona were present, but she never skipped meals. They used that time to compare notes for the day.

"How should I know? This house has been so cold today I spent the day in bed. Alone," Fiona complained, tossing a pouty look toward Quil.

"I had important matters to attend to," Quil said.

"Your wife is an important matter," she said.

"Very."

"And I felt neglected." Another pout and Quil ate it up, promising to spend extra time together, perhaps a trip.

The expense of those trips added up. He should say something to Quil, but it would only lead to an argument. His brother would hear nothing negative about his mate.

"She said she was cold and wanted to warm up in the bathhouse," Charl said.

"And you didn't stop her," Talen accused.

"That was an hour ago. She had time to return before the snow arrived."

Outside, snow already fell but did not yet coat the ground. The wind had yet to arrive. Georgia was still out there, possibly unaware of the severity of the storm. If she did not return to the house soon, she would be trapped in the bathhouse, a structure with no door and a ceiling that opened to the sky. Staying there offered as much protection from the elements as standing in a field.

His worry took a dark turn. She could have slipped or fallen on the stone steps and fractured a bone. Humans were fragile. They broke so easily. He saw plenty of broken human legs and arms in the Navy. The sailors put on a brave face and never admitted the pain. Georgia was a civilian. How would she tolerate the pain? She could be unconscious, passed out and bleeding.

Blood would attract predators, particularly mornclaws. Violent storms often uncovered egg clutches, causing them to hatch and seek prey. That was another reason to secure buildings from flying debris. Mornclaws would seek out the heat of a home, especially in the winter.

"I have to find her."

He grabbed his coat and a powerful flashlight and headed out the door. He shouted but heard no answer. The wind stirred, cold against his face. In thirty minutes, the storm would arrive full force. Maybe an hour if the stars were kind.

Thankfully, he did not find her in a broken heap on the stone stairs. She was in the bathhouse, floating in the coppery water, eyes closed in serenity. The pale tips of her breasts crested the water, along with the swell of her belly and her thighs. Her dark hair fanned out around her, like some enchanting sea creature. Snow drifted in from the oculus in the ceiling, melting into a fine mist when it hit the warm air.

"My mate!" His shout echoed off the stone walls. Startled, she splashed, sinking down in the water. "Apologies, I didn't mean to shout."

Submerged in the water from her chin down, the green water obscured her form. She watched him with narrowed, suspicious eyes. "Can't I have a little bit of privacy? And I'm not your mate."

"We don't have time to waste on that tedious argument. The storm is nearly here." He normally enjoyed teasing her, just to see the flush of color in her complexion, but they had no time for such flirtation now.

"Then stop bringing up that tedious idea that I'm property you can trade like... like I don't know, something tradeable. Goats or some shit."

Spying a thick towel and a pile of her carefully folded clothes, he extended the towel toward her.

She kicked and swam away from him. "The snow's not that bad."

Spoken like a novice. "The snow is not the issue. It is the wind," he said.

She dipped under the water and reemerged, slicking back her wet hair. "Two ideas," she said. The coppery green water hid her form. Only the tops of her shoulders were visible. "We should rent out the house for functions and events."

"We rent rooms to guests." He would fail if he tried to rush her, understanding that his mate was a stubborn one. She'd dig her claws in and hang on tightly. They still had some time to return to the shelter of the house safely.

"Yes, and the house is amazing. It was built to entertain, you said. People will pay good money, a lot of money, to hold weddings and parties here. You even have a ballroom."

"That requires refurbishment." But he could see the potential.

She dipped under the water again. "Then we hire some people to get it finished. The conservatory is a photogenic and intimate place to exchange vows or hold a small event. In the summer, we can set up a marquee on the lawn."

He made a non-committal noise.

"We have ten rooms if people want to stay the night, which is perfect for smaller events. For the larger ones, we're not that far out. Besides, I've been looking at the market, and there's nothing comparable in Drac. If someone wants to get married and have a party, they do it in their backyard. It's a good idea."

The confidence in her voice was unmistakable.

"And the other idea?"

"We should fuck," she said.

CHAPTER 9

GEORGIA

G,

Get it.

-Freema

This wasn't like her. This was rash and impulsive, a bad idea in progress, and her heart raced with excitement.

The way he looked at her, like he wanted to toss her over his shoulder caveman-style, made her shiver, in a good way. Naked and wet, she wanted him to throw her down to the floor—okay, maybe onto a towel on the floor—and fuck her senseless.

The day had been so frustrating; she just wanted to feel good. Despite being introduced as the house manager, the window installers refused to follow her directions. Every question, every decision, they just ignored her and ran off to Talen, only to have him repeat her words. The shitshow took twice as long as it should have, resulting in the windows running way past the estimated three-day installation. With the storm setback, it'd take a week, easy. She had to cancel guest bookings, which was lost revenue and a black eye to the house's reputation.

If she'd been on Earth, she'd order a pizza, eat ice cream right out of the container, and wallow in self-pity.

But she was tired of wallowing. She came to Corra to do something different, something exciting, and right now that excitement stood in front of her and had a sexy-ass tail.

"I like you," she said, feeling the need to explain herself. "And I've been thinking about you, that way, since day one. I know this is a bad idea because you're my boss—"

"I'm your mate."

"And I'm not staying. I've tried to be good and follow a life plan, but that didn't work. I tried to be spontaneous, and that didn't work. So maybe I should just enjoy myself? Today was bullshit and I should have some fun." The words spilled out. If he said no, fine. She'd have an answer and would stop thinking about him every night, wondering. "Can't two adults who are attracted to each other have fun without commitments or any expectations? No strings attached, that's what I want. Me. You. Naked. Sweaty. Fucking."

He stared at her, his tail frozen and his ears back.

Not exactly the reaction she expected. Her face burned so hot with a blush, she thought she might burst into flame. That was as explicit as she'd ever been in her life and she desperately wanted to claw the words back. "I'm sorry. I thought… but I misread. Obviously. You don't think of me that way." She swam toward the edge of the pool, where he still held out the towel.

"I do think of you that way," he said.

"It's nothing, probably just proximity and hormones." The attraction couldn't be real. The more she thought about it, the more obvious it became. "Forget I said anything."

She grabbed the towel, but he did not release his hold. For a moment, they both tugged on the cloth.

"Listen to me, my heart. Yes, I agree. You have many clever ideas, about which I am very enthusiastic, especially the last one. But now, we need to return to the house before the winds pick up. It is already snowing heavily." He pointed to the ceiling, where fluffy flakes came in fast but melted immediately. "Now please dry yourself and dress quickly."

She climbed out, momentarily worried about what he would think at the squishy roll of her waist or the jiggling of her butt, but she ignored that moment of self-doubt. If he didn't like the look of her fat ass, better to know now.

Still damp, she tossed her sweater on and wiggled into her jeans. Shoving her feet into her boots, she peeked at Talen, gratified to find him watching her with a ravenous expression. If she had any doubts about his attraction to her, the cockstand he sported cleared that up.

Okay, not turned off by a fat ass.

He hadn't been joking about the wind. The moment she stepped out of the shelter of the bathhouse; the cold wind tore through every layer of clothing until she felt like she wore nothing at all. Hard pellets of frozen rain mixed with snow hit her face.

"Take this," Talen said. He fastened his coat over hers and grabbed her by the hand.

Carefully, she made her way up the slick stone steps, one hand gripping the railing and the other holding onto Talen. Her foot slipped and she felt herself fall back. His grip tightened as he pulled her back from disaster and steadied her. Visibility had fallen and she could barely see past her nose. She held onto the railing, sliding her hand up incrementally and feeling the steps out with the toe of her boots as she went. Coming out before the storm was irresponsible and losing track of time bordered on stupid.

Finally, they reached the top of the stairs. She felt frozen solid. Definitely no feelings in her toes or her fingers. The gloves worked like a charm on a normal day but did nothing against the wind. Talen swung her up into his arms and she let him carry her back to the house.

The warmth of the kitchen surrounded them, and Georgia shivered, feeling the cold in her bones. Bright and Charl's conversation abruptly ceased. They had to be a sight, Talen snowed over like a yeti and carrying her like a prize.

No, not a prize. He carried her like a dumb lamb that wandered off in a snowstorm. Embarrassment flooded over her.

"Put her by the fire," Bright said. "Where did you find her? She looks frozen."

"I feel frozen too," she said, teeth chattering. She shed the coat, crusted over with ice pellets, which clattered as the pellets hit the floor. "I'm sorry about the floor. I'll need a mop or some towels."

"We'll worry about that later. Now, get those clothes off." Talen held up a towel, indicating that she should strip and dry herself.

She grabbed the bottom of her damp shirt and hesitated, keenly aware of the eyes watching. "I can do without the audience."

"Humans are shy," Charl said, somehow speaking while shoveling food into his mouth.

The condescension in his tone rubbed her the wrong way. It had been a long, hard day of dealing with workers who didn't like taking orders from a human woman and had to run everything by Talen. She wanted a few minutes of peace and quiet but apparently, she couldn't do that right and had to be rescued from freezing to death in a blizzard, so the four-armed alien could take his know-it-all attitude and fuck right off.

"Not wanting to flash my bare ass to the world ain't being shy," she snapped. "It's called not being a pervert. Scram."

"Leave us," Talen said.

Chairs scraped against the floor as everyone left. Charl took his plate with him. Bright gently touched her arm and gave her a concerned look. Georgia nodded, which seemed to pacify the older woman's concerns.

She stripped, eager to get the damp clothes off her body. Talen rubbed her down with a towel and discarded that one before producing another. She wrapped it around her and moved a chair closer to the fire. She carefully towel-dried her hair while he rubbed her feet.

His warm hands brought life to her numb toes as he rubbed and kneaded the digits.

"Is it wrong that this makes nearly freezing to death worth it?" she asked, leaning back in the chair.

"I'm enjoying the view," he said, the hint of fangs in his grin, "but try not to make it a habit." She gave a slight shove with her foot before he switched to the other foot. He continued speaking, "The thought of you lost in the storm was too much. Please, my heart, have mercy on me. My heart could not survive without you."

His words were sweet, but they couldn't be sincere. He didn't have to butter her up since he was already getting laid.

His hand moved up her leg. "I like how you are hard here," he said, caressing the muscles in her calves. "And soft here," moving his hand to her inner thighs. With a hand on either knee, he spread her legs and moved between them.

Georgia lifted her hips, waiting for a brush of fingers, for hot breath, for anything, but nothing happened.

"Everything okay down there?"

Talen stared into her pussy like it was a complex puzzle to be solved.

Shit. When was the last time she groomed herself? Her bush had to be a jungle by now.

Mood: ruined.

She sat up, scooting back in the chair. When she attempted to close her legs, his powerful grip kept them open.

"Human physiology is different," he said.

"Different good or different bad?"

"Your clitoris is external," he replied, not answering the question at all.

"Yeah."

"Is it pleasurable when stimulated?"

"Oh yeah."

"May I?" His amber eyes watched her, waiting for permission to touch her pussy.

This doofus.

For an ex-Navy guy, he was surprisingly chivalrous. She expected him to swear more than her, be vulgar, and just take his pleasure, not thoughtfully study her body because he wanted the experience to be good for her.

For someone who agreed to a no-strings-attached fling, he

made it hard not to fall for him. He was close to perfect in a lot of ways, but that could just be her being horny. A good fuck and she'd get over it.

"Talent Achaval, if you don't get your face in my pussy right this second, I'll snatch your ears right off your head," she said.

He huffed with mirth, the fucker. "Is that what humans call your cunt? Slang for a feline?"

"My twat, beaver, cooter, snatch, and muff. I don't care what you call it."

He leaned in, her inner thigh aching with the stretch. A breath away from her flesh, he said, "And what do you want me to call this beauty?"

"I don't care. Call it what you want," she said, voice plaintive.

Did he want her to beg? He certainly enjoyed teasing her. If he thought she wouldn't give him a taste of his own medicine, he had another thing coming. If she could get that big cock of his in her mouth, she'd suck it like her new favorite lollipop and draw it out, not letting him come until he grabbed her by the hair and pistoned into her face, losing that chivalrous veneer and showing her his lusting heart—

"Mine. I'll call it mine," he said, derailing her thoughts of teasing out revenge as he licked her silky folds.

She melted from the combined warmth of him, the rough texture of his tongue, and the strength of his fingers gripping her thighs. His claws pricked against her skin. She'd have a bruise in the morning, maybe even puncture marks, but she didn't care. Her hands dug into his mess of hair, nearly pulling out clumps as she came fast and hard.

He leaned back on his heels and licked his lips, eyes dark and full of feral desire.

She panted, desperate to catch her breath. "I'm sorry. I came too fast. That was really, really good." She stumbled over the words, aware that nothing could express how that brief encounter was the single best sexual experience of her life.

"More," he growled. Holding both her wrists in one hand, he steered her over to the table. His free hand swept aside the dishes, making a spot for her. Her belly pressed against the hard edge of the table and she felt his heat behind her.

He planted his hands on either side of her, caging her in. His claws popped and flexed, gouging the polished wood surface. All she could think of was her defiled desk in the study and how everyone ate their meals at this table. They traded jokes and stories, teased with such affection as they passed around platters. She'd never be able to eat her breakfast and not remember Talen's claws digging into the table as his cock dug into her and anyone who noticed the fresh marks would also know, which was basically everyone.

"Wait," she said.

He growled and did not move, waiting.

"Not here."

He backed away immediately. "Have you changed your mind?"

"Oh no. This is happening, just not on the kitchen table," she said.

A grin spread across his face. "We do have perfectly serviceable beds upstairs."

She glanced at the door and wrapped the ends of her damp hair around her fingers. "Is there any chance we can make it upstairs without being seen?"

He crowded against her. His hands rested comfortably on her hips, like they belonged there. "Are you shy, my mate?"

"Not your mate and not shy." She lightly pushed him away, slipping away to retrieve her partially dried clothes. "We just don't need to advertise what we're doing. Some things are private."

"I believe it is best to assume everyone knows." He took the damp clothes away and wrapped her in a large towel. Tenderly, he tucked the ends in, securing it.

"They don't know for sure."

He huffed but did not argue.

A blush rose to her cheeks. Everyone knew. Of course they knew. She and Talen had been eye-fucking each other since she arrived on Corra and he hadn't been subtle when he told everyone to leave.

She needed to say something. Anything. He was about two seconds from asking her why she blushed, and then she'd stammer out something about this not being a big deal, how it was just sex with no strings, and she'd try to sound convincing even though it would the first time she had sex in over a year and with the only person besides Kevin, so it was a big deal and she refused to freak out.

"The floor is cold," she said as a weak excuse, shifting from one bare foot to the other.

Gathering up their boots and clothes, his tail wrapped around her wrist and he led her up the stairs.

Talen

WITH THE TASTE of her on his tongue and tantalizing glimpses of her ass peeking out from the towel as she climbed the stairs, Talen would follow his mate to the blackest reaches of deep space and back. The moment they crossed the threshold to her room, he pushed her to the bed. Their clothes lay in a discarded heap on the floor and he couldn't care less. His mate lifted her hips, presenting her swollen pink cunt to him.

"So perfect," he said, carefully stroking the globes of her ass. His fingertips itched and burned as his claws demanded to extend. If he was not careful, he would shred his mate's delicate skin.

"Talen," she mewled.

He retrieved the claw caps from his nightstand and divested himself of his remaining clothes. Georgia twisted on the bed, watching him as he opened the container. He had hoped to be able to control his reflex to claw, but he did not want to hurt her. He'd happily take a decrease in sensitivity to spare her pain.

"Let me," she said. Slowly and deliberately, she licked the length of his fingers before placing the caps.

"Your lips will look so pretty around my cock," he said.

She hummed happily as she finished both hands. He flexed his fingers. "How do they feel?"

"Odd, but not as odd as I expected." The flexible material warmed to the shape of his body. He would grow used to the sensation in time.

"You've never used the caps before? I'm your first human?" She smiled, pleased with herself, and Talen had to confess that the smugness charmed him.

He leaned forward, pushing her back onto the bed, and planted a hand on either side of her. He loomed over her; a hunter fixed on his mark. She licked her kiss-swollen lips. "My mate. My only human," he said.

"I'm not your mate," she replied softly.

"But you are my human."

"Yes." No hesitation. No denial.

His.

Happiness rumbled in his chest. Enough talk. He flipped her over, stomach down, and climbed onto the bed. His thighs straddled her, and he gripped her ass cheeks, parting enough to push into her warm cunt. He held onto the generous curves of her bottom, pulling her toward him, and he pushed forward.

She bit her lip, trying to hold back her moans even as she lifted her hips with every thrust. He lost his rhythm and fell forward, hands on either side of her, caging her in. With the new angle, he hit the perfect spot. Her moans became outright cries of ecstasy.

His mate. No matter what she said, he claimed her.

He leaned forward; mouth pressed to the shell of her ear. "You feel so good on my cock," he said. "Tight. Made for me, my lovely human."

Her entire body shivered at his words and her cunt gripped him tighter. She pulsed around him, squeezing, as she found her climax.

An electric spark coiled at the base of his spine, signaling his own release. With a growl, he pumped deep into her. The feral part of his mind wanted to coat her womb with his seed, to plant a kit in her, sink his claws in and mark his mate. His fingers flexed, digging into her soft, yielding flesh.

No doubt his civilized self would have some pangs of guilt about the bruises tomorrow. A male his size needed to be careful, to be mindful of how he touched his mate, but for the moment he was inordinately pleased. He wanted her to feel him tomorrow, to remember how he possessed her and made her come undone.

As their bodies cooled, sated and relaxed, he held in his arms. His tail curled possessively around her ankle, desperate for any bit of contact.

His human.

His mate.

His heart.

Georgia

TALEN RUBBED his hand up and down her arm, unable to get enough of her. "Why did you come?"

"Angle and position, I imagine. Technique had something to do with it. Plenty of clit stimulation, so thank you for that. Good job. I rate this a satisfactory experience."

He rolled onto his back, huffing with amusement. Yeah, she knew he meant why did she come to Corra, but found it too hard to give an honest answer when he looked at her with those puppy dog eyes. Wrong turn of phrase. Kitty cat eyes? No. Bedroom eyes, yes. Heavy and hooded and sparking with desire. Eyes that made her brain short circuit and forget the question.

"I'm sorry," she said. "It's easier when you're not looking at me."

"Yes. I find myself inspecting the floor or the ceiling often in your presence." He gave a gentle nudge to indicate no hard feelings.

"It's not that you're too good-looking, but you're too good-looking," she started.

"Much obliged. I often worry if I'm too attractive," he said dryly. Then, he added in a serious tone, "I'm not Quil."

"Thank heavens for that." She twisted her fingers in her hair. "I worry about what people think and if I don't look at you, then I don't have to worry about what you're thinking."

"Fascinating ceiling. Plaster and wood. There's a damp spot in the corner. Is that new? I'll check the attic and see if the roof is leaking," he said.

They lay side-by-side, nearly touching. Wind gusted around the house and whistled down the chimney, but the warmth of the fire—and the company—drove away thoughts of the storm.

"My mom died of cancer," she blurted out. "That's why I came to Corra. I mean, that's why I signed up for the agency. I thought I had cancer too." She sighed, taking a moment to calm herself. "My mother died of cervical cancer when I was sixteen. I didn't have any other family, so I went into foster care."

She took a breath, gathering her thoughts. "Nothing terrible happened in foster care. You hear stories of bad homes and abusive parents, but the worst that ever happened to me was that I was alone. No one cared." No extended family, aunts or cousins or even a long-lost grandparent, emerged after her mother's death. Georgia had to learn to take care of herself because no one else could be bothered. That was probably the birth of her obsessive need for the security that having a life plan provided. She couldn't blame her sixteen-year-old self for finding the adult world intimidating.

"That is too young to be on your own," he said.

"A little more than a year ago, I fell ill. More than a year, I guess. Being sick sneaks up on you. When you feel lousy for long enough, that just becomes normal. Anyway, the doctors thought it could be cervical cancer, like my mom."

"Was it?"

"No. I had polyps, a growth in my uterus, but it wasn't cancer." She reached up to toy with the ends of her hair again but paused.

Talen covered her hand with his and gave it a reassuring squeeze.

"It scared me," she said. "I want a family. Kids. All that. But I had this plan, like a timeline. Then I realized that my mom was only a few years older than me when she died, so maybe I needed to accelerate the timeline." She glanced at Talen, who kept his gaze fixed on the ceiling. "The worst part is I debated how to tell all this to my boyfriend, the man I thought I was going to marry, when I found him fucking someone else."

His hand squeezed hers, but he said nothing, allowing her to continue speaking at her own pace.

"Playing it safe didn't work out for me, so I decided to do

something wild. Unexpected. That didn't work out so great for me, either."

It brought her to him, she wanted to add, but Georgia held her tongue. It didn't matter. She wanted casual, she said. She wasn't staying.

CHAPTER 10

GEORGIA

Most sentient life in the known universe can consume the cuisine of other planets with no ill effect, excluding specific allergens. Flavor profiles vary by culture and some spices may not be suitable to everyone's taste, but any food can be consumed without worry.

-Guidebook to Life on an Alien Planet

"Stop the car!" Georgia flung the door open and took two steps before barfing up her lunch. A soothing hand rubbed her back. She tried to keep her hair from her mouth, but the wind fought her, and tendrils caught the bile on her lips.

So gross.

Stomach finally empty, Bright handed her a bottle of luke-warm water. She rinsed her mouth, trying to wash out the taste of garlic sausage and stomach acid.

"Better?" the older woman asked, watching her with deep consideration.

Georgia took a deep breath, trying to judge the tenderness of her stomach. "I think so."

"Are you with kit?"

"What? No." She climbed back into the vehicle, ignoring the older woman's concerned gaze as she fastened her seatbelt. "I'm not."

"The way you've been carrying on, it's a natural assumption."

"I've been carrying on? It's not just me *carrying on*, but that doesn't matter, because the answer is still no." Like what she and Talen got up to was any of Bright's damn business. They hadn't started on a discreet note, with Talen practically ordering everyone out of the kitchen so he could bang her on the table. "Besides, I had the birth control shot before I left Earth. That's good for two years."

"This is the second day in a row you've been sick," Bright said.

"I think the sausage I had at the market was spoiled or something. It tasted funny." She assumed the funky taste was due to the unfamiliar blend of spices, not that the sausage had gone bad. She enjoyed wandering the vendor stalls at the weekly farmer's market in town. The delicious aromas always brought her to a new favorite and she never hesitated to try new food.

Just remembering the savory, pungent smell of the

sausage stand made her stomach turn. She covered her mouth and fought back the urge to gag. "It was a bad sausage. That's all."

Bright snorted. "Bad sausage. That's one way to put it."

Georgia blinked, unsure if she really heard the older woman, the woman who Talen considered his mother, make a dick joke.

"I'm old, not blind. Or deaf," Bright said. The afternoon light created a silvery crown out of her white hair.

Georgia blushed. "Can we not talk about this? I'm not pregnant."

The vehicle shifted into motion. For a moment, her stomach tumbled and she almost begged Bright to pull over again.

Everything stayed put. Stupid actual-sausage-and-a-not-a-crude-dick-joke-sausage.

"A kit would be nice, don't you think? I miss the sounds of little ones," Bright said.

She'd be lying if she said that the promise of marriage and kids hadn't prompted her to change her life and come to Corra, so she kept her mouth shut.

"THIS IS A CLASSIC OF TAL CINEMA," Talen said. He settled against the headboard. He propped up a tablet on a pillow and it projected onto the wall.

A Tal male, dressed in a fussy silk military uniform with very tight pants, stood heroically on a—

"Is that a mountain of skulls?" Georgia settled on the bed next to Talen, dragging a blanket over her.

"Mount Penlo. That's not accurate, though," he said.

"It's a metaphor? The giant mountain of skulls is a metaphor for how kick-butt this guy is?"

"No. The actual Mount Penlo is much larger. Prone to collapsing, though. It's not the most stable mountain of skulls. That's what happens when you take no pride in craftsmanship."

Georgia twisted to face Talen, searching for any sign he was serious. His face remained placid, even sincere. The tail twitch gave him away.

"You're fucking with me," she said. "No pride in crafts-manship."

"Your face! You were looking at me like you thought I lost my mind." He grinned broadly and she couldn't help but smile too.

"So, what's this movie about?"

"It's based on a historical novel. An innocent female gets lost in a forest on a school trip and is rescued by a noto-rious rogue and scoundrel."

"How young are we talking? Because I'm not interested in watching some male fantasy about deflowering virgin schoolgirls. It's gross."

"Deflowering? Do humans actually say that?"

"Well, it's a bit prissy and old-fashioned, but yeah," she said.

"I never suspected you of being prissy."

"Shut up. Now, what else happens if Lord Creeper isn't creeping on underage girls?"

"Lord Avarice—"

She snickered at the name.

"Be quiet. Do not mock my culture," Talen said.

"No, tell me more about the notorious rogue and scoundrel, Lord *Avarice*." She pressed the back of her hands to her cheeks. Her face hurt from smiling.

"Lord Avarice is a gentleman. They meet again in two years' time."

"When she's conveniently a legal adult."

"Yes, because he is not such a gentleman their second night together."

"Okay, where does the mountain of skulls come in?" she asked.

"No," he said, folding his arms over his chest. "You will have to watch to find out."

"Come on."

"No."

"Come on…" Her fingers brushed the tip of his tail, which

jerked away. He regarded her with a look of scandal on his face.

Oh shit.

She was just playing but went too far. Talen never grabbed her boobs or her ass when he teased, so why would she grab his tail? "Too much? I'm sorry. Was that a bad touch?"

He tossed his head back and laughed. It echoed off the bedroom walls and she was certain the entire house could hear him. "Twice! You are too easy."

"Are you really sitting in my bed and calling me easy?"

He gestured broadly to the room, subtly implying that the situation did point toward her ease and accessibility.

No one had ever accused Georgia of being easy. Uptight. Frigid. A goody two-shoes. Never easy.

Finally.

She couldn't wait to tell Freema.

"Okay, start the film. I won't make fun of it if you actually answer my questions without the bullshit," she said, adjusting the pillow behind her back as she leaned against the headboard.

Talen placed an arm over her shoulder like it belonged there, like they had cuddled and watched a dozen films. "Deal."

TALEN'S CLAWS dug into the wood paneling. Georgia gave a melting moan, grinding back against his hard cock, not caring that they'd have to repair the damage.

Add it to the list.

"I want you, wife," he said, practically purring into her ear.

"I'm not your wife," she protested.

This was their game. He made a statement of what he wanted; she denied it but absolutely wanted the same thing. Talen never took more than she would give.

"And I don't want you."

I want you.

They both knew their marriage license wasn't worth the paper it was printed on. Soon the courts would dissolve the farce and they'd go their separate ways. Until then, nothing said that two adults couldn't have fun together. It was just sex, not love. Amazing sex, yes, but not anything to keep her on this backwater planet.

His hands skimmed down her arms and back, pausing to squeeze her butt. He rucked up her skirt, revealing the lacy boy shorts.

"Get your filthy paws off me," she said.

Touch me.

"These are very pretty. Did you wear them for me?" That voice, smoother than silk and so deep it reverberated through her body, made her ache. Purr didn't begin to describe the effect Talen's voice had on her. She shouldn't want him this badly. He wasn't her husband, not really, and these games, while fun, would come to an eventual end. But she couldn't resist him. She was human, after all.

"They're not for you." *Only for you.*

"I think you wore them for your mate and I think you want your mate to take them off." His fingers hooked under the waistband, the tips of his claws scratching at her. He had claw caps and had even offered to wear them for her protection, but Georgia enjoyed the scrapes and abrasions of his love marks.

"Don't, please." *Please, please, please.*

He tugged the panties down, exposing her to the cool, damp air. He crouched down and paused, drinking in the sight of her. She practically vibrated with need.

She could remove her hands from the wall. She could push him away and stop the game at any time, but she didn't want to. She wanted her husband-by-a-technicality to do all the filthy things he promised. Besides, it's not like they were emotionally invested in each other. This was just sex.

His tail brushed up her inner thigh. She shivered and pushed her ass back, hoping he'd get the idea. What was he waiting for? The corridor wasn't in a high traffic part of the house but with her luck, someone would blunder down the hall soon and see her with her ass on display.

Maybe Bright had been right to tease her. They were hardly subtle, but she found she didn't care at the moment. She spun in place, intending to push Talen to the ground and climb on top.

Talen, her almost fake alien husband, knelt at her feet, his pupils blown wide, obscuring the amber of his eyes. His ears twitched and his tail wrapped around her waist, tugging her close.

"Georgia, I want you."

This wasn't a game anymore.

Oh, fuck.

He looked about a moment away from doing something dumb like pledging his everlasting devotion or proposing that they make their not-marriage real.

She pushed him down to the hardwood floor and climbed on, distracting them both with sensory overload. He gripped her hips, but his claws did not puncture her skin. Their love was fast and loud, and anyone could turn the corner and discover them. The pair was so self-indulgent it was embarrassing, and she might have been if she hadn't liked the way her body shivered with need when Talen reached for her.

They were still learning each other and exploring their limits. She never would have guessed a year ago that she'd have the balls to ride a man in a dusty hallway. He made her reckless and she loved the heady exhilaration when he fixed those amber eyes on her, like she was exciting and not a stick-in-the-mud, like she brought him to life, like he felt a fraction of what she felt for him.

Oh, fuck.

They hadn't been playing a game for a long while now.

Talen

HUMANS HAVE a unique mating concept called "friends with benefits." At its core, it is mating for pleasure only, either for a limited time or at periodic intervals. It differs from a one-time sexual encounter, called a "hookup" or "one-night stand", in that the friend-with-benefits is a long-term acquaintance.

If a human proposes this relationship to the reader, the authors strongly advise against participation. Navigating this type of relationship is extraordinarily complex for the novice.

-So You Want to Mate a Human

"GOD, IT'S CREEPY UP HERE." Georgia stood in the doorway; arms wrapped around herself protectively.

Talen scanned the attic for any potential threats. The windows were secure, and the room was dry, if dusty. What did she sense that he did not? Perhaps the shadows alarmed her. Humans did not possess strong low-light vision.

"I detect no predators lurking in the shadows. You are safe," he said.

"No predators? Who says that about their own attic?"

"You are agitated."

"Oh, and getting more so by the minute." She pushed past him into the attic and stood proudly with her hands on her hips. "I'm not scared of any attic monsters."

"Of course." He adored the bravado in her voice.

"But maybe a little more light? It's too dark up here."

He handed her the solar lantern. "It's fully charged. Pick out the pieces you desire, and I'll bring them down."

She wandered through the disorganized maze of old furniture, a hand skimming along the dusty surface, leaving behind a trail. "Where did all this come from?"

"This was here when we took possession of the house." With the damaged roof and exposure to the elements, most items in the attic had to be tossed, but the items kept under tarps had survived largely intact. "With new upholstery, you'll never know it came from the monstrous attic."

She tossed him a sharp look over her shoulder. "Are you mocking me? A huge, dark attic filled with old furniture under drop cloths, a single bare bulb for light... This is classic horror movie stuff."

Another guest room had been renovated and another two were close to completion. Talen would rather utilize the old furniture in the attic rather than purchase new pieces, even if he did have to strip the varnish and reupholster all of it. The old furniture matched the soul of the house.

Georgia dusted off the seat of a hardback chair and sat at a writing desk. The thin legs seemed impossibly delicate.

The moment any weight was added to the desk, it should collapse.

She rested her elbows on the grimy surface, the sleeves of her shirt picking up the dirt. "This one."

"Are you sure? It is impractical."

"It's perfect. We'll call the room the secretary's suite." She frowned. "Okay, maybe not that, but it'll be decorated around this writing desk. That lamp there with the glass shade. An overstuffed chair and footstool. That bookshelf." She pointed to the objects as she spoke.

Talen marked each item with a piece of painter's tape. "And the bed?"

"I don't know. Not this one." She brushed a heavy headboard with the carved head of a boar clutching a ring in its mouth. Dust embedded itself in the crevices and coated the eyes, turning them white with age. He agreed. No one needed that beast watching them as they slept.

She twisted her fingers in the ends of her hair. "Actually, this is sort of ugly-cool. One of the other rooms can have a hunter's theme."

"Are you sure? I know I told you there were no monsters in the attic, but I may have misspoken."

A luminous smile graced her face and his heart swelled with joy, along with other parts of his anatomy. "You don't like it?"

"It is not to my taste."

"I swear the eyes follow you. Look." She moved to the right, then shuffled back to the left. "Weird."

"Weird? My mate, it is disturbing. That beast is unnatural." And now that she pointed out the trick with the clouded eyes following, he could feel them on him.

She rubbed the beast's snout and gave the ring a tug. "First, not your mate and it might be fun to hang onto, you know?" She glanced back over her shoulder at him and licked her lips.

"With it judging me? No, thank you."

The light giggle she tried to hide behind her hand delighted him beyond measure. Did she want to try it now? Sometimes, Georgia could be forthright with her desires, but other times, she left it to him to tease out what she wanted, either through words or by other means, also involving his mouth. And tongue. And lips.

He crowded next to her, staring down at her with heat. She backed away a half-step, still licking her lips, until she bumped into the bed. Carefully, he guided her down to the cloth-covered mattress.

Her legs parted without prompting and he settled himself in to cradle there. Trousers kept them separated but he knew from experience how quickly that barrier could be removed.

"Talen, did you lure me into the creepy attic to seduce me?" Her eyes darkened and color flooded her cheeks.

"Yes, I hoped to impress you by protecting you from the attic monsters and work up a sweat moving furniture."

"You'd have to take your shirt off if that happened, to stay cool," she said.

"It's very warm in here. It'd be necessary."

"I believe it is very, very necessary for you to remove your shirt whenever the spirit moves you."

His mouth claimed hers and she responded with eagerness.

He broke the kiss, his gaze landing immediately on the carved boar's head.

Watching him.

Judging.

"Talen," she mewled, lifting her face for another kiss. Her lips were swollen and dusty pink, so tender and—

The boar continued watching.

"I cannot." He rolled away.

"What? Why?" She rolled onto her stomach and looked up, directly into the boar's cloudy eyes. "Oh, God." She scrambled away. "That's terrifying. This bed is a total cockblocker."

"No, come back. Do not leave me alone with the boar of judgment." He held out a hand, gasping dramatically. Laughing, she grabbed his hand and tugged. She didn't have nearly the strength to pull him to his feet, but he took a wild step as if she had. His arms wrapped around her. "Thank you for the rescue."

"Let's agree that one stays in the attic. Under a tarp. With some chains and a lock," she said. "I'd say we should burn it, but we don't want to upset the curse."

Talen placed a drop cloth over the headboard, concealing the carved monstrosity. "What else?"

They walked through the attic, Georgia selecting the pieces they could use in the guestrooms. Each required a thorough cleaning, possibly even a full refinishing, but Charl was good at such tasks.

"I will move these to the workshop." He set up a workspace in the old stables, to keep the noise and fumes away from the house. "Would you like to watch a film later?"

"Um, not tonight. I just feel like reading." The mood shifted. The playfulness between them vanished, replaced by the cool distance in her eyes.

Talen flattened his ears, hating the feeling he had inadvertently upset her. "What is it?"

Her gaze wandered over his shoulder and her fingers twisted in her hair again. "Nothing. I'll leave you to it, then."

Talen started with the items he could carry himself, such as the writing desk and chair. After the third trip, his calves burned and his shoulder ached, which pleased him. He needed the distraction.

He didn't like the way Georgia avoided him. Something changed. On matters for the house, she remained as professional as ever. When it came to flirting, or sex, that also remained unchanged. When he asked for any piece of her time outside of work or sex, she ran away. She would gaze at his shoulder, like she searched for an escape route, and then dash off with an excuse.

That hurt more than he expected. He thought they liked each other. Yes, sex muddied the waters but even if he never touched her in that way again, they had friendship. That his friend couldn't stand to be around him if his cock wasn't involved distressed him.

He needed to prove to Georgia that they worked together on every level, not just in the bedroom.

This time in the attic was the most they had spoken with their clothes on and Georgia not rushing away in weeks.

"Talen, there you are. I've been looking all over for you."

Talen set down the chair he had been carrying. Fiona approached him down the corridor with a flurry of tossed hair and a cloud of floral perfume.

He sneezed. Rude, yes, but he couldn't help it. The stench made his nose itch. "What is that sten… smell?"

Fiona took a deep breath. "I don't smell anything."

"Your perfume." Another sneeze. He stepped back, away from the toxic floral cloud.

"Oh, roses. An Earth flower. Quil said he liked it."

His brother must be nose blind. "It is unique."

"Thank you," she said, fluttering her lashes like that meant something.

"Do you have something in your eye? I will retrieve the

eyewash from the first aid kit. Remain here and do not panic."

"No. Don't bother." She frowned, confused as to why her charms failed to captivate him.

He knew why but he wouldn't share. For one, she stank of Quil and Earth roses. For another, her personality made him want to run in the opposite direction.

Patience. Kindness. He needed both.

"You wanted to see me," he prompted.

"Oh, yes. I wanted to talk about Georgia." She flung herself in a chair and immediately sprang up. "Why is this filthy? Ugh." Fruitlessly, she wiped her hand on her thigh.

"What about Georgia?"

"Well, this." She waved to the chair. "Standards have fallen, haven't they? God, that thing looks like it hasn't been cleaned in years."

"And that's Georgia's fault," he said, unsure what angle the female attempted to work.

"You tell me. She's the house manager, so yes. It is her fault. And what do we even know about her?"

Talen flattered himself by thinking he knew Georgia fairly well, but he didn't know why she pulled away from their friendship, so he said nothing. Better to say nothing and be mistaken for wise than open your mouth and be known as a fool, his father said once in a rare moment of insight.

"I'm just concerned that we know nothing about this

woman, and we let her live with us. She could murder us in our sleep."

Talen highly doubted that. It had been nearly three months with nary a whisper about middle-of-the-night murder sprees. "We knew nothing about you when Quil dragged you home, and we let you live with us."

"Yes, but I'm Quil's wife," Fiona said, as if that vouched for her character. Quite the opposite.

"Until the marriage is annulled by Earth authorities, so is Georgia."

"She is not!" Fiona stomped a foot. A hand fluttered to her chest and she smiled. "Mercy me, please excuse me. The idea of that woman laying a hand on Quil makes me so vexed. Positively vexed."

"I can honestly say that I feel the same," he said.

"Good, because I think she's only interested in our money. We shouldn't trust her with the accounts."

"Our money?"

"Quil's. Mine. Ours." She lifted her chin, a stubborn look on her face.

"Do you know something in particular or is this all slander?" He folded his arms across his chest.

"Slander? No, this is *concern*. Genuine concern." She laid her hand on his forearm, peering up at him with wide, beseeching eyes. "I don't trust her. She's up to no good."

He stepped back, distancing himself from the female. He

couldn't even begin to unpack everything wrong with Fiona's insinuations. Truthfully, the house ran smoothly with Georgia at the helm and the accounts had improved.

"Georgia has only improved the quality of this house since she arrived. Hiring her on was the wisest decision I've made in years," he said.

"Fine, but when you wake up one morning and all the money's gone, don't say I didn't warn you!" With another stomp of her foot, she stormed off. In the distance, he heard doors slam.

"What the hell was that about?" he muttered, lugging the chair out to the workshop.

CHAPTER 11

TALEN

Fuzzy Britches,

Happy Annulment Day! See the attached document which annuls that shitshow of a marriage contract. The agency apologizes for the "profound misunderstanding" but I'm more interested in a refund.

-G

"You are thinking of your female," Charl said.

"I am not." He was, but he refused to admit that to Charl.

"You're smitten as a kitten." Charl grinned, pleased at his joke.

"That's not amusing," Talen grumbled. He wasn't thinking about Georgia, much, or the shift in the dynamic between them.

"Yes, it is. Very. I am extremely clever. You, being an uneducated heathen, can't possibly appreciate my wit."

"You think a boot to the ass will show you my appreciation? Get to work. I don't actually pay you to mock me."

Charl laughed. He sat on the floor; a chair overturned in his lap as he delicately wove the strands of cane to repair the seat. His four arms especially suited him to the task, one hand weaving, the other holding the cane in place, another pulling the binding cord taught, and another ready with a hammer. All four limbs worked with frightening speed.

"You're staring," Charl said.

"Just admiring the way you're not smashing your fingers with the hammer. You've got three hands to keep track of and I can barely manage one."

Charl shrugged. "It is normal for me. I am amazed at the way you cope, being deformed as you are with only two hands. So brave."

"Asshole," Talen said, laughing. His tail swished merrily behind him.

"Would you like me to tie two hands behind my back, so you do not feel so inadequate?" Charl teased.

"No, because I pay you to work with four arms, not two. Stop trying to cheat me."

Charl's mouth quirked up at the corners. Almost a grin. The male had a sense of humor after all. "Try not to trip over your own tail when you're thinking about your female. Or at least share what is worrying you," he said.

The male was Talen's closest friend, had been since the first day of basic training when they stood next to each other in line waiting to be issued gear, wearing nothing but boxer briefs. As much as he valued Charl's friendship, he had never seen the male take an interest in anyone romantically, male or female. Charl had never been in a relationship, as far as Talen knew, and the male remained silent about much of his life before the Navy.

Talen watched the male weave the thin cane reeds with skill and dexterity. He knew so little about the Gyer male, who knew absolutely everything about him. Charl lived with his family, was like a brother—better, actually, because he wasn't a scheming little fraud—and could probably read Talen's mind if he wanted.

"Right now, you're wondering if I'm qualified to advise you on your mate," Charl said.

"Ha! You are wrong." Only because Talen hadn't arrived at that thought yet, even though the course had been charted.

"So, you do not doubt my qualifications."

"Oh, I doubt. I've never seen you look twice at… anyone." Talen stumbled as he found the correct word.

Charl snorted. "I was mated. Once."

"You have never said," Talen said.

"I've never said anything," Charl clarified.

"True enough." His friend never spoke of his past, of his family, of life on Gye or why he left his homeworld. Talen's history was a painfully open book and in one embarrassing case, an actual book titled *The Lost Princes.*

Stupid book, filled with only the worst gossip and rumors. He'd like to punch the author in the nose. Beyond the gossip-mongering, the book was highly inaccurate. The heir of a duke is a marquess and a younger son who would have been an earl. Honestly. Everyone knew that.

Talen waited in silence while Charl continued to weave, but the male shared nothing else about himself.

The mystery of Charl's past would remain for another day.

"She is scared," Charl said, breaking the silence.

"Of what? Did she tell you that?" Jealousy flared in his chest that his mate would share her fears with Charl and not himself.

"Hold your stones. She didn't have to tell me. It's obvious."

"Is telepathy a common ability for the Gyer?"

"No. Why would you ask such a dumb question? Did you hit your head again?"

"Because unless she told you how she felt, you don't know shit. You're not some magic four-armed guru, doling out wisdom," Talen said.

"You don't know what she's feeling either, but you're happy to ruminate in your ignorance over there."

Talen grumbled, because Charl was correct.

"What was that? I couldn't hear you."

"I said she's been avoiding me," Talen answered reluctantly.

"So, make yourself unavoidable." Charl waved a hand dismissively at Talen.

"And how do I do that, exactly? She leaves the moment the conversation becomes..." He searched for the word. Not serious. The other day in the attic was playful and far from serious. Perhaps meaningful.

With that as context, their encounters took on new significance.

"You're a clever male. Figure it out."

Georgia

BUSY WEEK. Georgia authorized work on the ballroom and music room once she received estimates. The contractor didn't want to provide an estimate, as he was the only operation in town and felt the business was guaranteed. After a few casual comments about how the next town over wasn't too far to commute for a new project, a reasonable and competitively priced estimate arrived.

With the rooms prepped for renovation, she set about finding tables and chairs. If she planned to sell Achaval House as an event venue, they needed to provide the basic accommodations, like having somewhere to put your butt.

The attic had a matched set of backless loungers and an incomplete set of chairs with broken seats. Those went out to the makeshift workshop in the stable. She combed the local markets for more furniture, deciding to go with an eclectic decor. Honestly, tablecloths would cover old and battered tables and slipcovers would hide mismatched chairs. Appearances didn't matter as much as the chair just needed to not collapse the moment someone parked their butt on it.

Super boring, right? She hadn't gone off the deep end of event hosting, but it was easier than thinking about the way Talen looked at her.

The crazy thing was that she couldn't describe the way he looked at her, only the way it made her feel like she was at the apex of the first drop on a rollercoaster. Anticipation coiled through her, ready for the fall, clinging to the safety harness but brave enough to let go for a moment and scream with delight.

Yeah. It was bad, already half in love with him and terrified. She thought she had loved Kevin, but she never felt half the eagerness and excitement she felt for Talen. Was that love? Or just lust?

She wanted to claim that hooking up had been a mistake, but they had the most explosive sex. What she had before didn't compare. Nothing compared. Talen consumed her, drove all thoughts and worries from her mind, and made her feel at peace. He felt like home.

It terrified her.

Home never lasted for her. The people she needed always left. Even Freema, her best friend, planned to leave her for a colony. Everyone left, even sexy feline-esque aliens who liked books and made her laugh. Especially those.

She was tired of being left behind, tired of opening her heart and being disappointed. She could only rely on herself.

"Can you explain to me why we have no bookings for the next month when I know we did?" Talen's voice pierced her musings. He stood opposite the table, every inch of him dripping with pheromones or whatever witchcraft that made her lose her damn mind and start her mouth watering. Opened at the collar, he had rolled up the sleeves of his shirt to the elbows.

Witchcraft.

She looked down quickly, wanting to avoid torturing herself with his sexy arms.

Too late.

"I canceled them." She focused on assembling the cleaning bot. "Before you get all huffy about the lost income, we're starting renovations in the ballroom tomorrow. It's better to take the loss than deal with noise and dust complaints."

"You really think so?" His tone sounded like a challenge.

She looked up, meeting his glare. "Yes, otherwise we'd lose money on refunds and get a slew of negative reviews."

"That is acceptable," he said at length. "What is that?"

"Cleaning bot. I want to see how this little guy works in the drawing room." When they were ready to host events in the summer, they'd need to either hire to increase the cleaning staff or kit out the rooms with bots. Either way would be an expense. Retrofitting cleaning bots to an older house without a centralized computer was difficult, so she'd start small. One room at a time.

"They are expensive," he said.

"Cheaper than hiring new staff," she replied.

"You didn't ask my approval."

"Do I have to run everything by you? You hired me as the manager, not your assistant."

His tail swayed behind him and he leaned forward, planting his hands on the table. "Georgia, I—"

"I'm really busy. Can it wait?" She looked back down at the bot, its internal workings exposed, and compared it to the setup guide.

He stood by the table for several minutes before eventually leaving. She swallowed the feeling of disappointment.

She wasn't staying, she reminded herself. She was leaving

him before he had the chance to leave her. It was better that way.

THE BED SHIFTED. A familiar presence crawled under the blankets and snuggled next to her.

"Talen, I'm not in the mood," she said, voice thick and groggy.

"I can't sleep." He pulled her into him, her back against his bare chest.

"So, you thought you'd wake me up?"

"I sleep better with you." His hand rested where her hip blended to her thigh, fitting like it belonged. A brush against her ankle had to be the tail.

"You've slept without me your entire life." Too heavy to open, her eyelids fluttered.

"Yes, and now that I know a perfect night's rest, I can't go back to that. It's uncivilized."

Sleep must have impaired her judgment because she giggled at the scandalized indignation in his voice. "All right, but keep your paws to yourself, mister. Now let me sleep."

He pressed a kiss to the back of her neck.

Yup, her judgment was totally impaired because she smiled.

. . .

Talen

HE HELD his mate in his arms, but she might as well have been a thousand lightyears away.

CHAPTER 12

GEORGIA

Freema,

I am so sick of snow.

-G

"Explain to me why we're doing this again," Georgia said. She couldn't feel her nose or her fingers. Any heat from the thermal warmer in her pockets was long gone.

"It's MidWinter. We need to decorate the house," Bright said. Using a pair of pruning shears, she cut clippings from an evergreen. The wide leaves were a waxy green with violet berries that reminded Georgia of the juniper bushes outside her childhood home. The prickly bushes provided the perfect hiding spot for a young Georgia. Despite being allergic to the bush, she loved wiggling her way in under the branches.

"Is there a holiday?" she asked.

"Everyone has a MidWinter holiday," the older woman replied.

"I'm not comfortable with broad generalizations." Georgia shifted the basket to the other arm. Bright added more clippings, increasing the weight.

"You do say the most interesting things. Earth must be the only planet in known civilization that never felt the need to lighten their spirits when the days grew short. That seems fairly remarkable." Bright's tail swayed behind her as she moved to another evergreen. She had a way of speaking that made Georgia feel like she had been scolded for naughty behavior and given a piece of candy for good behavior simultaneously.

"It's called Christmas and falls on December 25th, which I guess is around the winter solstice. Well, Earth actually has a few, but that's the one I celebrated." Planets in the Interstellar Union followed the same standard IU calendar. Christmas Day was Christmas Day, whether on Earth or one of the colonies. Corra followed its own calendar, which did not neatly align with the IU standard. It messed with her sense of time. None of the pamphlets the agency sent mentioned that.

"How do you celebrate human Christmas?"

"We decorate a tree. Sing holiday songs. Exchange gifts. Santa Claus brings presents for good boys and girls."

"Claws?" Bright chuckled. "How does Claws determine who is good and who is bad?"

"Oh, parents totally snitch on their kids. They have to be good all year long, or Santa will find out, and then they'll get nothing but a lump of coal."

"Seems like a bribe for good behavior."

"It totally is," Georgia agreed. Her last Christmas had been spent with Freema, lasagna, a bottle of wine, and a Christmas movie marathon. "But waking up on Christmas morning and racing to the tree to see what Santa brought you? It's the best. What do you do on Talmar?"

"Light candles to drive back the dark. Decorate with greenery to represent life in the middle of the barren winter. We bake small cakes. Each has a charm that will signify your luck for the coming year."

"That sounds nice."

Once Bright was satisfied that they collected enough greenery, they moved into the formal dining room. A cloth of rough canvas covered the table and Bright showed her how to create a simple swag of ribbon and the evergreen boughs. Once satisfied with her skill, Bright instructed her how to weave a wreath. The sharp edges of the leaves pricked her fingers, but Georgia grinned in triumph at her first wreath, complete with golden ribbon and jingling bells. All the while, she babbled about making popcorn garlands to decorate the tree with her mother. She stuck her fingers a lot then, too.

Soon, they had festooned the foyer and the drawing room. Each room had a small centerpiece of a candle surrounded by greenery. A fresh smell of crushed leaves filled the house, accompanied with beeswax candles and spices.

Quil wandered in, fascinated by the idea of humans decorating a tree. "Do you want a tree? What size does it have to be? Can it be any tree or is it a ritual with a sacred tree?"

In the end, he dragged a potted palm—not really a palm, but it had fronds—from the conservatory and arranged it in the corner of the drawing room. They decorated it with the leftover golden ribbon and bells.

"We need a star or an angel for the top."

"The tree needs a hat?" Quil scratched behind an ear in thought.

Once the word *hat* came out of his mouth, all she pictured was a red and white Santa hat on top. It'd be perfect. She raced to her basement office, found the appropriate sheet of paper, and raided her bathroom for cotton balls. Carefully, she glued cotton balls around the base and finished with one on top. With a flourish, she balanced her creation on the highest fronds of the tree.

"This is the best Christmas alien palm tree ever," Georgia declared, quite proud of herself.

***

THE NEXT MORNING, Georgia couldn't open her eyes. Seriously, not being dramatic. Her face felt puffy and sore. No matter how she squinted and blinked, her eyes were swollen shut. Careful prodding at her nose and cheekbones convinced her it was like the time she had been stung by a bee when she was seven.

The rest of her body itched and burned. Running her fingers over the back of her hands and arms revealed bumps. It felt like poison ivy—her mind flashed back to the fragrant evergreens she gathered with Bright—and touching the inflamed spots would only make it worse.

Wonderful. She was in the middle of an allergic reaction to an alien plant.

She scratched at the base of her throat.

Maybe Bright had a home remedy, calamine lotion or something.

Georgia reached for her robe and faced the general direction of the door. Her sense of direction was strong enough that she could stumble her way around, but Charl had been working in the hallway yesterday. The corridor would be a minefield of trip hazards. She'd be lucky to find the stairs without breaking her neck.

What then? Shout down the hall for help? The closest person was Talen—

Georgia sighed, knowing what she had to do. Their connecting door lay directly opposite the foot of her bed. She took careful steps, hand outstretched, until she felt the wall. Fumbling, she found the doorframe.

Was he still asleep? He was an early riser but she didn't know the time. Carefully, she listened. The birds were silent, so it had to be before dawn. He'd still be in bed.

She knocked lightly. "Talen? I need your help."

The door opened. She couldn't see him, but she felt his

presence, still warm from sleep. She bet his hair was rumpled too.

"What happened to you?" he said, hands landed on her shoulders. He tugged at the robe, exposing her rash-covered skin.

"That bad, huh?"

"Were you bitten? Do you have a fever?" He pushed the robe away and lifted the hem of her tank top.

Georgia batted his hand away. He didn't need to inspect her. "It's an allergic reaction."

"You need a medic."

"Yes, I do. Can you take me?"

"Can you breathe? Your throat?" She felt the heat of his hand as if he reached out to stroke her throat but held back.

"Yeah, that's fine. I think it's just on my skin and my eyes," she said, forcing herself to keep a sunny attitude. The day had started off on the wrong foot; being grumpy would only make it worse. Talen made no reply. "I look that bad, huh?"

"Alarming, yes, but not bad. You never look bad," he answered.

She wanted to know what his ears were doing and if he told the truth. "You don't have to fib to make me feel better."

He huffed. She scratched at her forearm. "I have a lotion, if you are itching, but does not smell pleasant," he said.

"Yes, please. Anything."

With his hand on her elbow, he guided her back to her bed. "Remove your clothes," he said, before leaving to fetch the lotion.

She stripped, eager to discard her pajamas as they were probably contaminated with whatever pollen or oil that caused the reaction. Anything she touched yesterday— doorknobs, furniture, her toothbrush—would have to be cleaned thoroughly. She had no idea how extensively her skin had been damaged; she only knew she felt like she was on fire everywhere.

"Here," he said, placing a bottle in her hands.

"Umm." She fumbled until she opened the cap. "Can you?"

Starting at her hands, the cool lotion instantly soothed the itch. He worked his way up her arm, dabbing at her shoulders and collarbone.

"That feels amazing," she said. Then she sniffed. And sniffed again. The unmistakable odor of fish tickled her nose. "What is it?"

"It is derived from algae. It is good for your skin."

"It smells like fish." And dank ponds.

"It is also good for enforced solitude," he said.

"Leave-me-alone stink goo?"

He huffed, amused. He lifted her hair and worked the lotion onto her shoulders. His touches were soft but clinical, no lingering brushes or appreciative squeezes. Which was fine. She did not feel sexy, and seduction wasn't high on her list of priorities.

With a tap, he indicated for her to stand. Her lower half had been clothed—yay for layers—so the only patch he found was on the top of her feet. How she got it on the top of her feet, she had no idea. Maybe when she kicked off her shoes.

"I'm going to have to clean everything, aren't I?" If the reaction was to pollen or oil from the evergreens she collected yesterday, then everything she touched needed to be wiped down. All her clothes and bedsheets washed.

"Bright will see to it," Talen said. "Done. Now let's get you dressed."

He dressed her carefully in a loose-fitting tunic and leggings. The fabric pressed against the drying lotion.

"Thank you," she said, as he slipped shoes onto her feet, "for helping me. You didn't have to." He could have fetched Bright.

He huffed again. She wished she could see his ears and have some idea of his mood. Was he annoyed? Irritated? Or tolerating her for the moment? His thoughtfulness was unnerving her.

"The hour is still early," he said. "You will eat before we go to the clinic. The journey is not long, but you need your strength."

And just like that, everyday Bossy Talen replaced Thoughtful Talen.

"I really appreciate the way you ask me what I want to do and then immediately tell me what to do. It's cute," she said with a grin. Another huff, no doubt offended at being called cute. "I'm not particularly hungry, anyway."

"You must keep your strength up. Your body will need the energy to heal."

She sensed from his tone that there was no winning the argument. "Fine, but don't laugh at me if I spill my porridge on myself. Actually, I think toast is all I want." She considered the logistics of buttering and adding jam to her toast. "Just dry toast today."

With no warning, Talen scooped her up like she weighed nothing.

"What? Put me down," she said.

"Your vision is impaired. I assume you do not want to stumble down the stairs, which is why you knocked on my door."

"You could hold my hand and guide me."

"This way is faster."

"I wouldn't brag about that. Faster isn't always the way to win over the ladies," she said automatically. Gah. Was that flirting? She was covered in a rash and stink-lotion, with her eyes swollen shut, and she had the gall to *flirt*? Get your priorities straight, girl. "What did you dress me in? My ass isn't hanging out, is it?"

She winced at her choice of words. Talking about her ass was so much better than flirting.

"Your ass is appropriately covered." Amusement colored his voice.

They descended the stairs. "What did you do to Georgia!?" Bright gasped.

"I did nothing. She came to me this way," Talen grumbled.

"I think I'm allergic to the evergreens we used for decorating," she said, raising her voice to speak over Bright and Talen.

"Well, don't just stand there," Bright scolded. "Take her to the medic!"

No time for breakfast then. Just as well. Georgia didn't want to eat or drink anything just in case her body decided that today was the day for exciting new food allergies.

They exited the house without drawing an audience. Talen grumbled the entire way. "Does she believe I cart you around for my entertainment? Of course I'm taking you to the medic."

He pressed her closer to his chest as he opened the vehicle door. With little fuss, he sat her inside and fastened the seat belt.

"Thank you, again," she said, blindly reaching for his hand. "I know you have things you'd rather be doing than carting me around."

He huffed, this time sounding less agitated. "I would not trust Quil to do this."

"I wouldn't either. He'd probably get distracted by something sparkly and leave me stranded on the side of the road."

No response. For a moment, Georgia wondered if she pushed too far. Then, he burst into laughter. The driver's side door opened, and the vehicle shifted as Talen sat down, still chuckling.

The day wasn't so bad, all things considered.

Talen

GEORGIA LOOKED wretched but never uttered a complaint about her obvious misery. Angry red splotches and tiny bumps covered her pale skin. Scratches marred her fingers and hands, possibly from the evergreen she handled yesterday, or possibly from vermin. He did not see any obvious bite marks, but he could hear the vermin moving in the walls at night. He had difficulty believing such a radical transformation was an adverse reaction to a plant.

The condition of her eyes alarmed him the most. Whatever substance she encountered, she rubbed her eyes at some point and Talen hoped she would not lose her vision.

Humans were too fragile. Georgia could be blinded

because of a sweet-smelling plant used for home decorating. The oil that made the leaves fragrant did not irritate Tal skin. Obviously, human skin was more susceptible to damage. He mentally made a list of everything that would have to be cleaned, such as furniture she may have touched, including doorknobs.

He drove carefully, aware of every bump in the uneven road. A herd of *hipi* unhelpfully blocked the road. He honked the horn, but the stubborn creatures would not move. Frustrated, he climbed out of the vehicle and guided them back onto a pasture, cursing the entire time. When he returned to the cabin, Georgia smiled.

"Tough day at the office, dear?" she asked.

"*Hipi* are stubborn," he said.

"At least they're cute and fluffy," she said with a slight laugh. The tension eased in his chest. If Georgia could find the energy to laugh, even at his expense, then she must not be in too much pain.

The wait at the clinic to see a medic, only thirty minutes, was unacceptable. Talen paced the waiting room, tail lashing violently. This town never had enough medics. The population had grown but the only thing that had grown in the clinic was wait times. The staff and building size remained the same as when Drac had been a simple mining outpost.

They should move to the closest, largest city, or a town with adequate medical facilities. Damn Quil and damn the house. None of it mattered if he could not provide his mate with the care she needed.

Eventually, a staff member escorted them to a private examination room, where they continued to wait.

"I am Belith. What seems to be the matter today?" A tall blue-skinned Fremmian female entered the room. The medic's gaze went directly to Georgia. "A human. How delightful. I have much experience with humans, so do not worry. I am an expert at this point. I don't think there's anything I haven't seen your little brown bodies do."

Talen's top lip curled back. He disliked the thought of anyone seeing Georgia's *little brown body*, even if it was more beige than brown. "My mate has been poisoned. Do something at once," he said.

"Not your mate," Georgia said. "I'm having an allergic reaction to a plant, I think. Contact dermatitis."

"You certainly appear to be suffering from contact dermatitis," the medic said. "Do you have any vision?"

"Not really," his mate—no matter how she denied it —said.

"I will need to touch you as I examine you. Do not be alarmed. Tell me, what plant did you encounter?" Belith took Georgia's hand and turned it over, inspecting the rash of red bumps that ran up her arm.

"An evergreen with purple berries," Georgia said.

"The *meyen* bush," Talen said, supplying the name.

"Hmm. The oil from a crushed *meyen* berry is normally not caustic, but human skin is delicate," the medic said.

Talen nodded in agreement. "Several in the family handled the *meyen* clippings but had no ill effects."

"I'm assuming the rest of the family is Tal."

"We have another human."

"Two humans." The medic clucked her tongue, amused. "How extensive is the rash?"

"My hands, face, arms, and chest," Georgia said.

"Also her waist," Talen added.

"Basically, anywhere you touched when your hands were contaminated. That sounds right," Belith said. "Any known allergies?" Georgia shook her head. "I'm going to administer an antihistamine injection now to reduce the swelling around your eyes."

"Okay. Tell me when." Georgia turned her head away, but the gesture made no sense as she could not see a needle anyway.

Sometimes he did not understand how his mate's mind worked.

"I will not." Belith inserted the needle with practiced ease. "You will tense up and the jab will be more painful. There. Did you notice anything?"

"I noticed being manhandled by a doctor." Georgia rubbed her arm at the site of the injection.

"Manhandled. That is clever. Now, open your mouth." The medic conducted the examination. Every device filled him with worry. He demanded to know the results of every reading and what it meant for his mate.

Tired of his foolishness, Belith snapped at him. "If you do not stop, I will remove you from this room. I am not inclined to tolerate witless males."

"She called you witless, Talen. It's like she knows you," Georgia said with a grin. The return of his mate's humor bolstered him.

"Now, I suggest you use this particular soap to soothe your skin," Belith said, writing on a notepad. "Clean any surface the *meyen* oil touched and launder your bed linens. Do not expose yourself to the oil again. I will prescribe an oral and topical steroid to reduce the itching and help with healing. Do not worry. The steroid will not adversely affect the baby."

CHAPTER 13

GEORGIA

Humans are remarkably fertile. Females have a fertile cycle once a month and males continually produce viable sperm well into old age. Humans are also genetically compatible with many alien species.

Redundant forms of contraception are recommended unless the reader wants a human hybrid child.

-So You Want to Mate a Human

old the phone. Pregnant? Impossible.

"I'm sorry. I'm not pregnant," Georgia said. The swelling had reduced around her eyes enough that she could see, even if her field of vision was squinty.

Talen gripped her hand. He practically vibrated with excitement. Or rage. She twisted on the exam table, trying to see more with her squinty vision. His tail danced madly behind him. She had no idea what that meant.

"You are. Approximately three months." The blue-skinned giant of a doctor wore a white lab coat. Amazing how that white lab coat was universal.

"But that's not possible. I had the birth control shot. That's good for two years."

The doctor gave a patient smile and looked from Georgia to Talen, still gripping her hand. "It very much is possible between mates."

"But—"

"You're certain it is Tal-human?" Talen asked.

Georgia turned back to Talen, yanking her hand out of his grip. "What the hell kind of question is that? How many people do you think I've been sleeping with? Of course, it's your baby, fuzzy britches."

He looked suitably embarrassed, but wow, that question. They were going to have a serious talk about what he thought she got up to.

"The birth control shot is very reliable but certain medications can alter its effectiveness," Belith said, ignoring the tension between Georgia and Talen. "Do you take any maintenance medications?"

"No. There was a bug on the ship before I got to Corra, though. I took a course of antibiotics but that was weeks before, you know—"

"Yes, you and fuzzy britches," Belith said with a nod.

"That moniker is never going away," Talen grumbled.

"Antibiotics can impact the effectiveness of birth control. Did the medic fail to give you a list of potential side effects?"

Georgia found herself reluctant to admit that the ship's medic may have given her such a document, but it had been written in Corravian. Talen placed his large hand on the back of her neck, which soothed her.

"Even if I had read it, I had an upper respiratory infection. I couldn't breathe. I couldn't sleep. I would have taken the meds anyway," she said.

Belith rolled a cart over with a large scanner and screen. "Lift your shirt. Let's examine the child."

She squirted a cold gel on Georgia's stomach and rubbed a wand over her abdomen. The blank screen distorted into a gray and white image. Slowly, the image of something that looked more like a fish than human—or Tal —emerged.

The image moved. Her breath caught in her throat.

No. She took back the fish statement. Those were fingers, teeny-tiny fingers. No sign of a tail, though.

"When does the tail develop?" she asked.

"Soon. It can be hidden in this position, but the tail does not always develop."

Belith said the baby appeared healthy for its stage of development. "Human-Tal kits take nine months to gestate. Most pregnancies occur with few complications. I will prescribe vitamin supplements and I expect to see you again in a month for a check-up."

A baby.

Her baby.

Georgia had spent many nights drifting off to sleep, imagining the family and life that awaited her on Corra. Whenever her fantasies took her to this particular moment, she assumed she would burst into tears of joy. She'd have her husband by her side, not her casual hookup.

Only he hadn't felt like a casual hookup for some time now.

Talen's amber gaze fixed on the monitor. "Our kit." He grinned, fangs exposed, but if the dancing his tail did was any indication, he was thrilled.

She didn't know if she felt the same.

The situation was completely backward. She had everything she thought she wanted, and it wasn't right. At all.

Talen

"I DON'T THINK we should tell anyone just yet," his mate said.

She sat at the edge of his bed. Until her room could be thoroughly cleaned, she had to make do with his bed, which pleased the feral part of his brain. That hungry beast wanted his mate in his bed every night.

When they arrived home, he hustled her upstairs, walking straight past a curious Bright. Soon the older female would burst through the door, bearing a tray laden with a meal, and demand updates.

Before she could say another word, he pushed her against the closed door and knelt, pressing his ear to her belly.

His mate. His kit.

He wanted to believe he could hear the kit's heartbeat but settled for the gentle thrum of his mate's heart. Gently, he lifted the fabric of her tunic and rubbed his cheek across her bare skin, marking her with his scent. She smelled of lotion and medicinal soap.

Her fingers tangled in his hair and she sighed. "Okay?"

He withdrew, unsure if she asked after his well-being or if he would refrain from shouting his joyous news. He'd bet on the latter. "I will try, but I have never been able to keep a secret from Bright," he said.

"It's not a secret. At least it won't be for much longer. I just need to think." She scratched the back of her hand, the skin red and raw.

"I will draw you a bath," he said, setting a glass of water down on the bedside table. After the bath, he would apply the ointment the doctor prescribed. He took a thick bathrobe from the wardrobe, as any garment of hers might be contaminated. When he placed the robe next to her on the bed, she remained in the same position along with the pill waiting next to the glass.

"My mate, you must take your pill."

"Yes, Daddy," she muttered. The color leached from her face, making the red splotches around her eyes and on her cheeks that much more vivid and grotesque. "I didn't mean it like that."

"Medicine. Bath. Then we talk."

He ran the water in the tub until it was warm, and then he plugged the tub. Slowly it filled. He added a packet of powder that promised to soothe itching skin to the water. He doubted the claim, but it smelled pleasant enough.

Georgia stood in the door, wearing his bathrobe. The sight pleased him to no end. His mate, carrying his kit, wrapped in his scent. His chest rumbled with happiness, the closest he had come to a purr since he was a kit.

"What did you mean, 'Is it Tal-human?' You don't think this baby is yours?" The hurt in her voice obvious, even to one as foolish as himself.

If he could go back in time and take back those damaging words, he would. "I spoke before my brain had a chance to process," he explained.

"It was very hurtful." She clutched the lapel of the robe, drawing it closed over her throat. "I've only ever been with two people. I told you this."

"I know the kit is mine. I think I wanted to know if the kit had my ears and tail and it came out the most horrid way possible."

"The dumbest way possible," she clarified.

"Without a doubt. Now, will you take a bath before the water gets cold?"

She gave him a dubious look but climbed into the tub. He took the bar of soap and worked a lather on her back. Her muscles relaxed with the heat and his gentle touch.

Four months ago, he had been content to be alone and overworked. All that changed in a heartbeat, but he also knew it had been changing slowly. He only realized it as he tried to discern the features of his kit on a blurry screen. Now he wanted more than anything to watch his mate swell with his kit. He positively itched with anticipation to hold his kit in his arms.

"I am sorry," he said.

"It takes two to tango. This is as much my doing as it is yours."

"About the *meyen* berries. I asked Bright to decorate the house. I thought it would please you."

"It did." Her wet hand gave his a squeeze. "I sincerely had fun yesterday and I can't wait to have one of those cakes with a charm in it. Next year, I'll leave the wreath-making to the Tal in the house."

Hearing her speak of plans for next year gave him a sense of inordinate pleasure. Next year they would have a kit, barely more than a newborn.

While she bathed, Bright arrived with a tray groaning under the weight of a meal, just as he knew she would. "Well?" she asked sharply, setting the tray down on the bureau.

"Contact dermatitis from the *meyen* berries. We must clean any surface the berries encountered and anything she touched."

"The cleaners come in tomorrow. I'll strip her bed now, but the rest can wait until the morning," Bright said with a nod. "I assume she will stay with you tonight?"

Talen tucked his tail close to his body. How much did Bright suspect? What other secrets would she drag from him without even trying?

Bright shook her head. "Silly kit. I know you've been courting Georgia. Everyone knows. You've hardly been discreet with the way you've been carrying on. And I also know she finds you agreeable."

"Stop gossiping about me," Georgia called from the tub, followed by a splash of water.

"Do you need anything?" Bright asked.

"A nap."

"Well, I'll leave you to it then," Bright said, a smile ghosting across her lips.

As Bright left, Justice dashed through the door. Immediately the *wuap* patrolled the room and gave little humming calls. Once satisfied, she jumped onto the bed and curled up to sleep.

Georgia emerged, her head wrapped in a towel and holding a bottle of lotion. A green paste covered the front of her, fading as it dried. "Can you get my back, please?"

"How are your eyes?" he asked, taking the bottle. She knelt in front of the fire, presenting her back to him.

"Better. Good enough to see that my bathroom is much nicer than yours."

"I had to replace damaged tiles in mine," he said. He rubbed the lotion between his hands to warm it. She sighed with relief as he applied it across her shoulders. "Finding tiles that matched took too much time. It was only for me and I do not mind if it is not aesthetically appealing."

"The color on the original tile is lovely, though. It's like a summer twilight sky." The tension in her back eased as he applied the lotion. "I don't want to talk about bath tiles."

He capped the bottle. "All finished. Sleep. Anything you want to say can wait 'til the morning." And he'd appreciate the time to gather his thoughts. He knew what he felt—wild excitement. He knew what he wanted—Georgia. Always.

"No." She twisted in her spot on the carpet to face him. "I'll never be able to sleep until I get this out of my head." She took a deep breath. "I want the baby. I really, really do. Like so much it scares me."

"Yes," he agreed, ears perked.

"I never wanted to be a single parent, but I will." She put a hand on her stomach. "I didn't even know about this kid three hours ago and I already love it more than anything. How is that possible?"

He felt the same.

"But that's not what I'm trying to say. You might not want to be a dad, so I understand if you don't want any part of this."

"Georgia—"

She continued to speak, at the rapid-fire pace that indicated nervousness. "But I'll stay on Corra if you want to be involved. If we could stay here until the baby is born, that'd be good. I'm sure I'll need the help, but I can move out if you want. I don't want you to feel like I trapped you. I didn't have much of a father and it sucks not having one, but I'd rather the kid's dad be fully invested rather than disappearing—"

"Georgia." He sank to the floor in front of her and took her hands. "You carry my heart and now you carry my kit. There is nowhere you could go where I wouldn't follow. I will be by your side until the light leaves me."

"This was supposed to be temporary. No strings attached."

"No one said that but you." He placed a kiss on her forehead, the only part of her face not covered in the pale green lotion. "This has never been temporary for me and not for you, either. Not for some time, I think."

She blinked, her eyes glossy. He suspected she might cry but she took a deep breath and looked away. "I can stay?"

"If you leave, I will follow." With a finger under her chin, he guided her gaze back toward him. "I hope you find my face pleasing, because you will see it every morning and every evening until the end of our days."

"I suppose the house is big enough for all of us."

She did not understand him, either purposely or he failed to express his intentions.

"Georgia, I want you for my mate," he said.

"Don't say things you don't mean."

"I do not know how to make it plainer. You are my mate, Georgia Phillips."

"I'm not—"

"You are." He kissed her lips, softly just to quiet her reflexive denial. "You have been since the moment you walked off that shuttle. I do not care what brought you here. I am sorry for the pain it caused you, but I am not sorry that it has led you to me. There is no one else who fills me with joy. There is no one else I want to spend my days with and no one else I want to pull my leg."

She snorted, the laugh thick, and her eyes watered. "Jesus Christ, Talen. Go easy on a girl." She pressed her index fingers to the corners of her eyes. "I'm naked, covered in green goop and a rash."

"You are lovely."

"You're such a liar." Her lips twitched at the corner.

"We've already established I'm a terrible actor," he said. "The green goop complements your eyes. They are like the buds of spring."

That earned him a proper smile. His chest swelled with happiness to the point he felt he would burst.

"Someone promised me breakfast and didn't produce. Feed me," she said.

He set the tray between them and they had a picnic in front of the fire.

"When do you want to tell the rest of the family?" he asked. Honestly, he did not trust himself to keep the kit a secret for long. Excitement fizzed and bubbled inside him. He wanted to tell his brother. He wanted to witness Bright's shrewd, all-knowing gaze soften for a moment at the news of a kit. Even Charl would lower his defenses for a moment and clap Talen on the back.

"I think Bright already suspects," Georgia said. "I barfed on a market day. That must have been morning sickness."

"When you are ready, but not too long. You've already established that my acting abilities leave much to be desired."

"Not too long," she said.

"And marriage? Will you be my mate?"

She studied the fire, the light casting shadows on her face. "I'm not saying no," she said at last, "but give me some time."

CHAPTER 14

GEORGIA

G,

Don't you dare have that baby without me.

-Freema

After two days, the general misery of constantly itching abated and her skin cleared somewhat. Angry red patches still graced her hands and arms. She applied the anti-itch cream in a thick layer, pushing up the sleeves of her sweater while the cream dried.

The steroids made sleep impossible. Exhaustion had a tight grip on her but even when she lay down in her comfortable bed, she couldn't sleep.

The enforced bedrest was worse than the itching and the sleeplessness. Having nothing to do but watch films or read sounded delightful, but nothing held her interest. Her mind kept drifting to the baby—the kit.

First impression: fear. She wasn't a grown-up or responsible and under no circumstances should she be allowed to be in charge of another person, especially an infant.

Second impression: excitement. This wasn't the plan. It was an accident, chance, luck, and a fluke.

And she liked it.

So that's where she was, deciding that the pregnancy was scary but good. Lots of expecting mothers probably felt the same. She and Talen still had lots of decisions to make, but she had a client meeting. The baby drama could wait.

Georgia opened the door to her office in the servant's quarters, slapped the control panel to turn on the lights, and shouted, "Oh shit!"

As if by magic, Talen thundered down the narrow stairs. "What? What has happened? Are you injured?"

She held her hand out like it was poisonous, because it was. "Did anyone clean the office? I didn't tell you I went in there, but I did to make the tree topper. Shit. I re-exposed myself." More itching. More angry red splotches on her hands.

"Do not panic. We will handle this," he said, and she believed him.

He led her upstairs to the scullery adjacent to the kitchen

and carefully washed her hands. He patted the skin dry and applied a layer of the prescription cream.

"Let that absorb. I will clean all the surfaces in the office." He grabbed a container of cleanser and disposable towels. "Is there anything else you touched?"

"The banister on the stairs. The light switch in the hall." She sat at the worn kitchen table, her arm extended, and palm turned upward, inordinately angry with herself. She knew better. Had she taken a moment to think, she'd be organizing price quotes and not being such a useless lump.

"I don't like that look. Stop thinking negatively about yourself," Quil said, settling into the chair next to her. He plucked a bright green citrus fruit from a bowl and pierced it with a claw. The tang of citrus filled the air. "It does no one any good."

"You don't know what I'm thinking."

"Right now, you're berating yourself because, in all that has happened in the last forty-eight hours, you forgot to clean a lamp or a tablet. Am I right?"

"A doorknob."

"Slice?" He offered her a segment of the green fruit. She took a piece, knowing it looked like a lime but had a much sweeter, mellow flavor.

"So, have you considered baby names? Because I'd humbly suggest that Tranquility is an admirable name for an infant, especially for tired parents who desire sleep. I'd be honored, of course, and flattered."

Georgia dropped her half-eaten piece of fruit. "How did you know? Talen swore he wouldn't tell."

"Relax. He has not broken your confidence." Quil popped a segment into his mouth and chewed slowly, drawing out the moment. The man lived to make drama. She really hated him at times. "Who do you think picked up your medications? The pieces were not difficult to assemble."

"So, you know." Which meant that Fiona knew, which meant everyone in the house and the surrounding countryside knew.

"In all fairness, Bright had her suspicions weeks ago."

"Yeah. I told her it was impossible," she said.

"I'd make some thinly veiled comment about family vigor and tenacity, but why bother? Self-flattery is so vulgar."

"But you love it."

He grinned. "I adore it and I adore you."

She sat up straight in the chair, easing herself back.

"Not like that." He waved a hand. "You stink of Talen. While it's nice you smell like family, you also smell a bit too much like my brother. My admiration is strictly chaste."

"Pro-tip, don't go telling ladies that they stink. It's like you have zero people skills." She took another piece of the offered fruit, juice dripping down her fingers.

"May I touch your abdomen?"

She wiped her hand on her pants. "Okay, but don't make it weird."

"An uncle cannot express interest or joy in a kit?"

"That's what I'm talking about. That's making it weird."

He grinned and crouched down beside her chair. Cautiously, he placed a hand on her belly, over the sweater. He leaned in, much as Talen did the first night, and pressed his face to the knit fabric. "Hello, kit. I am your uncle and I cannot wait to meet you."

Georgia balled up her hands, resisting the urge to place a hand on Quil's head. For a moment, she believed she fell through some portal into an alternate dimension. This was what she had wanted months ago, Quil at her stomach, cooing to her unborn baby. This could have been their baby, their life, but Quil fucked it up, and everything about it felt wrong, like trying to shove her feet into too-small shoes.

"I don't like you," she said.

His tail thumped against the chair and her leg. "Despite your bitter exterior, I like you."

"I'm serious. If we were married, if we had stayed married, I don't think we'd have gotten along." So much of his irreverent, self-aggrandizing personality rubbed her the wrong way. He was tolerable as an acquaintance, but he grated on her nerves. "We'd make each other crazy."

"And not in a good way," he said.

"No, so that's why I'm glad you fucked everything up, Quil. Thank you."

He buried his face into her soft belly, hiding his pleased grin. After a moment, he stood. "I still think Tranquility is an admirable name, and a fine expression of your thanks."

"Oh, fuck off," she replied, grinning. "I haven't even thought of baby names."

"Would you consider family names? We've had an Evanescence in nearly every generation."

"No, absolutely not."

"Discretion? I believe we had a great aunt who caused quite the scandal—"

"I think baby names is something I should discuss with Talen, not the crazy uncle."

He nodded. "I will send you a list. See? I am already very helpful. I will be a good uncle."

Georgia had no doubt in her mind that he'd be the fun uncle.

"Is he trying to convince you to name the kit after himself?" Talen asked, ascending the stairs.

"He's giving me horrible suggestions so that Tranquility sounds like a good idea," she answered.

"And human names are better? Mildred. Sound mildewy. Bob." Quil over-pronounced it, sound popping on the B. "That is not a name. That is a motion. I will help. You'll love my name suggestions. Just wait and see."

"WHAT DO you know of the *zasten*?"

"A coming of age ritual to mark the transition from youth to adulthood," Georgia said, reciting the words she memorized that afternoon.

She escorted the human woman, holding a toddler on her hip, and the Tal female adolescent through the foyer into the conservatory. The adolescent was all long limbs and angles, her head swiveling as she took in the ornate details of the room.

"You did your research." The woman had a British accent, softened by her time on Corra.

"Just the basics. If you explain to me what you need for your event, we'll make it happen," Georgia said.

"Kalini! I found it." Another adolescent, this one male, dashed through the foyer, waving a plush doll.

"Thank you, Dare." Kalini gave the plush doll to the child, who happily jammed it into his mouth.

The baby was a human-Tal hybrid with pale stripes and the trademark Tal ears and tail.

"He's adorable," Georgia said, unable to help herself.

"She, actually. Felicity." As if sensing she was the center of attention, she buried her face against her mother. "She's a bit bashful."

"How old?"

"Eighteen months."

Georgia felt herself go all gooey for the baby, for what she and Talen had made.

"You look familiar," Dare said, addressing Georgia. "Did Aunt Amity yell at you at the café?"

"Your aunt is the madwoman who runs the café?" That had been such a spectacle. She had politely requested not to have cilantro in her dish because it tasted like soap to her and received a lecture about understanding the complex flavors and how dare she question a professional chef. Yeah. Good times.

"She yells at everyone. Don't be embarrassed," he said. "Are you looking for a cook? I have experience and I've worked with Aunt Amity for a long time. No matter who you have running your kitchen, I guarantee I'll be able to work with them, no problem. Dare Isteimlas, by the way." He held out a hand.

Her first impression had been wrong. This was not an adolescent, but a young adult who had not entirely grown into his frame. He was tall, on the lanky side, but he would fill out in a few years. "I wasn't planning to interview today, sorry."

"That's not a no."

"Dare. Enough." Kalini handed him Felicity. "Make yourself useful and watch your sister."

Georgia continued the tour. They went through the conservatory, past Quil elbow-deep in dirt, through the formal dining room and the unfinished terrace, admired the snowy landscape, and finished at the ballroom.

With the subflooring exposed and the plaster walls unfinished, Georgia realized her mistake. She should have finished with the conservatory, as it was the most impressive space in the house. "I know it looks rough, but the major work has already been completed. We've completely upgraded our electrical and environmental system. The subflooring was replaced but once the plaster is patched and finished, the new flooring will be installed. Everything is right on schedule and it'll be ready for your event."

"Seems a bit grand," Kalini said.

"How many people do you expect?" She already knew. Kalini had already contacted her, expressing worry that even though her family was small, they had to invite all her and her husband's coworkers, Clarity's friends, and neighbors. The crowd would simply be too large for their home. The event was practically in the bag, but still, Georgia worried. This would be their first hosted event and it had to go smoothly, starting with assuring them that the ballroom would have a floor.

"This is perfect!" Clarity clapped her hands together. "Can we use the terrace?"

"Weather permitting." And if the stonework got patched. She'd bump that up on the to-do list. "The far windows can be folded open, so you'd have direct access to the terrace."

Kalini sighed. "Her heart's already in it. Are you sure all this will be finished in time?"

"Work is scheduled to be finished next week, so yes." She fudged the dates. The work should be finished in ten days, barring a disaster. "Would you like to review the menu? We have a very talented cook who makes wonderful desserts."

"I'm afraid we have a chef in the family. She'll make our lives miserable unless we let her cater. Will that be an issue?"

"Not at all." Catering the event would have been good practice for the kitchen, but perhaps it would be best to just focus on the basics of hosting the event. Tables and chairs needed to be arranged, as well as serving the food and drinks.

"What do you require as a deposit?" Kalini asked.

Fantastic. Her first booking.

CHAPTER 15

G eorgia quietly turned the lock to the library door. Talen sat on worn wood treads of the staircase to the upper level, like he pulled down a book and immediately fell into the story. He was oblivious to her and her very short skirt, and the rest of the world.

For some reason, he did not wear a shirt and she heartily approved. The discarded garment sat on the floor, near the fireplace.

He was too handsome. He was all muscle and bulk, sitting with his elbows on his knees and a book cradled in his large hands. It just wasn't fair that the universe made someone that good-looking and that intelligent.

"Ahem." She cleared her throat dramatically.

He lifted his head. "What are you wearing?"

She plucked at the buttons at the front of her white blouse, exposing the pale pink bra underneath, before hiding her hands behind her back, which thrust her chest forward. Demurely, she twisted the tip of one of her shoes against the floor.

"I've been bad," she said.

Talen snapped the book closed with one hand. "What have you done?"

"I don't want to tell you." She licked her lips, aware that his eyes tracked the motion.

"You do or you would not be here." He stood, bare feet padding down the steps, and his thighs flexing and straining his trousers.

"I took a book from the restricted section," she breathed.

He paused, brow furrowed. "You are welcome to any book in my collection. It is not impressive by any means, but nothing is restricted."

She pressed a finger to her bottom lip and blinked her eyes. "It was a naughty book."

"Is something in your eyes?"

She fisted the front of her shirt, tugging it down to expose the bra. "It had pictures. They made me feel funny."

He looked at her with a blank expression.

"Funny. Down. There," she said, stressing each word. "Could you help me feel better?"

"Your attire appears inadequate for the temperature. Warm yourself next to the fire and I will fetch you some suitable garments." He picked up his discarded shirt and draped it over her shoulders. "Wear this."

"For crying out loud, Talen," she said, tossing her hands in the air and dislodging the shirt. "Haven't you ever played Naughty Librarian?"

"Oh! This is one of your games." He grinned, finally having caught on.

"It's just a little roleplay. It's not weird," she said defensively. "Never mind. I'm not feeling it anymore."

He perched on the edge of a sturdy table, setting the book down beside him. As he folded his arms over his chest, the movement of his dark amber striations mesmerized her. Too handsome and too smart, he watched her with sharp eyes. "Explain this game to me."

"I'm not in the mood now."

He sniffed the air and his tail twitched. He didn't have to say anything. They both knew she lied.

"Fine," she said. "You're the sexy librarian." Obviously. "And you're very protective of your books."

"I am."

"And I've been a naughty student. I read books from the restricted section; books I can't possibly understand."

His ears went back. "No. I will not listen to you besmirch your own intelligence. I refuse to believe you did not understand."

Oh boy. She had her work cut out for her. "It's a fantasy, so I'm pretending."

"By being unintelligent? No," he repeated.

"Okay." Her fingers twisted into the bottom of her hair, thinking. "The book was forbidden. It had pictures. Pornographic pictures."

His posture changed and he sat more rigidly. "Explain this."

"For this fantasy, I'm a student, right?"

"I will not play if you are pretending to be a kit."

She fought the urge to roll her eyes. Instead, she started with the basics. "I'm in university and a perfectly legal age, but I'm inexperienced." His tail lashed behind him. "I spend all my time studying," she said, letting her voice grow soft and wistful. "I'm too busy to have a boyfriend or to be interested in males, because I'm always in the library."

She stepped closer and walked her fingers up his bare chest, savoring the warmth and hardness of him.

"Libraries are where students should be," he said, his voice deepening.

"There's this male who works there. A sexy librarian. I like watching him and his tail as he shelves books," she continued.

"You like his tail?"

"I love his tail. I wish I was brave enough to pull it." His chest rumbled and she grinned. "And I like his voice. It's so deep and firm." She licked her lips. "Especially when he tells off the noisy students. He likes his library to be in order and you can just tell that he'll discipline anyone that breaks the rules."

He growled, low and so perfectly tempting. "And you broke the rules by going into the restricted section."

"Yes," she breathed.

"I will help you understand the reading material."

Thank fuck for that.

Talen

HIS MATE LICKED her lips and he could hear her heart accelerate.

He moved to the lounge chair and patted his lap. "Fetch this book and show me."

A look of confusion furrowed her brow. "But—"

He patted his lap. "We will read this forbidden book together."

"Oh." She looked around the library, clearly not prepared for this possibility. His mate loved to play bedroom games and he loved the awkward way she tried to explain her fantasies as he feigned misunderstanding.

Naughty librarian. That game was universal and one he held in great affection.

She grabbed a book at random.

"Not that one," he said. "I want you to read for me, my heart."

With his trousers unfastened, he took his member in hand, already hard, and worked his length while she pursued the shelves. This might be one of his mate's games, but he wanted to hear the progress she made teaching herself to read a new language.

"This one," she said, pulling down a book with a colorful cover.

"Show me."

She brought him the book, holding it out for inspection.

"Good," he said. "Now lift your skirt and show me your panties. Are they wet for me?"

She sucked in her breath and complied, raising her skirt just enough to see the white lace undergarment.

"Turn around. Good girl." His fingertips brushed against the damp fabric. "Now take them off for me."

She eased the lace panties down slowly, revealing the luscious curves of her bottom.

"I could sink my fangs into you," he said. Her breath hitched in response. "Now take a seat."

He guided her down, teasing her entrance with the head of his cock.

"Talen, I don't know—"

"You can take me," he said, as she sank down onto his length. She groaned, stretching around his girth. He smoothed down the back of her skirt, covering where their flesh joined.

She rocked her hips, searching for friction.

"None of that. Read for me." His hands on her hips kept her immobilized. Her warmth surrounded him, taking all his concentration. He wanted to drive up into her, to make her gasp and shudder with pleasure, but he restrained himself.

She opened the book to the first page and read aloud.

He thrust upward and she stumbled on a word. Slowly he moved, enjoying the way she held him tightly as he pushed into her. Another thrust, harder, and the book fell to the floor.

"Please, Talen. I need—"

"Tell me, my heart." He stroked his hand down her back, admiring the way she leaned back into his touch.

"I need more. I need you to move." She rocked her hips and gave a frustrated moan.

"You want me to fuck you," he said, a statement not a question. He wrapped her hair around his fist and moved it to the side, baring her neck.

"Yes, please."

"I only fuck good girls," he murmured, pressing a soft kiss

to the back of her neck. "Bad girls get to keep my dick warm."

"Talen—"

"Have you been a good girl?"

"Yes," she said, her voice breathless.

He tightened his grip on her hair, causing her to yelp, and forced her to look toward the floor. "A good girl does not throw books on the floor. A good girl does not take books from the restricted section." His free hand smacked her bare ass. Her cunt tightened around him in response.

"I'm sorry. I want to be good."

"I believe you, my heart, but you won't learn your lesson until you've been punished." He thrust upwards by a tiny fraction and she gasped in response. His mate, lost in her game of fantasy. "I take no pleasure in this," he said.

Georgia

"PLEASE, let me be your good girl," she begged.

Her alien acted all innocent, like he never thought of role-playing, but he delivered a knockout performance. Damn.

His arms tightened around her, holding her back to his bare chest. He filled her, hitting the sensitive spots, and a hand slipped down to her clit. He rubbed and rocked into her, teeth on the back of her neck, pressing but not biting.

The light prick of pain made everything else that much better.

This had to be the pregnancy hormones. She was always turned on, always ready for him, and she felt like they could be joined like this for hours. If she listened to her body, she'd never leave the bed and die of dehydration.

"My female, my heart," he whispered in her ear, lips brushing the sensitive shell.

Her skin tingled and a warm, glowing feeling spread from her stomach. Soon, the sensation was too much, every touch and information overload, and she gasped as her climax broke.

He released deep in her, filling her with his seed, and gave a few more pumps until he stilled. He relaxed his grip on her. Tension left her body and she melted back into his warmth.

"I'm sorry I dropped the book," she said. That hadn't been her intention, but she had been distracted and her grip slipped.

"We're doing this again. You can fling any damn book you please."

CHAPTER 16

GEORGIA

Sister,

Obedience is a name that has a fine history in our family. I suggest you give it proper consideration.

-Quil

Georgia studied her cards, looked at her diminishing stack of chips and back to her hand, and decided her meager pair of nines was not worth the risk. They played for bragging rights, but still. She had her reputation to consider. "I fold."

A gust of wind tossed rain against the window. The fireplace kept the drawing room warm, casting a cozy glow over the wood-paneled room. Georgia found herself drawn to the arch of the fireplace. In lieu of a mantle, gold leaf covered the ornate scrollwork framing the opening. It gleamed and promised a warm haven from the soaking rains outside.

Little wonder they used the drawing room as the guest lounge. Everything from the plush overstuffed furniture to the thick carpeting was designed to be comfortable and cozy. Fresh bouquets of flowers from the conservatory decorated the tables, perfuming the air with a heady floral aroma. It was the perfect place to snuggle up and read by the fire or spend an evening chatting over drinks.

Winter kicked and gasped but finally released its icy hold. They had a day of warm sunshine, followed by a week of rain, but thankfully no snow. The day had started promising enough with a bright morning, but gray clouds rolled in, bringing a cold spring rain to soak the grounds. Tomorrow's forecast promised more of the same. Georgia looked forward to seeing the sun once the rainstorms finally broke. She didn't realize how much she enjoyed sunlight on her face until she didn't have any.

After dinner, Quil suggested they retreat to the lounge for cards and a brandy-like alcohol. With the house void of guests during the ballroom construction, she saw no harm in an evening of cards and drinking. Well, a non-alcoholic beverage for herself.

Poker, despite its Earthly origins, gained rapid popularity in the Interstellar Union and beyond. Travel was long and slow, especially in the early days when humans first left Earth, and a deck of cards were the perfect traveling companion. The other members of the IU had their own games, but the standard fifty-two-card deck soon infiltrated every ship and station. That illustrious history of colonizing the stars with spades, clubs, diamonds, and hearts explained why Georgia sat at a table playing poker with three aliens, one of whom she was certain cheated.

She played a few hands until Fiona arrived and complained about never being included. They dealt her in, even though she knew nothing about poker and constantly demanded Quil's opinion on her cards.

That totally defeated the purpose of poker, but Georgia kept her mouth shut. Eventually, Fiona grew bored and wandered off to the plush sofa to watch a talk show on her tablet. The scandalized hoots and calls of the audience drifted over from the device.

Georgia nursed her drink—apple juice—determined to enjoy herself. The juice was cloying and left a sticky residue in her mouth. She missed booze, not that she had ever been a big drinker, but nothing compared to the way liquor spread through her like soft, liquid fire, leaving her with a pleasant heat. She needed to relax but it was so hard because everyone got on her nerves.

Pregnancy hormones swung her rapidly from overly senti-mental to raging asshole in an instant, and it sucked. She hated being out of control of her own emotions.

"You need a refill," Talen said, topping off her glass.

She took a sip, aware of his gaze on her mouth. Her tongue licked up any stray drops on her lips and his eyes tracked the movement. The moment stretched between them, as soft and sweet as the drink itself.

She still hadn't given him an answer yet regarding his

marriage proposal. In that moment, she saw how desperately he needed an answer and she saw his struggle to be patient. She wanted to say yes. She wanted to believe that a kit would bind them forever and no one would ever abandon her again. The desperate longing made her choke up, like she needed to sob and scream all at once.

Yup, those hormones were playing with her head.

Quil cleared his throat and spread his cards on the table. "I'll call. Straight flush."

Georgia stared at the nine of diamonds, an impossible card for Quil to play as the nine of diamonds was in her hand.

She set her glass down, the heavy cut crystal making a satisfying clinking noise. "You sure you want to play that?"

"Oh, that's interesting," Talen said in a tone that was at the same time playful and threatening, like a tiger toying with prey. He leaned forward, his tail brushing against her leg. "Why wouldn't he want to play those cards?"

"Because I had them first," she said, flipping over her hand. She leaned back in the chair, smiling broadly. "Someone's been a naughty boy."

Quil did not protest but instead fished out the suspect card. "I'm out of practice."

"You're shameless is what you are," Georgia said, not bothering to suppress a grin. He had all the moral fiber of a wet paper bag, but he was entertaining.

A moan came from the sofa. "Ugh, stop flirting with my husband. It's tiring and so not cute," Fiona said.

"I'm not flirting." At least not with Quil. Gross.

Talen leaned in and whispered, "I think it's cute." Another brush of his tail, this time feeling as intimate as if he held her hand.

"Not. Flirting," Georgia repeated.

Fiona slinked across the room and perched on Quil's lap. When she snuggled in and his arms automatically went around her, she gave a triumphant smile, like she won some prize.

For a moment, with the firelight turning her chestnut curls into a riot of a warm chestnut, Fiona looked like she belonged in the stately home, cradled in the lap of her handsome mate. Only for a moment, though, because Fiona's practiced smile transformed into a smirk and the illusion shattered.

Whatever. Georgia rolled her eyes.

"Then what do you call all that?" Fiona waved a dismissive hand toward Georgia.

"All what?" She looked down, finding only her cards and a glass of sweet golden apple juice.

Fiona arched a brow. "Your décolletage? It's a bit low-cut, don't you think? Girls your size should know better than to wear anything too revealing."

A hand instinctively went to the vee neck of her sweater and tugged it up. The sweater wasn't that low-cut, but it drifted down at the end of the day. Fiona smiled smugly. Georgia's frustration grew. Fiona was such a petty bully, and they were having a lovely evening until she flounced in and had to be the center of attention.

"You think a bit of cleavage is flirting? Wow, your skills are remarkably unrefined. Is that a demonstration of the high-class techniques you employed to snag Quil? Just flopped your tits out and gave them a shake?" The crude words spilled out of her.

"You're just jealous that I have him and you don't." Fiona pushed Quil's face directly into her own cleavage.

"Jealous? Of you? Over him?" All winter long, she bottled away her frustration and tried to make the best of a very shitty situation, but now the cork had been removed. All that frustration was ready to spew forth directly onto Fiona.

Charl and Talen discreetly pushed away from the table.

"Yes, jealous of our happiness. Jealous that I'm mistress of this house and you're just the hired help."

"Okay," Georgia said, letting out a long sigh. "Let's unpack this. First, your precious boo-boo is a cheater." Fiona opened her mouth to protest but Georgia kept talking. "He cheats at cards—"

"I do," Quil said with a nod.

"And he cheated on me with you," Georgia added.

"I knew you weren't over that," Fiona said with an air of

triumph. "You just have to accept that Quil-boo wants me and not you."

"Quil-boo?" Talen muttered.

"I know you're staying on because they felt sorry for you, but I really think you've worn out your welcome. In fact, when Quil-boo and I start our family, I think it'd be best if you found another position. We'll give you a good reference, of course."

Georgia tried to stay calm. She was a grown adult, calm and rational. The worst thing to do was to yell and fling insults. Her bad behavior, no matter how much Fiona goaded her into it, would only confirm the worst things Fiona claimed.

But this bitch did *not* just try to fire her.

If she wore earrings, she'd be taking them out and handing them to Talen.

"Quil-boo signed a marriage contract with me," Georgia said, her tone even but as cold as the rain pounding the window. "He found a loophole, yes, but when he decided to marry you, that makes him at best a scuzzbag and, at worst, a bigamist. And this house you're so proud of? He signed that marriage contract a month before winning it in a card game." Georgia leaned forward, arms on the table, unconcerned about her cleavage. "Which means he got this house for *me*. You're just here because boo-boo Quil has a lot of flaws, including being impatient and easily distracted by cheap and gaudy things."

"That is also true," Quil said.

"Shut up," Fiona snapped, turning her ire to Quil. "Are you just going to let her tell lies like that?"

"She has only spoken the truth so far," he answered. "And I'm curious as to what she'll say next."

She had nothing else to say. As much as she tired of Fiona's constant barbed comments, she took no satisfaction in her words. Fiona was a shallow, petty person who only understood shallow, petty words, and Georgia felt disgusted that she lowered herself to Fiona's level. She should announce that she was going to bed, but instead finished her drink.

"You're trying to steal my husband because that one won't have anything to do with you or your bastard." Fiona jabbed a finger in Talen's direction. "You're not going to trick my man into marrying you, you slut."

The room fell silent.

"Apologize," Quil said, voice barely louder than a whisper.

"I won't," Fiona said.

"Apologize! Your behavior shames me. Georgia is family and we treat family better than that."

Georgia felt the brush of Talen's tail against her leg, offering comfort. Whatever ugly things Fiona said about her, she knew his heart.

"She's not family," Fiona said, voice rising in pitch. "She's just the help that got knocked up. You should be taking my side, not hers." She fluttered her lashes but Quil sneered, finally seeing her for the pile of human garbage she was.

That was definitely the hormones talking.

"If you won't defend me, I'm not going to stick around and be spoken to in such an undignified manner," Fiona announced, moments before flouncing out of the room.

Georgia felt the burn of three sets of eyes on her. "I think I'll head to bed too."

"No one thinks that. You're as much a part of this family as I am," Charl said, the most he had spoken all evening.

"Thank you." Tomorrow, Georgia would pay the price for her sharp tongue, but she intended to savor this moment.

Talen

BY MORNING, Fiona was gone, along with the cash box from the office, assorted items that could be resold easily, and the jeweled music box.

"All our money?" Quil raked a hand through his hair.

"All your money. And the household account. She did not have access to my personal accounts," Talen said. Fiona took quite a lot of money, but they had a cushion. A tiny cushion.

A call to the bank would freeze any additional with-drawals, but the household account had already been emptied.

He paced the length of the library, passing by the empty display case. Shattered glass from the case littered the floor, crunching underfoot. He didn't care about the money—well, he did in the vague way that he did not want to lose the house and be a pauper—but his focus was the missing music box.

"This is my fault," Quil said.

Talen did not have to affirm that statement. It was obviously his fault. He knew nothing about that female before he brought her into their home. He gave her access to their money with no more reference than a pretty face and a warm cunt.

Fiona played them. Not even skillfully. Every bit of doubt she cast at Georgia, every accusation, was projected from her own schemes. She had literally been telling them what she planned to do, and they ignored her because she was vain and shallow.

They would have to sell the house, if they could sell it at all. Who would be so foolish enough to purchase a money pit and toss another fortune into that same pit?

Talen glared daggers at his brother.

Who besides Quil?

"Your damn cock got us into this mess," Talen growled.

"My cock brought you your mate and your kit, so you're welcome."

Quil stepped right up to Talen, nose nearly touching nose. Their ears flattened and they snarled. Talen's claws itched, wanting to be unsheathed. No, correction, wanting to be covered in the hot, sticky gore of Quil's blood.

Patience. Forgiveness. Kindness.

The virtues offered him little comfort.

"You are impossible," he said, shoving Quil back a step. "You never accept blame and you never apologize."

"And what would you have me do, brother? Cover myself in ash? Parade through town for all to see my shame?"

"Take ownership of your shit! Stop expecting me to fix everything."

A cough at the door interrupted them. Georgia had a tablet cradled against her chest. "Have you called the police?"

"No police," Talen and Quil said simultaneously.

"They could post a bulletin and stop her from leaving the planet."

"No," Quil said, slouching in a chair. "She is my mate with full access to our shared bank accounts and family heirlooms. The police will only consider this a nuisance and not theft."

Georgia shook her head. "Fine. A single human female isn't too difficult to track. A shuttle left Drac two hours ago for the province's capital. She was on it. Any clue where she would be headed?"

"To spend money," Quil grumbled. Then his body snapped to attention. "I know where she would go. If I find her, I may be able to recover some of our funds. She would sell the music box, so you should look in pawn shops," he told Talen.

If she transferred the funds to an anonymous credit account instead of spending every cent, they weren't ruined. Talen cared less about their possible ruin than the recovery of the jeweled music box. An item like that would be difficult to fence, even knowing its history. Few pawn shops could offer anything close to the music box's true value. Feeling out collectors would be better, but Fiona needed credit fast. She might be desperate enough to accept a pittance.

"Agreed," Talen said.

CHAPTER 17

GEORGIA

T he first thing Georgia noticed was the rare peek of winter sun glimmering on the river. The second thing was bridges, so many bridges. The provincial capital was a rusting industrial town seated at the merger of two large rivers.

They drove past shuttered factories and closed mills.

"What happened?" Economic depression could happen anywhere, which made it a ridiculous question in her mind, but the whole section of the city had such an air of abandonment to it that she had to know the culprit.

"It's the labor shortage. It's easier to ship raw material off-planet than process," Talen answered.

"But that makes everything more expensive in the long run." Listen to her, like she was an expert on economics. Georgia rolled her eyes at her own damn self.

"Yes, and modern factories use robotics. They're more efficient than those old heaps."

"And we're here in the shadows of these old heaps why?"

He grinned at her turn of phrase. "Because this is exactly the type of neighborhood you could hock a priceless work of art and avoid too many questions."

"What if she sold it to a collector, like you said?"

"Then the sale was arranged ahead of time. We'd have no chance."

"Right." The music box would go into a private collection, never to be seen again. "What makes the music box so special? Besides the obvious gems."

"Ever heard of the jeweler Adoration? No? Adoration was a goldsmith, jeweler, and designer on Talmar. Very famous. Created intricate pieces, each one a masterpiece," he said.

"And the music box was made by Adoration? Seriously? You kept it in a glass display case."

"It was locked."

"Which was circumvented by smashing the glass," she retorted. He kept a priceless artifact out on a shelf like a trinket. Honestly.

"I suppose you're going to tell me I should have locked it away? A security deposit box, perhaps?"

"Yes! Since you say it's a unique, one-of-a-kind piece of art, then yes."

The car pulled off the road and came to a stop in a parking lot. A squat building, covered in faded and peeling paint, had a light flickering in a window. Georgia recognized the characters meaning "open."

He turned off the engine and turned to face her. "My father commissioned it for my mother. It was meant to be seen and heard. If I locked it away, then it'd be like locking them away." The meaning was clear in the tone of his voice. He loved that gilded music box, not for its monetary value or famous maker, but for pure sentimentality.

"You're such a marshmallow," she said.

"I am no such thing," he protested.

"All sweet on the inside. I can't believe they didn't make fun of you in the Navy."

He opened the door, visibly uneasy.

"They did!" Georgia bounced out of the car. "Was it Charl? He doesn't say much but when he does, I bet it's biting."

Talen's ears went back. "Enough. That trinket is all I have of my parents. I smuggled it off Talmar when I was a kit. I will not be mocked."

"Oh." She hurried forward and placed a hand on his arm. He did not speak often, or ever, about his parents. She knew they were murdered, and he had to leave his home planet as a child. All this had to be dragging up unpleasant memories. "I'm sorry. That was a shitty thing for me to say."

"Yes, it was," he grumbled, and then he ran a hand through his hair. Somehow, he looked better for the mess.

"Fiona needs quick cash, so she'd try to sell the items she took."

"She won't get a fraction of the music box's value if she pawned it."

"Hopefully, neither she nor the pawnbroker will recognize what she has."

Georgia saw no value in adding that they needed a lot of luck for that to happen, so she kept her mouth shut.

Fiona hadn't visited the first pawn shop, or the second, nor had they heard of a human female trying to sell a gaudy music box. At the fourth shop, they found some of the silver serving pieces that Fiona took, but no music box. At some point, Fiona must have realized what she had, or at least thought she could get a better price elsewhere.

Georgia called jewelers, thinking maybe Fiona tried to sell the music box in parts. No human female with chestnut hair wandered in with flawless sapphires and diamonds that day.

By mid-afternoon, all they had to show for their efforts were sore feet, a cranky disposition, and zero leads.

"You take me to all the best places," she grumbled, sliding back into the vehicle.

"We'll stay the night. I'm too tired to drive back," Talen said.

"We can try again in the morning."

"No. She didn't pawn the music box. Perhaps she did have a private collector lined up."

His shoulders slumped with a look of defeat. She wanted to squeeze his hand, stroke behind his ear, the way he would never admit to enjoying but made his tail curl and comfort him. The words *only a material possession* were on her lips but she knew how crass that would sound. In the grand scheme of the universe, one music box wasn't as important as a loved one, but that same music box represented all his lost family.

Fuck it. She could offer comfort and keep her mouth shut at the same time. Stranger things had happened.

"It's a stupid thing to be upset about, isn't it?" He leaned into her hand, eyes closing as her fingers worked behind his ear. "Did I tell you it was a courting gift from my father to my mother?"

"You said he had it made for her." The jeweled *objet d'art* seemed a bit much to her, but she kept her snarky comment to herself.

"She hated it. Said it was a waste of good money."

Georgia tried to swallow her laugh. "I think I would have liked your mother."

"I believe she would adore you." He pulled away, the light catching fire in his honey-amber gaze. "Enough chasing ghosts. Fiona can keep the blasted thing. Food first, I think, then there's somewhere I want to take you."

"Sounds good."

Dinner was a simple meal at a riverside diner. They ambled down the boardwalk, past boutiques and specialty shops, eventually stopping at a narrow brick building painted blue.

"Here we are, my favorite shop," he said, which turned out to be a rare bookshop.

"You really do take me to all the best places," she said, genuinely meaning her words this time.

The clerk at the counter recognized Talen when they walked in.

The shop smelled of aged leather, dusty pages, and beeswax. With bookshelves crowding the floor, creating a maze, and the odd chair tucked into unexpected nooks, this was exactly the sort of place she expected Talen to love.

A familiar cover with two young Tal children caught her eye: *The Lost Princes*. This time, however, she could understand the tagline under the title which read, Talmar politics and the aristocracy. It looked interesting.

"This is garbage," Talen said, plucking the book from her hand.

"Hey, you don't get to tell me what to read. Maybe I like hot garbage." The book just became a thousand percent more interesting because he disliked it. "I'm not leaving here without it."

He gave a weary sigh. "It is gossip and speculation and holds little academic merit."

"Stop. You're selling it too hard," she said, her tone sarcastic. She drank in the sight of him, such a massive man holding what seemed to be nothing more than a scrap of paper in his large hands. Even though he professed to despise the book, he held it with care. Even books of mostly gossip and little academic merit deserved respect, and she loved him for that. "You're such a book nerd."

"More sweet words of affection? Have mercy, my heart, for my ego cannot take the strain."

He smiled down at her, the book between them, with warm affection in his eyes. All the reasons for rejecting his offer of marriage—the kit, coercion, future regret—fell away. She didn't care. Those reasons were petty and this feeling between them was big. Important.

She licked her bottom lip. "Talen, I need to tell you something."

"Yes." He leaned down, the book-free hand cradling the back of her neck.

"I can't wait to read this." She plucked the book from his grip and danced away, snickering. He gave chase as she slipped around a corner, slowing to let him catch her. His arms wrapped around her, holding her tight, and this was where she belonged.

"Exciting news," the clerk, a Corravian male, said, interrupting. "I finally sifted through all the damaged books you brought me, and most of them were beyond saving."

"I wouldn't call that exciting news," Talen said, leaning on the counter.

"Oh, you'd be wrong. One of the books was thought lost." The clerk took down a flat box from the shelf behind the counter. Inside the box sat a book badly swollen from water damage. "It is damaged, but you're looking at a very rare copy of *The Descendent of the Eclipse*."

"Is it notable?"

"The author was well known at the time but generally considered a hack." The clerk removed the book and laid it on the counter. He gently opened the front cover. "This was published just before the Crisis and had not yet been distributed to the general public. The books were stored in warehouses until the release date, but the Crisis happened. From time to time, one will turn up."

"Are there no digital copies?" Georgia asked. Talen's obsession with physical books remained beyond her understanding. The words of the story interested her more than the book itself.

"Of course." The clerk made a scoffing noise, clearly thinking little of digitized works.

"Is the condition a problem?" Talen asked.

"It's not ideal, but it shouldn't matter. A serious collector will want it, no matter the condition. I'd suggest not rebinding. The original cover may fetch a higher price. That is, if you were interested in selling." He licked his lips, clearly wanting Talen to sell the book.

"I'm not sure. It belongs with the house," Talen said. They

could use the money, no doubt, but even Georgia knew not to appear too eager.

"I've already had buyers express an interest."

"It is not a decision I can make on my own."

The clerk nodded. "I was able to locate the book you want. One moment." He disappeared into the back.

Georgia leaned against the counter, mirroring Talen's posture. "You're going to sell the book?"

"I don't have a choice," he said in a near whisper. "I'd sell the entire contents of the library if I thought it'd buy us another month in the house."

"Wow." He loved that library, even with the mostly bare shelves.

"Found your order." The clerk returned with a stock of seven books. She recognized the series immediately. "Apparently these are quite popular. Never heard of them, myself."

Georgia grabbed the top book, a blue cover she had stared at for hours when she was young. "They're in English."

"Is that a problem? I could get you a Tal translation but it's not available in Corravian, unfortunately," the clerk said.

"English is perfect," Talen said. He opened the closest volume, flipping through the pages. "I wanted our kit to read your favorite story in the original language."

Georgia hugged the book to her chest and launched

herself at Talen, smashing into him with the book. "It's perfect. Thank you so much."

Talen

BROTHER,

I have given your mate several good suggestions for naming the kit and she refuses to take me seriously. Correction is a wonderful name. I can see how Unwanted is not fashionable, but it is traditional. Well, we just have the one great-great-and-so-forth called Unwanted, and by all accounts, he was a bastard, so perhaps that was not my best suggestion. Be that as it may, Correction remains a wonderful name.

-Quil

"HOW FAR TO THE HOTEL?" She turned up the collar on her coat. The air held a brisk, muddy smell from the river. Having lived her entire life never more than an hour from the ocean, the water smelled wrong. Sounded wrong. The gentle lapping of the river against the embankment had its charms, though. Her hand trailed along the top of the railing, all that separated the pavement from the water's edge. Lights from the city reflected on the dark water. Further upriver, commercial shipping continued no matter the late hour.

"Tired?"

"Yes," she said.

"Fortunately, it is nearby."

"That's not what I meant." She leaned her back against the railing. Her feet ached, and she knew that she'd pay tomorrow for the day of constant walking. "We should get married. Yes. I accept."

Talen swung her into an embrace, lifting her right off her feet. The scent of warm citrus and spice, undeniably his scent, surrounded her. The bag of books fell to the pavement, momentarily forgotten. "It was the book, wasn't it? I knew the right courting gift would open your heart."

The book sealed the deal but wasn't nearly all of it. "I can't believe you remembered me talking about that book. I don't even think I told you the title," she said.

"I didn't do the legwork. I just described what you told me. Maxis did the rest."

"I'm sorry it took me so long to give you an answer. I already knew, really. There was never any doubt, but I was scared. Everyone leaves. Everyone. My father. My mom. My stupid ex-boyfriend." She huffed, torn between the urge to laugh and sob. Speaking her fears made them seem so small, trivial even. "Quil left before he even had a chance to meet me. It's like something innate in me."

"You are wrong." His arms tightened around her.

"If I used the baby to bind you to me, you'd end up hating me. When you left anyway, it would hurt too much. I couldn't bear it." Ah, the truth at last. "I love you. I think I have since the bookstall in the market."

"You carry my heart," he said, and she wanted to believe.

"But only because of the baby." He loved her now, but the excitement would fade and then what would they have?

"I think since that first morning when you yelled at Quil."

"Oh God," she groaned. "Not my finest moment."

"I disagree. I was fully prepared to clean up my brother's mess and tend to a broken-hearted female. To be her champion. Instead, I found a female who was her own champion, saying everything I wanted to say and saying it so much better. My very own Persistence come to life."

Her heart thumped. He was talking books and it was the sexiest thing she ever heard. "I don't recall Persistence having a temper."

"She gets riled up. It is one of her challenges." He tucked her head under his chin. "Now you see how serious this is for me."

"Comparing me to the main character in your favorite book? Yeah, I see."

"I can never leave you, for you carry my heart. I will be at your side until the light leaves me and I will keep repeating this until you believe me."

"Thank you. I love you more than I can say." She intended to show him.

CHAPTER 18

GEORGIA

"We will marry today," Talen announced the moment her eyes cracked open.

"Okay? I mean, sure, let's get a license." She yawned, stretching and rotating her feet. "I don't particularly want a big fuss. We can get a justice of the peace. Do they do that here?"

If they went to the courthouse and applied for a marriage license that day, they could schedule an appointment with a judge, but she had no idea what was a reasonable amount of time to expect to wait. A few weeks, most likely. Maybe she'd find a dress, not that she wanted a fancy wedding gown, but it would be nice to be married in something other than yesterday's sweater and leggings.

They went to the courthouse and had an appointment with a judge that afternoon. Amazingly.

Georgia sat at the café table, nursing her cup of tea. The brew was a rich, sugary, black tea that zipped through her veins. She recognized the sweet ambrosia of caffeine at the first sip. She'd keep that revelation to herself, lest Talen take the cup away, but she wouldn't have more than one cup. Moderation was fine. Freema, a genuine human doctor, said one cup a day would be safe.

She inhaled the aroma, enjoying how it was the opposite of lawn clippings. Maybe she could get some to take home.

Talen drummed his fingers on the tabletop, ignoring his own cup.

"It's getting cold," she said.

"I have two confessions," he blurted.

Something akin to dread curled in her stomach. They were getting married, he asked, she said yes. Now he had something to tell her and it couldn't be good. "You better not have another wife." She blinked, surprised at herself. "Sorry, I thought I was over that."

He looked around the café and leaned in conspiratorially. "Talent Achaval is not my birth name."

As far as secrets went, that was a dud.

"I knew that," she said with relief.

"How?"

"Well, you told me that your parents were murdered. You fled your planet and moved around a lot. I assumed a new identity was part of all that." She kept her voice low and confidential.

He nodded. "My parents did name me Talent. That remains true."

She didn't ask for his original family name. As hard as it was to imagine danger in a bright, sunny café with the perfect cup of sugary tea, there could be danger yet in the events that took his parents two decades ago.

"Do you want to know who I am?" he asked.

"I know who you are." The father of her child. Her husband. Her love.

The noise of the café surrounded them, the murmur of voices and the clatter of dishes. A door opened and cool air wafted in.

"You carry my heart." He reached across the table for her hand. "I am honored you have chosen me. My spirit is filled with joy. Every day I think this the happiest a male could be, but I am wrong because what I feel today pales with my love for you tomorrow. And I am terrified of being a father."

Not a dud secret. Not even a little bit.

His grip on her hand tightened, waiting for her response.

"I'm scared, too," she said. "Being a parent is scary."

"But I do not know how to be a father."

"Well, no one really knows until they do the on-the-job training." She stroked her thumb across his wrist and his grip eased. He was such a large man, absolutely massive. Sitting at this tiny table, in a tiny chair, drinking from a toy-sized cup, he should have looked ridiculous, but he didn't. He looked like a man who was comfortable with himself and his place in the world. She couldn't imagine a stronger, safer person, or a better dad. "You're going to be a great dad."

His tail thumped against the thin legs of the table, rattling the cups sitting in saucers. "I would sit with my father while he worked, as long as I remained quiet. How is that enough? Maybe I would have seen my father more if I was older, but I don't think he spent much time with Quil, either."

"But he was there, and he wanted you there." Which was more than her father ever did.

"He tolerated my presence when I was old enough to sit quietly. That is not the kind of father I want to be."

"I think that counts for a lot, knowing your strengths and weaknesses. Usually, people just imitate what their parents did," she said. Her father yelled, stank of beer, and came and went with the seasons, sweeping chaos into their lives. Her mother endured with tired eyes until he left for good. "I don't want to be the kind of parent my parents were, either."

He stared at her as though she just babbled nonsense. "My parents were no parents at all. They hired a nursemaid."

"There you go. Do that."

"No! I will not hire a stranger to raise my child," he said, genuine anger seeping into his voice.

"I mean ask for help, fuzzy britches." She nudged his

shoulder. "We're not alone. Bright raised you. For all intents and purposes, she is your mother."

"I suspect she will monopolize the kit."

"And Quil will be a good uncle."

He huffed.

"Not for discipline. Can you imagine? He's going to teach our kid to cheat at cards and then drag them to every garden and arboretum on the planet." She placed a hand on her stomach. "But no one is going to love this kid harder than Quil."

"This is true and Charl is a suitable challenge for a curious kit to climb."

She grinned, imaging Charl as a very surly, four-armed jungle gym. "We got this."

His communicator chimed and he checked the device. "Five-minute warning. Ready to be my mate, officially?"

Yes.

Talen

LATER, once he became a properly married male, he stretched out in the hotel's bed next to his mate. The room felt stiff and formal, the bed too soft, and the blankets scratchy. It wasn't home but as long as he heard the beating of his mate's heart, he was home.

Georgia propped herself up on one elbow. Her hair, a delightful, bed-rumpled mess, framed her face. "Why do the Tal kiss?"

"We like it. Why do humans kiss?"

"Was that a rude question? Sorry."

"Not rude." Unexpected, not rude, considering he had first kissed her months ago.

"I was curious, because some cultures don't," she said. "So, is kissing a thing that Tal do or is it something you picked up on the street?"

Moonlight spilled through the window, casting a soft glow over half her face. He searched for some hint of amusement or an indication that she teased him.

"You're serious," he said.

She flopped down onto her back. "Never mind. Ignore me. I get all goofy and day-dreamy after sex. I got to stop blurting out everything that pops into my head."

"No, I like that about you." He pulled her to him, her back to his chest, and nuzzled her hair. The scent of sleep, sex and dreams clung to her. "It's biology," he said, rubbing his jaw and pheromone glands along her bare shoulders. "Your poor human nose is completely blind but mine detects pheromones. I want to mark you with my glands."

"How delightfully savage of you," she said and squirmed. He growled a warning for her to stay put until he was done marking her.

"Kissing is one way to mark you," he said, placing a light kiss on her shoulder. "And it's pleasurable."

"I just thought the fangs might get in the way."

His fangs... might get in the way? His mind blanked on a response. "I have not been that clumsy since I was an adolescent." And even not then, not really. "Do humans have that problem?"

"Oh yeah." She rolled to face him. "First kisses are notorious. No one knows what they're doing so it's like they're trying to eat your face." She snapped her blunt, harmless human teeth.

"You jest."

"I'm not! My first kiss was terrible. Our teeth kept bashing into each other and there was way too much tongue and it was gross and slobbery."

He hated that someone else had her first kiss and possibly shared in other first experiences with her. Such jealousy served no purpose. His mate was a grown female, beautiful, clever and desirable. The male before him had been a fool to toss her aside—and he distinctly ignored that his brother had been the male before him—so he should not feel jealousy over the opportunities the fools had squandered. He should be thankful.

All he could manage was a growl.

Georgia placed a hand on his chest. Green eyes, bright and clear as spring leaves, watched him. "Hey, that was a long time ago. You're the only man I want to kiss."

"I'm not your first."

"And I'm not your first, either."

"I will be your last," he vowed.

"Okay," she breathed.

Then he kissed her, because it wasn't their first or their last but simply one of a million brief moments that tied them together and that was reason enough to rejoice.

CHAPTER 19

GEORGIA

My mate,

Quil will try to convince you that Erection is a traditional family name, having to do with standing tall and with pride.

He lies. It is an elaborate ruse and I refuse to allow our kit to be named after a dick joke.

-Talen

Georgia slept late the next day, slept during the two-hour drive back home, and then took a nap in the drawing room. Climbing the stairs to her own room seemed an impossible feat and curling up on the fainting sofa was a much better idea.

"I don't know why I'm so tired," she said, pulling a quilt over herself.

"You are with kit," Talen answered, because that was the

correct answer. She wore herself out the last two days and paid the price today.

"Tomorrow, I'll get back to work." Just contemplating all the things on her plate exhausted her.

"You will sleep if you need to sleep."

Snuggling down, she considered that a day off wasn't a bad thing before she drifted off and woke in darkness. She slept the entire day away.

She folded the quilt and draped it over the back of the sofa, before wandering out. Moonlight streamed through the windows, casting pools of pale light against the floor. Conversation drifted from the direction of the kitchen and she followed the sound.

White blossoms caught her eye and Georgia found herself pulled into the conservatory. Moonlight combined with round lanterns strung from the ceiling created patches of luminous greenery and deep shadows. The moon violets blossomed, their pristine petals turning toward the moon.

During the day, the cacophony of sight and scent overwhelmed the space. The color green and the lush floral aromas threatened to overpower her. At night, it was peaceful. Still.

"Hiding?"

Georgia raised a hand to acknowledge Quil. He joined her, standing at a respectful distance, and they admired the moon violets.

"Any luck?" she finally asked.

"Not in any of her usual haunts." He looked tired; it had been a long two days with little sleep. "Though I did find a few debts she skipped out on."

"Did you just return?"

"Still have dust on my boots."

"Mud, more like." She refused to worry about the state of the floor on her day off. Muddy floors would be there in the morning.

"I know you were not flirting," Quil said.

"Good. I wasn't. You were cheating, badly. I'm disturbed by the lack of quality."

"Standards have fallen." Amusement slipped into his voice but vanished quickly. "She planned her exit."

Georgia wanted to protest that Fiona didn't seem the type for planning or plotting, but that would be buying into the shallow, empty-headed persona she obviously honed. Fiona slipped away too easily, vanishing off the planet when she should have stuck out like a sore thumb. "I suppose she did."

"I've ruined us."

Georgia tossed him a sharp glance. "As much as I'd love to watch you heap abuse on yourself, cut yourself some slack. You're tired. I'm sure there's something tasty in the kitchen that Bright would be more than happy to shove down your throat. I'm all for it if that keeps you quiet."

He gave a thin-lipped smile. "Such tender maternal instincts."

"Oh, fuck off already." She rolled her eyes. "I'm not interested in your pity parties. People make mistakes and trust the wrong person all the time. You're not special."

He huffed. "Talen is right. Your brand of affection is harsh."

"Stop trying to flatter me. Now, let's eat."

Talen

TALEN CLIMBED into bed next to his mate. "I think we should share this room and let the kit have mine. Your bed is much nicer than mine."

"Of course, it is. Your mattress feels like it's stuffed with rocks. Are you ready to sleep?" She partially closed the book, marking her place with her index finger.

He cringed at the unneeded stress to the spine but felt pleased that she read his gift. The clerk at the bookshop assured him that the series was popular and locating a copy in Georgia's original language took no effort. Georgia could mistreat that book and he could replace it a hundred times over.

His bibliophile gut cringed at that. Perhaps he could procure a set for display purposes and try to ignore his mate's mishandling of the books.

"Read to me, please. I want to know the story of the orphaned wizard."

"I'll start at the beginning." She held the book in one hand, in such a manner that put too much pressure on the spine.

He tried to look away. He tried to focus on her voice and the story, but his eyes kept drifting back to the book's spine. It would crack. The glue and binding would come undone.

"Hold it like this," he said, moving her other hand to the book. "Both hands."

"You're so fussy tonight," she grumbled but held the book correctly.

With that minor atrocity rectified, he fell into the story. Georgia briefly had to pause and explain the physical appearance of a Terran owl and how they were wild predators, not suited to deliver mail. After two chapters, her voice grew thick from use and she closed the book, using a scrap of paper to mark her place. He barely noticed, really, but left a stack of suitable bookmarks at her bedside.

"Hairy seems an unusual name," he mused. He lay on his back, staring at the ceiling.

"It's pretty common, actually."

"Why would humans wish their children to be hairy? It is a strange aspiration."

"Not hairy like hair." She touched her own chestnut hair. "It's short for Harold. Maybe Harrison."

"Would you consider it a good name for the kit?" He

rolled to face her. Without thinking, he placed a hand on her stomach. Visually, her stomach appeared only slightly more rounded, but the tactile sensation had changed. Before, his mate had been all softness and pliable. Now, her belly felt denser. He thrilled to feel the changes in her body as the kit grew and could not wait to see her grow large.

"That's sweet. Harry is a lot nicer than Correction or Obedience," she said.

"Those are no longer fashionable. Names tend to be more hopeful now, rather than disciplinarian."

"Discipline isn't bad," she said. "As a name, I mean."

"It most certainly is."

"I could be persuaded on Erection."

His mouth fell open. "No."

She smirked and then bit her lower lip in an effort not to laugh, a battle she quickly lost. "I think it sounds rather noble."

"You can't even say that with a straight face."

She cleared her throat but couldn't utter the words without giggling. In that moment, the universe did not exist outside the space they shared. He could live there forever. Her joy, pure and simple, filled him with such devotion. They would have a lifetime of laughter, of teasing and smiles. They would have tears and pain, too.

He wanted it all. Every moment. Every smile. Every tear. Forever would not be enough.

CHAPTER 20

GEORGIA

Freema,

If I have to swallow one more cup of herbal tea, I'll scream. I want caffeine. I want sugar. I'm prepared to throw a tantrum if they try to take away my dark chocolate.

Please, please, please, use your medical knowledge for good and tell them one cup a day is fine.

-G

Six months pregnant was no joke. Her slight baby bump grew, seemingly overnight, and now nothing fit. Not her black pants, the professional suit jacket or white blouse she planned to wear for the Isteimlas party. The gray-and-blue-striped wrap dress would work, even if it felt too casual.

She fussed with the belt and the fabric gapped at the front of the dress. Her boobs were definitely bigger. A safety pin kept her modesty in check, but she disliked the gleam of metal against the fabric. Maybe she'd grab a flower and make a boutonniere or whatever the equivalent was on a dress.

Rubbing her hand over her belly, she dreaded how big she'd get in the coming two and a half months. She had a few maternity dresses of Corravian design, super cute with an A-line that allowed the fabric to swing over a massive belly, but she stubbornly wanted to wear pants as long as possible. The spring air still held a chill, and her bare legs did not appreciate the cold.

Time to suck it up, buttercup.

She drained a cup of tea and smeared some jam on toast. The tea tasted like lawn clippings and mangoes. She hated the brew but drank the vile stuff because Bright cut off the coffee when she learned that caffeine could be bad for the kit. No amount of arguing that one cup a day was safe would sway the woman.

Downstairs, the house hummed with activity. Construction finished on time and on budget. The newly renovated rooms sparkled with the gold leaf detail in the ceiling and the smooth polish of the floor.

The ballroom had been opened to the terrace, to take advantage of the mild weather. Talen and Charl set up tables and chairs outside, and a long buffet table for dining. Inside, plush rugs and pillows had been artfully arranged for seating around the perimeter of the room. Guests would lounge in the Tal fashion. A *wuap* had made itself at home, napping in the sunshine. Georgia didn't think she'd be able to sit down or get up gracefully from the pillows if she tried, but she wouldn't have much time for sitting today.

Flower arrangements arrived. She directed the deliveries to the terrace. Quil created a photo backdrop with specimens from the conservatory. She checked on the flower arrangements and found a goat nibbling on a centerpiece.

"What the ever-loving hell is that?" she shouted.

There was a goat. In her ballroom. Eating the centerpieces.

She stared at the animal and it stared back at her, its flat black eyes empty and chewing on green leaves.

"That's a goat," Quil said helpfully. "A very common domestic animal."

"Here? What's it doing here?"

"Oh, well, now that it's spring, I thought Consumption would be useful to clear out all the overgrowth on the grounds."

"You named the goat Consumption." Of course he did.

"Clever, yes? I am good with names," he said.

"Just get it out of here before it messes up the floor." Her perfect, pristine floor. As he led the goat away, she shouted, "And I'm still not naming the kit Tranquility!"

The caterer arrived, using the long counters in the butler's pantry to set up along with the ovens in the kitchen. She ducked into the kitchen to make sure they had everything they needed.

Dare trotted up, wearing a crisp white apron emblazoned with a moon violet, the logo for the house. "You look like you're about to fall over. Have you had anything to eat?"

"Um, toast for breakfast," she answered.

"Hours ago. Right, sit." He pulled out a chair and gave her a pointed look until she sat down.

He was a child—okay, technically an adult but still so young—but he barked orders with a commanding presence. She dared not disobey.

"Anything in particular you're craving?"

"Salt. Mountains of salt," she said.

"Rest your feet, have a cup of tea, and I'll make you a batch of chips." He moved about the kitchen with efficiency, pulling a container of already cut fries from the cooling unit. He drained them and patted them dry while the fryer heated.

Her instincts about needing an event venue proved true and they had enough bookings to justify hiring staff. Dare had been the first. For his interview, he made french fries, even though he called them chips. She'd been impressed with making fries from a local root vegetable. The moment the salty fries, still hot from the fryer, touched her tongue, she groaned with delight and hired him on the spot.

Best decision ever.

He seemed charmed by the historically preserved kitchen, was bossier than Bright when it came to his domain and was forever feeding her. It was amazing she hadn't ballooned up already, honestly.

"Oh, good. Dare's got you taken care of," Bright said, carrying a stack of freshly laundered linens. She sat at the table and rolled silverware and napkins into neat bundles.

"More tea," Georgia said, accepting the cup. "Yay." Keenly aware that Bright watched her, she took a sip and forced a smile. Lawn clippings and mangoes. Delicious.

The fries arrived, salty and still sizzling, and delivered her straight to greasy food heaven. Before long, the birthday girl arrived and would need a room to change into her outfits. Plural. Apparently, the *zasten* celebrated a child's coming of age and required at least two wardrobe changes. Understood. She never had a Sweet Sixteen party herself but if she had, she would have wanted half a dozen different dresses, all as flouncy as possible.

She set the Isteimlas family up in a guest suite on the ground floor and checked the schedule once again. The pieces fit smoothly together as the setup finished and the first of the guests arrived. In the foyer, Quil directed guests.

"Where's Talen? I need him to keep people off the second floor," she said. She stood at the foot of the stairs, blandly smiling as guests tried to climb the steps, before redirecting them to the party.

"I was changing," Talen said, from the top of the stairs. He wore a white suit made of an expensive fabric. Fastened with closures trimmed with golden thread, the coat front cut away over the abdomen, revealing a navy sash tied tight and low across his hips. The same rich navy fabric lined the coat. Knee-high boots in a soft white leather over tight tan trousers completed the look.

"Do you approve? It is my naval dress uniform. This is the only formalwear I have," he said.

"I approve." Very much so.

"There's also a cloak that goes with it but that seems a bit much." He brushed the front lapels, smoothing an imperceptible wrinkle.

She climbed a few steps and they met halfway. "I need to see your butt in those pants. Right now. It's super important."

With a chuckle, he turned. Coattails covered his ass, sadly, but the vent at the back allowed his tail free range of movement.

"I guess there's always room for improvement," she said, sighing dramatically with disappointment.

"That's a strategic military decision," he said. "My ass is the perfect weapon, so it's covered until the moment it's needed."

"Can't have civilians become desensitized to the mighty military ass? I really don't think that's a problem. Show me."

"Alas, it must remain shrouded in mystery." He stepped back, climbing a step.

"Talen, please. I need to see." She laced a comedic tone into her voice, exaggerating the whine.

"Hmm. I am intrigued by the design of this garment." He tugged lightly at the belt at the side of the wrap dress. Georgia knew nothing stood between her nude body and him but a layer of knit cotton held in place by one belt and a single tie on the inside of the dress. He played with the edge of the dress, pushing back the fabric to reveal her thigh. Her breath caught in her throat.

"You will show me later," he purred.

"I think that's a good idea—"

A familiar voice called out at the entrance, drawing her attention away from the shameless flirting. Fiona stood in the foyer, wearing a large sunhat and sunglasses, luggage at her feet, like she returned from a holiday and had not run off with a priceless family heirloom.

"She can't be here," Georgia whispered, clutching Talen's arm. The event needed to be perfect, the house needed to be perfect, and Fiona could ruin everything with a single tantrum.

Torn between the need to ensure the event ran smoothly and finding out what the hell Fiona was playing at, she glanced around the room. The Isteimlas family greeted guests and music poured from the ballroom. The occasional server with a tray of beverages or appetizers wandered through the crowd. Everything appeared to be under control. Even the damned *wuaps* behaved and watched the crowd calmly. No one would miss her.

"Take her to the library. I will bring Quil," Talen said. He planted a reassuring kiss on the top of her head before vanishing.

"Fiona—"

"Where's my honey bear?" Fiona untied the scarf under her chin and removed the hat.

"We weren't expecting you." To come back after you ran off with their money. Ever. Georgia kept the second half of the sentence unspoken.

"You sound like you're not happy to see me."

"You have no idea."

Fiona gave Georgia's outfit a scrutinizing look. "You got fat."

"I'm pregnant." Christ on a cracker. This bitch right here. "I know where we can find Quil. Follow me." She turned down the corridor to the library.

"Actually, there's something outside I need to show you." Fiona tossed a glance toward the open door to the ballroom. Music and laughter spilled out.

"Outside?"

"It's important, okay? It's why I came back." She grabbed Georgia's hand and tugged. "I'm not stupid. I know everyone thought I ran off with the family jewels or whatever, but this is important, so will you please stop being a stubborn bitch and follow me?"

Georgia glanced down the empty corridor. If Talen didn't

find her in the library, he'd go searching for them. It shouldn't take him too long. "Okay. Let's go to the workshop."

"Perfect."

They exited through the kitchen. Dare gave her a curious look as she opened the door to the garden, pointing in the direction of the converted stables. There. Talen would find them quick enough.

She pushed open the door to the workshop, the scent of varnish and wood dust heavy in the air. A Tal male stood leaned against the far wall. His head was down, superficially conveying casualness, but the tension in his body confessed that nothing escaped his attention. He looked familiar but Georgia had met so many people new people in the last few months, she couldn't place him.

"What's going on?" Georgia asked, turning to Fiona. She realized her mistake a heartbeat later, but it was too late to help her.

Talen

Secrets always find a way to claw their way into the light.

-Persistence and the Secrets of the Shadowed Hill

THE FEMALES WERE NOT in the library.

"I do not believe we have time to discuss literature. Your

mate is very insistent that we be available to serve the whims of our clients," Quil said, tail swaying with delight.

"You'd think that as much as you enjoy spending money, you might be interested in earning it," Talen replied.

"Why did you bring me here?"

"Fiona returned." He could not bring himself to honor that thieving female as his brother's mate.

Quil's ears moved forward with interest. "What does she want?"

"I did not ask. Money, no doubt," he said, nearly growling with frustration. Despite the carefree facade Quil fronted, Fiona's departure wounded him. Talen heard a few frantic voice messages that Quil left, asking for a reason, for some justification for him to bring her home.

Talen sighed. No matter what Fiona said, Quil would welcome her back, if she were here to stay. He couldn't imagine why. She had already robbed them of their most valuable possession.

"Fiona would not wait in this room. She would want to be the center of attention," Quil said.

They found no sign of Fiona in the ballroom or mingling with the guests. Dare, in the kitchen, sent them outside, claiming to have seen them head toward the old stables.

The situation felt off. Fiona had no reason to drag his mate to the stable. That female craved an audience.

Despite Talen's jest that his time in the Navy was mostly reading in his bunk or scrubbing the ship for inspection, when bad shit happened, it happened fast. He learned to listen to his instinct.

"Go to your female," he said, pushing his brother toward the building. "Have her send out my mate."

Quil mumbled about not being a messenger but entered the building.

Five minutes later, no one had exited.

CHAPTER 21

GEORGIA

Quil sat on the floor next to her, his hands and feet tied with rope and covered in thick, silver tape. He scooted over to Fiona, where she was similarly bound. "You did not return any of my messages."

"Is now really the time?" Georgia hissed.

"I just needed a little me time. I was always coming home, honey bear," Fiona said.

"You emptied our accounts."

"What's the point of getting away from everything if I'm scrounging for pocket change? I wanted a break from stress, not to be stressed."

"Will you two shut the fuck up?" Georgia snapped.

"I'm having a private conversation with my husband," Fiona said, indignant.

"Really? Right now? We're in peril, Fiona. Peril. This is fucking perilous." She lifted her hands and wiggled her fingers, drawing attention to the rough rope binding her hands together. "Maybe you can cut the bullshit and just admit that you're a gold digger."

"Better a gold digger than knocked up and fat." Fiona tossed the glossy tumble of chestnut locks over her shoulder but the rope binding her hands marred the dramatic effect.

"Fiona, stop being petty," Quil said.

She frowned and pouted, sticking her lower lip out. "I see what's going on. I was gone for two minutes and you replaced me!"

"You were gone for two months," he retorted. "No contact. No indication you ever planned to return."

"Will you be quiet!" The unknown Tal male picked up a well-used mallet and slammed it into a wooden post. The timber shuddered and bit of plaster from the ceiling rained down, stunning his captive audience into silence.

The male crouched down in front of Quil. "You're him, aren't you? Tranquility? It's an honor, Your Grace."

"No, you're mistaken." Quil sneezed lightly in the male's direction.

"You're as rude as a royal." He tilted his head to the side as his tail lazily waved behind him. "Your Grace? That's how you address a duke, yes?"

"I'm not that male. I'm not royal."

A silver knife flashed and blood trickled down Quil's cheek from a small incision. "Huh. You bleed as red as the rest of us." The male looked to Georgia, his gaze lingering on her belly. "And the next generation."

"Oh, honey bear, is it true? I knew it!" Fiona practically bounced with excitement, ignoring the fact that the psychopathic male sliced up Quil.

"This male has told you falsehoods," Quil said.

"I want to be a duchess," she whined. She glanced at the unknown male and licked her lips. "He said he needed proof. He said the music box wasn't enough; that he needed DNA."

Talen

PATIENCE.

The assassin had his back to the window.

Amateur.

He lined up the scope on the rifle, waiting for a clear shot. At that precise moment, he was upset enough with Quil and all the trouble he brought along, that his finger might slip and hit his brother.

Tempting.

Perhaps too tempting.

He took a deep breath and counted the virtues, forcing himself to be still even as his body screamed to take action. Patience would ensure his mate's safety.

Patience was difficult to muster.

Music from the ballroom spilled into the spring night. He listened and waited for the assassin to move away from his hostages. Soon he realized that would never happen.

"I'm going to draw the assassin away." He handed the rifle to Charl. "Try not to murder my brother," he said.

"You are rusty," the four-armed mail said, accepting the weapon.

"I'm not rusty. I'm furious." Quil's female brought an assassin to their door and now his mate, heavy with kit, sat on a dirty floor with her hands and feet tied like an animal waiting to be slaughtered. Rage pounded in his ears and his top lip curled back with a hiss. "If you must sacrifice Quil, I'll forgive you."

While Fiona and Quil squabbled like cranky kits, Georgia grew agitated, shouting at them to be quiet. The assassin said nothing, watching with sharp eyes.

"Get your priorities straight, Fiona," Georgia said.

"I want to be a duchess, I think my priorities are just fine," Fiona said.

"A duchess doesn't steal the silver," his mate retorted.

"I was short of funds. I merely borrowed the silver. I was going to bring it back."

"I do not believe you," Quil said.

Enough of this. He had to draw away the assassin.

"I think stealing the silver was a pretty good indication she never planned to return," Talen said, pushing open the stable's doors. "What changed? Your buyer wouldn't pay for the music box? Where is it, by the way?"

With every question, Talen stepped closer to the assassin.

Fiona sighed. "He said he needed proof and he could pay me a lot of money for the right item. A ridiculous amount of money. But then he changed the deal." She tossed the assassin a glare. "He said it wasn't good enough, even though there's the royal seal on the bottom. Anyone can see that."

The assassin stood. A slight male of moderate height, Talen had no doubt that the male would prove remarkably strong and agile in a fight. "The heir and the spare," he said.

"You will divorce your mate," Talen told Quil. The female brought danger to their home. She only thought of her own greed and selfish wants. She was not family.

"Of course I didn't sell it," she said.

"Couldn't get a fair price, more like," Talen snapped. "Did the pawnshops turn you away? No one willing to front you the credit for obviously stolen treasure."

"No, it wasn't like that," she protested.

"Enough of the act," Quil interjected. "It would be more convincing if you didn't fleece me of every cent I had and if you had spent a little money in your normal haunts. If you did that, I'd believe you if you claimed you went on a gambling binge. That's how we met, after all."

"You dumped me for a gambling addict? Unbelievable," Georgia said.

"Enough," the assassin said, slamming the mallet into the wall just above Georgia's head. Talen's stomach lurched. He wanted this male bleeding out on the floor. When the room quieted, the assassin held out a length of rope. "Kneel."

Talen did not move.

"Kneel with your back to me, Your Grace, or I'll make a necklace out of your pretty little mate's ears." The assassin produced a knife and held it to Georgia's throat.

The room held its collective breath, waiting on Talen's response. He needed to draw the assassin away from his mate. Charl needed a clear shot.

"I don't understand what's going on," Fiona said in a stage-whisper.

"Oh, you fucking moron. The person you wanted to sell the unique, one-of-a-kind, highly recognizable work of art to is not a collector. He's bad news," Georgia said. Pride sparked in his chest at his clever mate.

"He said he's a writer. He wrote that book, with the two kits. You know. You have a copy."

"*The Lost Princes*. Holy shit," Georgia said. "Is that you? Are you the lost princes?"

That fucking book. "Lies and slander," Talen said.

"I don't know. It's well regarded as a popular history," the assassin said, never stepping away from Georgia. "Attitudes are shifting. The old families are being restored. Your mother was a very popular figure and history looks favorably on the work she did." He spoke in a bored, almost aristocratic tone. He could understand how that would convince Fiona she spoke to the author of that piece of flaming garbage.

"A prince is the son of a king. Our grandfather was king and our father the younger son. I had the courtesy title of marquess at the time and Talen had an earldom lined up for when he reached his majority. Of course, I'd be only a duke now, I'm afraid," Quil said, as casually as if they were drinking and playing cards.

"So, I'm a duchess?" Fiona asked.

"Alas, my sweet, no. There was an unpleasant little civil war," Quil said. "Our parents were murdered, and Talen and I fled, hiding from assassins for a good decade until we were declared dead."

"So, go back! You're not dead," Fiona said, like the title of duchess was a trivial item Quil could pick up at a shop and give her.

"You see, my sweet, a second cousin inherited. Esteem. We agreed to renounce our claim, change our names and never return, in exchange for not being murdered in our sleep," Quil said, eyeing the assassin's blade.

The deal changed, apparently.

"As I said, attitudes have shifted. His Grace feels the previous duke and his mate have grown too popular posthumously and the two lost princes have captured the public's imagination with that book. Now, kneel." The assassin gesture with his free hand, blade still at Georgia's throat.

"So, I'm not a duchess?"

"I'm afraid not, kitten," Quil said.

Fiona turned her hot glare to the assassin, displaying utter lack of self-preservation. "This is your fault! You said he was a duke! I just needed to give you the music box."

Momentarily, the male turned his head toward Fiona and the knife eased back a fraction. Quil lifted his bound legs, knocking the blade from the male's hands. Talen dove, sending the blade further across the floor.

The assassin nimbly jumped to his feet and grabbed an object from the workbench. He held a chisel, not the most lethal item but it would inflict serious damage. He towered over Talen, who moved to intercept the blow and protect his mate.

Glass shattered.

The assassin swayed on his feet. The chisel clattered to the floor and his body dropped, a discreet hole in his forehead the cause.

"What were you waiting for?" Talen said, retrieving the knife to cut through the silver tape.

"Someone wouldn't kneel and kept blocking my shot." Charl entered their makeshift workshop, the rifle leaning on his shoulder.

Blood and brain matter splattered across the floor and along the top of desk waiting to be refinished.

"We are out of practice," Quil said. "I practically winked and repeated the signal."

"I saw no signal."

"My sweet? Come on. I do not speak like that. It's undignified."

"As you say, honey bear," Talen said, and quickly cut the rope binding Quil's hand and gave him the knife. He ignored his brother's babbling. Quil chattered when stressed. He had a more important person to tend to.

"Don't look," he said, helping Georgia to her feet. He ran his hand down her arms, holding up her wrists for inspection and gently kissing the red marks. "Are you hurt?"

Stress hormones rolled off her, clouding his senses. He needed to see she was unharmed. He needed to inspect every inch of her delicate human skin.

"I'm okay," she said. "Who was that?" She shook her head. "I guess I know who he was. I mean why? Why did he want to kill you?"

"That was an amateur. He should have dealt with you one by one, rather than round you up for a show," Charl said as he went through the male's pockets. "At least, that's what I would have done. Better crowd control."

His friend really was a frightening male.

"Standards have fallen if Esteem is hiring cut-rate assassins," Quil said.

"But now?" Talen asked. After so many years had passed. The brothers had honored their end of the agreement, assumed new identities with the best forgeries money could buy, and never set foot on Talmar again.

"This may shed some light on your questions." Charl held up a piece of paper.

"How utterly primitive," Quil said, opening the folded sheet. "It's a list of names." He frowned. "I think these are family members. I'm not sure. Distant relations, maybe."

Talen took the list but recognized none of the names. "Our cousin Esteem is removing those who could challenge his title." That is what the assassin claimed.

"I know this name." Quil tapped the paper. "Uncle Forthright had a bastard daughter. She was an infant."

Fuzzy memories of holding a crying kit came to mind and a nursemaid scolding him for holding the kit too tightly. "What happened to her?"

"Presumably the same thing that happened to us. Forthright was a bit more perceptive than our parents and, hopefully, had enough sense to send the kit away," Quil said.

"We have a cousin? She's been alone all this time." They could have been searching for her. Talen and Quil had each other but this kit had no one. He couldn't imagine the hardship of being away from home, too young to remember anything or anyone.

Quil's hand on his shoulder interrupted his thoughts. "We barely escaped. We were too young to do a search and rescue. It took everything to keep us one step ahead of his lot." Quil gave the dead assassin a kick.

"Your cousin must be dealt with," Charl said. He held the assassin's communication device. "That list is not for a family reunion."

"Agreed." Talen gave the list to Charl. "You will handle this."

"You're my family and no one gets to order a hit on my family without consequences," Charl said.

"You are one scary fucker," Georgia said.

Charl never spoke about his time in the Navy, or his life before joining the service, but Talen knew that the male enlisted already equipped with several deadly skills. He was patient and precise. There could be no one better to solve this problem and keep Talen's family safe.

"Esteem will want proof that the assassin succeeded," Quil said.

"You are correct." Talen grabbed Quil roughly and slammed him, face first, into the stone wall.

"What the fuck! My nose!" Blood gushed down his face.

He clutched his broken nose, spreading the mess. "Why did you do that? We could have used paint!"

"Authenticity matters," Talen said, quoting Quil at his most intractable about doing repairs the expensive way for the house.

Charl muttered about brothers. "Lay on the ground and don't blink," he directed. Using the assassin's communication device, he took a photo.

Quil clambered to his feet and used a handkerchief to scrub at his face. "This is monogrammed and now it's ruined. I'll never get the stain out."

"Stop being so fussy," Talen said.

Quil finally seemed to notice his former mate, still bound and whimpering on the wood chip-strewn floor. "He's dead. Oh my God," Fiona sobbed. "How could you?"

"He was going to kill us," Georgia said in a serenely calm voice.

"You! Not me. We had a deal. I never got my money." More pitiful mewling, the eye makeup running with tears.

Quil remained unmoved by this sight, which pleased Talen. Perhaps his brother had finally learned his lesson. Too bad his choice in mate brought a viper into their den.

"Oh, for fuck's sake. Shut the fuck up, you selfish bitch," Georgia snapped. Her tiny fists balled with anger. "He was never going to pay you for the thing you stole, and he was totally going to murder all of us."

Fiona opened her mouth to protest but Quil placed his

hand over her face. "Perhaps it is wiser to be silent and observe."

"Can we just gag her?" Charl asked, holding a roll of tape.

"Not until she tells us where the music box is," Talen said.

"My bag," Fiona said and Quil searched through the bag.

The music box was just an object and if he never saw it again, he'd wouldn't miss it. That revelation surprised him. The jeweled music box held such sentimental value that he expected to be devastated if it were lost.

He looked toward his mate, who rubbed her sore wrists.

He possessed items of greater value now. The music box was a gaudy trinket, an exercise in too much money and too little taste, and nothing more.

"Ha! Found it!" Quil raised a fist in triumph, holding aloft the purloined music box. "Seems smaller than I remember." He wound the gear at the bottom and a few mechanized notes sounded. With a smile on his face, Quil looked up, remembering his audience. "Oh. No one seems impressed. Don't we care about this anymore?"

He handed the music box to Talen. "Don't be upset with him, Georgia. We were conditioned to never speak of who we were or our family, just in case someone with influence decided that we needed to be assassinated as well. But all of that was before the civil war. It's no longer ours, I'm afraid."

"You can go back and claim what's yours, honey bear. You

were lost but we found you. It's all waiting for you," Fiona said.

"The title of the book is misleading," Quil said. "We were never lost and a few years ago, we reached a settlement with the new heir of the estate."

Talen nodded. "A cousin took over the estate and eventually inherited after it had been declared legally. When the war was over, and not being dead, we received compensation."

"We renounced our titles and agreed to live in exile," Quil said.

The brothers exchanged a look. The cousin no longer seemed content to let them be in exile and wanted them removed from the picture.

"So, I'm not a duchess?" Fiona's bottom lip trembled.

Charl slapped the tape over her mouth.

Georgia

"ARE THE DRAMATIC REVEALS OVER? We need to do something... about this," Georgia said and waved toward the body.

"Most of the local Watchtower is in the ballroom," Quil said. "I'll fetch the scariest looking bastard I can find."

"No, wait." She frowned. How would they explain this?

Talen's warm hand rubbed the back of her neck. "We did nothing wrong. We were attacked in our home."

"Okay. You're right, you're right." Adrenaline coursed through her, muddling her thoughts.

"Are you well?" Talen asked.

She nodded, then shook her head. "I wasn't scared, you know, when he tied me up or threatened to cut me." She placed a hand over her heart and felt it thrumming in her chest. "But it's hitting me now." She took a shuddering breath, willing herself to be calm.

"Quil, fetch a hunter from the Watchtower. I'm tending to my mate," Talen said.

"And that one?" Charl pointed to Fiona, still on the floor with her hands bound.

"She is a thief and conspired with a murderer. They can decide what to do with her."

"And a debtor, too," Quil added. "Although I believe I'm technically responsible for those. Oh well. Another reason not to dally on getting a divorce. Sit tight, my sweet little thief." He blew an exaggerated kiss in her direction before leaving.

Georgia needn't have worried. The head of the Watchtower just so happened to be the father of the birthday girl, Clarity, and also from Talmar. He nodded as Talen gave a statement about his family's history, what the assassin said about the cousin sending him, and how Fiona lured Georgia away from the house to be held hostage.

"Politics," Merit said with a sneer. "I really thought I left that behind on Talmar."

"As did I," Talen replied.

Fiona had been taken back to the Watchtower due to a warrant for her arrest. Her sticky fingers and gambling habit caused quite a lot of trouble for herself.

The event went off without a hitch, Achaval family drama aside. Clarity changed into another dress, burgundy with gold embroidery. Music played. People danced. Wine flowed. As the clock approached midnight, guests headed to their rooms or for their vehicles. A few clusters of guests remained, camped on cushions and drinking coffee.

Georgia cradled a steaming mug of tea and sat on the terrace. Lights and sounds of the ballroom spilled out from behind her. The sweet, minty aroma of the tea helped ease the tension from her body. She felt exhausted but was too wired to sleep anytime soon.

"Are you well? I will send for a medic." Talen joined her at the balustrade, leaning on the stone lip.

"I'm fine."

"I can hear your heart racing and smell your stress."

Delightful.

She took a sip of the minty tea. "I just need to calm down but I've never been good at letting my anxiety go."

"And the kit? Stress can harm the kit."

"Constantly elevated high blood pressure, sure, you big

doof. One stressful night wouldn't harm the kit." Once she said the words, she doubted herself. Freema would tell her to see the doctor and Talen would drag the doctor to her if she wouldn't go to the clinic. "In the morning, okay?"

She needed to see the event through until the last guest left, because burying her emotions under physical activity until she was ready to deal was how she coped. Life skills.

He moved behind her, wrapping his arms around and pressed his face to the juncture of where her neck met her shoulder. "Such sweet words of affection, my heart. Pray never tell me the meaning of a doof, because I already know it means love."

She snorted, nearly spitting out her mouthful of tea. "That was a bit harsh. I'm sorry for calling names."

She looked across the dark garden. The moon hid partly behind the clouds and the stillness surrounded them.

"It went well tonight," she said. "No one was murdered, I can't believe that's a benchmark now, and our first event went off without a problem."

"You did well."

"*We* did well." Another sip of tea. "Fuck, I'm tired. I think I'm going to sleep in until noon tomorrow."

"You need an assistant."

"I'm fine. Don't be ridiculous." They were booked up but not out of the financial woods yet. She couldn't go spending money like mad.

"You will only grow more tired with the kit. Once our Hairy Correction arrives, you will require an assistant."

"We are so not naming this kid Harry Correction, so don't even joke about that." She set the cup down on the ledge and turned to face him. "Do you miss it? Talmar. Being royalty?"

He scratched behind an ear in a thoughtful gesture. "I was young and I remember little, that has always been true. If it was not for the photographs of my parents in that damned book, I don't think I'd remember what they looked like."

She made a humming noise in her throat. Her mother had been gone for over thirteen years now. While her memories were fading and getting fuzzy at the edges, she remembered her mom's smile and her long hair that always seemed to be tangled from the wind. She doubted she'd ever forget those details.

"That was the past. Those kits are gone," Talen said. His hands stroked the length of her arm, warming her in the chilly evening air.

"Don't you ever wonder what your life would be like if you could go back? If you had never left?"

"That is a cruel game to play. What purpose does it serve other than to make myself miserable?"

She gave a thin smile. That cruel game had always been one of her favorites, imagining the life she had if her father never abandoned his family, or if her mother beat cancer and lived. Sometimes she had even fantasized about what it would have been like to have been adopted when she was a teenager and in foster care. "I suppose you're right. That person wouldn't be you, and I'm pretty damn fond of this version of you."

"You carry my heart." His lips caught hers and the kiss deepened to last for always. "My future is here, with you."

CHAPTER 22

GEORGIA

G,

Customs on this planet is crazy. You'd think a bag of coffee beans was a controlled substance. Okay, technically it's a "mild stimulant" but it's just coffee. I had the pleasure of paying exorbitant fees. But hey, I got a sticker slapped on my coffee bag, so let's count that as a win.

-Freema

"Looks like someone is eager to meet the world. The kit is early but healthy. I predict an easy labor," Belith said. Her cheeks had a glow which indicated sincerity. Nice to know the doctor didn't feed her meaningless bull.

Georgia clenched her eyes closed as a contraction rolled through her. Nothing about the last two weeks felt easy. Her back hurt, her ankles swelled up like balloons and she had to pee all the damn time. The spring weather went from cool and damp to hot and sticky in the blink of an eye. She hadn't been comfortable in so long she had forgotten what that felt like. Had she ever slept an entire night without a pee break every two hours? A solid night's sleep felt like a lifetime ago and she wouldn't be getting rest anytime soon.

"Why is it so hot in here?" Sweat collected in the small of her back. The medical clinic should have air conditioning. The house's unreliable cooling system seemed to only make things marginally cooler but never cold. Never not sticky.

Talen shoved an ice chip in her mouth and handed her a glass of melted ice water and ice chips. "I will inquire about the temperature."

"Don't you dare leave me here," she said, grabbing his hand, which she promptly dropped. "Gah, it's too hot to touch. You're a fucking furnace. Go away." She sloshed the near-empty tumbler. "And I need more ice."

He gave the doctor a pleading look. "When will the kit arrive?"

"Soon."

Not soon enough.

"You have not yet fully dilated." Belith arranged the paper blanket over Georgia's legs. "We will continue to monitor."

More waiting. She was so ready for this to be over.

"Can you just take the baby out? I changed my mind. I don't want to do natural childbirth."

"We can perform emergency surgery if you or the baby are in distress," Belith said with a smile.

"But not because this is hell and I'm tired," Georgia replied.

The blue-skinned doctor gave her a pat on the arm. "Soon this will be over, you'll forget all the unpleasantness and you'll be planning your next child."

Not likely.

"We will name the next kit Endeavor," Talen said with a nod.

"Unless you're going to carry it yourself, I don't know what the fuck you're talking about," Georgia snapped. Another baby. What the hell was he smoking? She still had the first one wedged up in her like a watermelon in a tube sock.

"Have some more ice." Talen pressed another ice chip to her lips.

"Have you decided on a name?" Belith asked conversationally, sitting down near the bed like she was visiting a friend and not, you know, delivering a baby.

"Yes. Persistence Marie," Talen said, obvious pride in his voice.

"Like the books?"

"Yes!" He launched into a detailed explanation of how

they had been reading the books, which had always been his favorite as a kit, and could not agree on any name...

Georgia tuned him out. She didn't care about anything other than the watermelon up her tube sock and her current state of utter anguish. Oh, and getting the watermelon out. That was relevant to her interests.

Another contraction broke her from her spiral of misery with a fresh slash of pain.

Belith grinned and nodded. "Soon," she said.

"You've been saying that for an hour," Georgia grumbled, accepting another ice chip. She narrowed her eyes at her amber-striped husband, unsure if he was being supportive and attending to her needs, or shoving ice in her face to keep her from complaining.

"The kit will be here soon, my heart." Another ice chip. "You have never looked more lovely." Another. "You've made me the happiest male in the universe, my heart."

Yup. Totally trying to keep her from yelling at him.

Voices rose in the corridor.

"Let me in!"

"Only family is allowed," Belith said, blocking the door.

"Well, I am family and I'm her personal physician, now get out of my way."

Georgia knew that voice and had desperately missed her friend over the last year. Joyful tears leaked at the corners of her eyes. Talen dapped at them with a tissue and murmured soft words of comfort.

"I have been treating this female for six months. I am her physician," Belith argued.

"Then I guess we're coworkers. Dr. Freema Jones. Now step aside."

Freema strode into the room, a laminate ID badge hanging around her neck, and dragging a suitcase behind her.

"You look terrible," Georgia said, struggling to sit up comfortably. She grimaced at her sore abdomen and complaining back.

"Humanity can travel the stars, but airports still suck balls." Freema brushed back the hair from Georgia's forehead. "Hey you. Long time, no see."

"You're late."

"And that baby is early."

"Not my fault." A contraction rolled through her and she grabbed Talen's tail, squeezing hard. To his credit, his face remained placid and he did not utter a sound of discomfort. A little part of her was thrilled to inflict a fraction of the pain she felt but a larger part of her felt remorse and vowed to make amends.

When Georgia could finally open her eyes, she found Freema watching her with a goofy look on her face. "What?"

"I'm so happy right now my heart hurts," Freema said.

"Did you acclimate to the oxygen levels on this planet? Sounds—" Another contraction hit, derailing her snarky comment. There was so much she wanted to tell Freema and so many questions to ask, like was she staying on Corra? Did she get the post at the medical clinic in town or would she be on the other side of the world? Did she bring the damn coffee?

Belith lifted the paper blanket and made a pleased murmur. "Perfect. It's time."

"Let's make a baby," Freema said. "Where do I scrub up?"

"Sorry, only the papa is allowed in the room now. You can wait in the hall with the rest of the family," Belith said, snapping on fresh gloves.

Fifteen minutes later, or three hours, she really couldn't keep track of time, she held a slumbering bundle. Persistence Marie Achaval was perfect. Beyond perfect with her tiny little fingers and fingernails, little button of a nose, pink lips, slender tail, and triangular ears with a tuft of dark hair at the tips.

"Your ears don't look like this," she said, brushing the baby fine hair.

"Kit's fur. It will fall out in time." He sat on the bed next to her, brushing one large hand over his daughter's hair.

"Hello baby," she said, not quite believing this life she made; they made. She looked up at Talen, "We did this."

"We did," he agreed. One arm tightened around her and his tail waved happily.

The feel-good endorphins must have been flooding her brain because the recent agony of labor faded—which was a terrible trick for her body to play. All she could think about was her glorious daughter and how soon they could have another. "I think Endeavor is a good name for the next one."

EPILOGUE

GEORGIA

G,

Don't sleep in too late. Santa plans an early visit and wants those sweet cream buns for breakfast.

-Freema

L ittle feet pounced on the bed, waking her. Someone giggled in her ear. Tiny fingers—wet, how were they wet?—poked at her lips.

"Mommy? Are you awake?" More giggling.

Little monster.

"No. I am soundly asleep," Georgia said.

"But you're talking." A weight settled above her, sitting directly over her bladder and the fluffy end bit of a tail brushed at her nose.

"I'm sleep talking. It's a thing."

"But Santa Claus came! Please, can you wake up? Pretty please?" Persistence bounced and that was the end of that game. Georgia had to pee like her life depended on it.

"Get off me, munchkin. Go wake up your father." Georgia gently removed Persistence, dismayed to see her daughter wearing only her pajama bottoms; no top and no socks.

Justice, once sleeping and now disturbed, raised her head and hissed. She leaped from the bed and repositioned herself in front of the fire, curled up and determined to ignore the child shouting excitedly about presents and candy and Santa. Poor creature. Some of the *wuaps* adored the kit and followed Persistence about the house like a band of marauders, but Justice seemed to enjoy her quiet solitude and avoided the kit.

Correction knocked on the door and held up the missing clothes. "I'm sorry. She got away from me."

"No worries, Corie. Just give me a minute and we'll see about breakfast and then," she paused, then whispered dramatically, "presents."

"Presents!" Persistence bounced on the bed, her chestnut hair flying and tail thrashing about madly.

"No bouncing. Your father is old and fragile," Talen grumbled, sitting upright. Persi leaped toward him, fingers curled to sink her kitten claws into him. They tumbled on the bed, all giggles and growls.

Georgia used the facilities, splashed water on her face and ran a brush through her hair. The hour was abhorrently early and she needed coffee. When she returned to the bedroom, Talen had wrestled Persi into her pajamas and Corie stood awkwardly by the door with her tail in her hands, like she was trying to make herself small.

"Hey, Merry Christmas and Happy MidWinter," Georgia said. She gave her adoptive daughter a one-armed hug.

Four years ago, when Charl eventually returned from whatever he planned to do with the assassin's list of name, he brought an eleven-year-old Tal female home with him. Apparently, Correction really was a family name and this distant cousin had been recently orphaned. Welcoming the adolescent into their home wasn't even a question: she was family. As far as Georgia was concerned, Corie was her daughter; her very tall, moody teenage daughter.

"When did you get taller than me? Why am I just noticing now?" Georgia asked.

"You notice. You ask me to retrieve items from high shelves all the time," Corie said. All elbows and long legs, Corie would be sixteen that spring. She hadn't decided if she wanted a *zasten* party or not. Georgia suspected that her eldest was too shy to admit that she wanted a party. She wanted to throw the girl the biggest, most lavish party possible, if only to show Cori how deeply she was loved. Then again, a big, lavish party would mortify the quiet teenager. It was hard to predict how she responded. Georgia wondered if her mother struggled trying to decipher her teen angst.

"Can I have my stocking now?" Persi pointed to the red

felt stockings leaning against the fireplace mantle, too heavy for their hooks.

"You already have your stocking," Georgia said. The stocking in question lay abandoned at the foot of the bed, individually wrapped candy spilling onto the bedspread. Empty candy wrappers were tossed on the floor. "And you ate candy before breakfast."

"That's my first stocking. It was in my bed so it's mine and Uncle Quil says I have more to find," Persi said.

Georgia noticed how her daughter side-stepped eating candy for breakfast. "Why did Uncle... Santa leave candy in your room?"

"Because he's the best!" Persi followed her proclamation with more jumping on the bed.

"I think Santa Claus got carried away," Talen said. "He may have also mentioned a scavenger hunt."

Persi stopped bouncing, her eyes wide. "What's that? I want it."

"Why don't you give your sister her stocking?" Talen said, setting Persi on the floor and pointing her toward the mantle.

She fetched the stocking and ignored Georgia when she held out her hand, to read the gift tag. "I can read my name," she said proudly. They had practice writing her name in block print the day before. "This says Persistence, so this one is for Corie."

"Thank you," Corie said.

The two girls sat on the floor and emptied their stockings. Persi had a set of plastic building blocks that for sure would be scattered across the floor in no time. Corie opened a velvet box, revealing a silver necklace with a charm.

"That's lovely," Georgia said, admiring the tiny moon violet cast in silver.

"Do you think Santa left us more stockings?" Persi dumped the blocks onto the carpet and mashed pieces together.

Georgia shared a look with Talen. Quil had been in charge of filling one—one!—stocking for the girls and setting presents under the tree. Who knows what he actually did in the overnight hours.

"Let's have breakfast and we'll go hunting," Talen said.

"I already had candy. Let's go hunting now," Persi retorted.

"You spend too much time with your uncle."

Corie snorted, then immediately covered her smile with her hand, ears pressed back with embarrassment.

"Breakfast or Bright will have our ears," Talen said, but the stubborn kit remained unmoved.

"I heard that Santa liked the cookies and milk so much, that he's stopping by to have breakfast with us," Georgia said.

"He did?" Persi's eyes went wide.

"That's what he told me last night." Charl purchased a large red overcoat years ago and had been patiently waiting for Persi to be old enough to appreciate Earth traditions. Georgia hoped that Persi would be too impressed by the visit to not question why Santa had four arms.

Talen herded the girls out the door. As Persi and Corie clattered down the stairs, no doubt waking the entire house, he hung back and gave Georgia a heated look.

"Oh no," she said as he pulled her toward him.

"Temptress," he said, his voice low and rumbling.

Really? Her hair was a mess and she wore an old bathrobe. She hardly looked the part of a temptress.

Standards had fallen. "No time for that, fuzzy britches," she said.

"Always time for you, my heart." He placed a kiss just behind her ear and nibbled down.

"Mmm. A compelling argument but we got a three-year-old monster who's already eaten her body weight in candy. We should totally try to get her to eat a vegetable."

"As exciting as that sounds, I have an alternate suggestion. You, minus the bathrobe, on the bed," he said, already loosening the ties to the robe.

"There's no time." Story of every parent's life right there.

"Okay, keep the bathrobe." He stroked down her back, hand over the robe. "I like how soft it is."

"How about," she purred, "you unwrap your present later, after the kits have gone to bed?"

His teeth nipped at her neck. "Happy MidWinter, my heart."

Four years ago, they discovered a surprise pregnancy and everything changed, yet nothing had really changed. Their kit only made her aware of the love she had been too scared to admit. She loved her massive alien with his large hands and book collection. She loved the way he read to their daughter every night. She loved the smile with just a hint of fangs he flashed every morning. She loved him with her whole heart and would until the light left her.

"Merry Christmas, love," she said.

AFTERWORD

Thank you for reading Georgia and Quil's story. I hope they made you grin and if you wanted to punch Quil in the face, that's understandable. He has a very punchable face.

I have plans for Freema. Stay tuned.

This book is dedicated to my friend Sushma, who suggested the title, Pulled by the Tail, slightly more than "Tail of Two Kitties." I asked my friends (Nat, Del, YF and Jenny) for punny tail titles and they unanimously, unwaveringly suggested "Tail of Two Kitties."

Guys, that's such a bad title. Maybe for a menage but not this book. I endured months of "Have you considered A Tail of Two Kitties?" I'm a little scared to brainstorm with them for the next book.

I'd also like to thank my editors, Lynn and Aaron, who tolerate my rough drafts and my inability to know how commas work. And, finally, the GargGirls (Regine, Stacy, Tamsin, Stephanie and Abigail) who keep me focused with writing sprints and help when I'm searching for a word. Making the words is hard work but it's good to know I'm not alone.

ABOUT THE AUTHOR

Join my newsletter and get a FREE copy of Claimed by the Alien Prince.

Get it at here:

https://dl.bookfunnel.com/jektemqay4

I write fun, flirty and fast stories featuring sassy heroines, out-of-this-world heroes, all

the mischief they can managed and plenty of steamy fun. Hopefully you want to read

them too.

I live in an old house with my husband and a growing collection of cats.

Follow my Facebook reader group for early teasers and whatnots.

https://www.facebook.com/groups/895051017325998/

ALSO BY NANCEY CUMMINGS

Pulled by the Tail

<u>Valos of Sonhadra</u>

Blazing

Inferno

Taken for Granite (Khargals of Duras)

<u>Dragons of Wye (with Juno Wells)</u>

Korven's Fire

Ragnar

<u>Alpha Aliens of Fremm</u>

Claimed by the Aline Prince

Bride of the Alien Prince

Alien Warrior's Mate

Alien Rogue's Price